CHOOSE YOUR OWN ADVENTURE®

HEROES AND MONSTERS

NETFLIX

STRANGER THINGS

by Rana Tahir

**Illustrated by Patrick Spaziante
and Katherine Spaziante**

CHOOSECO®
WAITSFIELD, VERMONT

To all the dreamers, this is for you. Let your life be strange and wonderful like your dreams. To my younger self, your dreams are coming true. Thank you for getting me here.

Copyright © 2023 by Netflix Inc. All rights reserved. Published in the United States by Random House Children's Books, a division of Penguin Random House LLC, New York. Random House and the colophon are registered trademarks of Penguin Random House LLC. Stranger Things and all related titles, characters, and logos are trademarks of Netflix Inc. Created by the Duffer Brothers.

Stranger Things 4 written by Matt Duffer, Ross Duffer, Paul Dichter, Curtis Gwinn, Caitlin Schneiderhan, Kate Trefry.

ReadStrangerThings.com

ISBN 978-0-593-64474-4 (trade) — ISBN 978-0-593-64475-1 (ebook)

Printed in the United States of America

10 9 8 7 6 5

First Edition 2023

BEWARE and WARNING!

This book is different from other books.

You and YOU ALONE are in charge of what happens in this story.

There are dangers, choices, adventures, and consequences. YOU must use all of your numerous talents and much of your enormous intelligence. The wrong decision could end in disaster—even death. But don't despair. At any time, YOU can go back and make another choice, alter the path of your story, and change its result.

YOU are a high school student from California. You're preparing to attend a journalism seminar in a distant town over your spring break, when you suddenly meet a troubled student with a mysterious background. Do you choose to help her, or do you continue on your trip to Hawkins, Indiana? Whatever you choose, you will soon find yourself on an unexpected adventure that takes you into a world of secret government operations, psychic powers, parallel worlds and even vengeful monsters!

It is the beginning of the last day before spring break at Lenora Hills High, and you are stuck inside with the editor in chief of the school paper as he lectures on and on about your duty to the paper. You want to roll your eyes so badly, but right now you need to appear to be listening.

"You haven't turned in the name for your next new student profile," he says, barely disguising his disdain for you.

"Isn't there something else I could do? I'm a good writer, and I could really dig into a good story if you let me, instead of these fluff pieces," you remind him for the millionth time.

"Not this again." He frowns. "Look, either give me a name by the end of the day or you're off the paper."

With those last words, he orders you out of the room. You grumble as you leave, stomping down the hallway amid smiling faces eager for the break. The energy is contagious, and you feel lighter. At least you have something to look forward to over break: a real conference for student journalists in a whole other state! You'll get to travel by plane on your own for the first time and meet student journalists from all over the country. Maybe then someone will take you and your work seriously. You hope that will be your host and organizer for the conference, Fred Benson. For now, you head to class daydreaming of the conference waiting for you in Hawkins, Indiana.

Turn to the next page.

2

You head out to the courtyard as the day ends. You still haven't found a subject for the profile for the paper, but at this point, you don't really care. A yell pulls your attention; a crowd is gathered around some freshmen. One is on her knees after apparently falling; the smug looks of the girls standing by her make it clear she was tripped on purpose. The girl on the ground gets up and yells, "Angela!" She puts out her hands and screams. There is a moment of silence, and then the crowd breaks into laughter at the absurd spectacle. A teacher pushes through the crowd and pulls the girl, Angela, away as the kids start to move on. The strange girl is joined by a boy, who tries to comfort her as they pick up the pieces of a broken project. You catch a snippet of their conversation. "We can fix it together . . . ," the boy says.

Her doe eyes water, and your heart breaks. Aside from her bizarre scream, she seems helpless and afraid. You could just walk away; you need to go home and get ready for your trip. That has been the only thing keeping you going through the sluggish week. Still, you feel for the girl. You could go talk to her; it seems the boy she's with isn't able to comfort her. You realize she's new and you need a subject for your profile! Do you go to talk to her?

If you choose to talk to her, turn to page 4.

If you choose to get ready for your trip to Hawkins, Indiana, turn to page 74.

"Here, let me help." You bend down to pick up the severed bottom half of a clay man in a brown uniform and hand it to the girl. "I'm sorry for what happened. Bullies are a pain."

"Like mouth breathers?" she asks genuinely.

You laugh. "Yeah, you could call them that—a lot of bullies are mouth breathers."

"Like the boys who called Will Zombie Boy—"

"El!"

"Zombie Boy? That's a weird insult." You look at the boy, Will, quizzically. He clearly wants to avoid that conversation, so you take the hint. "You're new to the school, right?" They nod. "Have you read the *Lenora Hills Gazette*? We're doing a series of interviews with students here, just basic introduction stuff. Would you be interested in being interviewed? It's pretty cool." You start to see a glimmer of hope in her eyes.

"I don't think that's a good idea," Will blurts out. "Anyway, your boyfriend will be here over break." He starts to walk away.

"I never got your name . . . ," you say hurriedly, and reach out your hand for a handshake to stop her from leaving. She says her name is Jane. "Well, Jane, it might be cool for your boyfriend to see you being interviewed." Her eyes brighten. Bingo! You got her! "Yeah, maybe he can be in it too. We could feature a picture of you together."

Jane quickly agrees, and you make a plan to meet at Rink-O-Mania tomorrow.

Go on to the next page.

You spin me right round, baby, right round . . . The music thumps loudly at Rink-O-Mania but still doesn't overcome the sounds of laughing, squealing, and the occasional fall. The disco ball streams light around the rink. Jane leads Mike, her boyfriend, by the hand to the rink. You trail behind, trying to catch snippets of the conversation, but sticking close to Will, who follows the lovey-dovey couple miserably. "So you, Mike, and Jane all grew up together?"

"Uh, no," Will says distractedly. "Mike and I grew up together, and we met El— I mean, Jane, a few years ago, and then when Hop— I mean, when her dad died in a mall fire, she came to live with us and we moved here."

You notice Will calling Jane *El.* Will stays quiet watching Jane and Mike. There's a wistfulness in his eyes. You don't know what to make of it. Before you can ask him about the nickname, the group skates out of the rink to grab food.

"Milkshakes! Yum!" Angela approaches your table. "Where, oh where have you been hiding this handsome thing?" Before you can register what is happening, Angela pulls Jane toward the rink. Will looks panicked as one of the boys with Angela grabs a milkshake from the table and follows.

Turn to the next page.

6

You race to the rink. The lights fade, and a spotlight hits Jane as Angela leads a group skating menacingly around her. You try to push through, but it's too late! The boy throws the milkshake in Jane's face, and she falls flat on her back, to the crowd's amusement.

"Sorry you can't cry to teacher today," taunts Angela. "You'll just have to cry to your daddy instead. Oh, wait, you can't do that either." Angela skates away with a vicious grin.

You can't believe she went there, to make fun of someone's dad being dead! Jane grabs a skate. Jane marches in the direction of Angela. You chase after her. "Jane, don't!"

She smashes the skate in Angela's face. The wounded girl crashes to the floor, touches her face, sees the blood on her fingers, and cries. Mike and Will run up to Jane.

Her eyes look glazed over, as if she is somewhere else. You leave, not wanting to get more involved with Jane.

Go on to the next page.

Sunlight wakes you up. It's a bright day, and you feel hopeful about putting yesterday's events behind you. Your mom is already at work, so you're home alone, checking and double-checking that you have everything for your trip to Hawkins, when you hear a knock at the front door.

"Mom?" She probably forgot something. You open the door to find two police officers asking for you. "Is something wrong?"

"You need to come with us. You are under arrest for assault and battery," one officer says gruffly as he pulls you out the door.

"Wait! There must be a mistake. I didn't do anything!" You pull back, trying not to let them take you.

"You were listed as an accomplice by the victim. You can explain at the station."

The next thing you know, you're in the police car. There are still some hours before your flight, and you hope that you'll get back in time to make it. You didn't do anything, after all.

Turn to the next page.

"Turn to your left."

You turn and try to hold your head high, but all you want to do is scream in frustration. The camera flashes, and your mug shots are finished. The officer leads you into another sparse room to wait for transport. Nothing you said in the interview helped, and you remembered too late that you probably should have stayed quiet and waited for a lawyer or a parent. How many times did your mother tell you to know your rights and use them? You sit on a hard bench and ruminate over it.

The door opens, and another officer enters, followed by . . . Jane. *Great!* When the officer leaves, Jane leans over to you.

"I'm really sorry," Jane whispers. "I tried to tell them you didn't do anything, but they said Angela said something different."

"Save it." You turn your body away from her as best you can on the rigid bench. "Everything is ruined now anyway." The defeat washes over you. So much for spring break. Once your mom bails you out of jail, she'll put you under house arrest.

"Time to move," an officer yells through the door before walking in and leading you and Jane out to a police van. You are going to jail! As the van pulls away, you see Mike standing on the road staring after Jane.

Go on to the next page.

You rest your head against the cold metal and stare at the road through the little sealed windows. At least you'll have a more interesting column than usual for the paper.

You are jolted when the van comes to a sudden stop. Pulling yourself upright, you yell in the direction of the driver, "What's going on?"

Jane tenses up. She looks ready to spring into action. You hear the lock click, and Jane pushes through the doors, knocking over a cop and landing face-first on the asphalt. Two men grab her, and she yells.

A kind-looking man stands before her and says, "Hey, kiddo." She stops struggling and walks slowly toward the man, as if in a spell. *Jane knows him?*

"What about this kid?" A stern-looking woman in a suit with short dark hair nods in your direction.

"This is a—" Jane looks back at you, then turns to the man. "Friend."

The man sighs and nods to the other adults. The stern woman offers you a hand and leads you out of the van to a black car. Jane follows the man to a different car.

"Where are you taking me?" The woman doesn't answer. It doesn't seem like you have much choice.

Turn to the next page.

You are driven to a small diner. Inside you and Jane sit with the man. A waitress takes your order. Jane asks for pancakes.

The man turns his attention to you. "I'm Dr. Owens. So you're Jane's friend?"

"Um . . . right."

"Well, you've got a choice to make, and I'm sorry I can't give you any more details than this. I need to take Jane with me, but she won't go until she knows what will happen to you. You've got two options—you can come with us, or you can go back to Lenora but not back to your house."

"Then where would I go?"

"The Byerses' place." He sighs. "I'm sorry. I can't tell you more than that." You can see a plea in Jane's eyes; whatever is happening, she is scared. After what Jane did to Angela, is it wise to go with her? And what is happening with the Byerses?

If you choose to go with Jane, go on to next page.

If you choose to go back to Lenora, turn to page 25.

The convoy transporting you and Jane stops in front of an anonymous concrete hut with a single door. They lead you inside to an elevator. "You didn't really think we were working out of a shed, did you?" Owens asks. The elevator stops, and the doors open into a large concrete hallway. "Do you know what an ICBM is?" the doctor continues. You all proceed past guards. Your mind flashes to old black-and-white movie reels of mushroom clouds in history class. "It's a big ol' empty space, so we repurposed it to house something much more powerful than a missile: you." Owens points to Jane. You want to ask Owens what he means.

"Hello, Eleven." Jane stops dead in her tracks, her face pale as she stares at the tall man in front of her. Jane's breathing gets heavier, and goose bumps appear on her neck as the man slowly gets closer; he knows she's scared of him. "Your gifts have been stolen. I believe I know why. Let us work together again, you and I. Daughter and papa."

Turn to the next page.

"I thought Will said your father died in a mall fire?" you blurt out.

"He's not my—" Jane struggles to speak. You finally understand what it means to smell fear.

The man puts his hand on Jane's shoulder. Jane pushes him off and runs back down the hall toward the elevator.

Without thinking, you run after her. Three security officers block her way and grab her. She struggles but is no match for them. A woman in a lab coat comes up holding what looks like a gun with a syringe attached. She stabs it in Jane's neck. Jane goes limp. "What are you doing to her?" you yell.

The tall man walks up and shushes you, then bends down to cradle Jane. "Everything's going to be all right. You're home." He lifts her up and walks away.

Go on to the next page.

Owens follows the man, but you pull on his sleeve. "Who is he? What has he done to Jane?"

"He's . . . His name is Dr. Brenner. For lack of a better word, he's—a colleague." A team of lab coats swarms around Jane, changing her into a white outfit with a matching cap that has wires sticking out of it. In the middle of the room is a large machine that opens up to a pool of water. You watch as the team lays Jane in the water.

"What are they doing?" You nudge Owens, who stares at Jane with a sorrowful look.

Brenner interrupts. "We're getting her gift back. This is the only way." He walks into a control room overlooking the machine. In the room are various screens and monitors. You can see Jane inside the tank and a small television that is blank.

"What do you mean, her gift?"

Brenner flips some switches, and the machine starts to whirr. The television in the control room begins playing. You see a small child, a girl with a shaved head, in what looks like a hospital gown.

"Is that—"

"Jane, years ago," Owens answers. You look from the television screen to see Jane, the real one, on one of the monitors, floating in a pool of water. "You should go. You don't need to see this."

Turn to the next page.

14

"You brought me here, remember?" you retort, your eyes never leaving the screen. There are other kids like Jane in the video—girls and boys of various ages, all with shaved heads and loose gray gowns. They are playing in a white room with a rainbow painted on the floor and along the walls. "What is this?"

"Surveillance tape from my old lab," Brenner answers.

"Well, well, look who finally decided to join us." A blond man in a white shirt and white slacks walks up to the young Jane on the television.

"Who is that?" you ask Owens. He doesn't answer. A machine started to beep slowly as it came online and started scribbling graphs on long paper. "What's that?"

"It's keeping track of her brain and heart activity," Owens says, then turns to Brenner. "She's rejecting it."

"Give her time," Brenner says calmly.

"We shouldn't have just thrown her in like this. She's going to drown in there." The surveillance tape is paused.

"Is she seeing the same tape we are?" you ask him.

"Not exactly." Owens turns back to you. "We're watching the tape. She's . . . she's reliving it. But she's rejecting the memory." Before he can say more, someone comes into the room and pulls him out.

Go on to the next page.

Brenner turns on a microphone and speaks to Jane and plays operatic music. She can hear him, but she doesn't seem awake. Brenner is telling Jane a story, but you recall Jane's reaction to Brenner earlier. You have never seen someone so afraid. And why did Brenner keep calling her Eleven? You remember Will calling Jane El. Is it some sort of nickname?

"A memory," the real Jane says, grabbing your attention.

"Very good." Brenner nods.

"How?" she asks.

"Never mind how." You wish Brenner answered her question, eager to know what he is doing to Jane and how.

Turn to the next page.

16

"Well, well, look who finally decided to join us." The tape plays again, showing the man in white speaking in his soft voice. "Someone's a sleepyhead this morning."

"I'm sorry." You hear both Jane in the tank and the younger Jane speak at the same time. "Am I . . . in trouble?" You can hardly believe what you are witnessing. You look over at the machines to see that their scribbling has slowed down. On the television a man opens the door to the room and walks in. It's a younger Dr. Brenner. All of the kids immediately line up.

"Good morning, children."

"Good morning, Papa," they say in unison, along with the real Jane.

Hearing Jane's voice with the kids on the screen is jarring. Is she remembering what she said? You wonder if, deep in the recesses of your own mind, everything you've once said is stored somewhere just out of your reach.

"Number Twelve, please get the door. Follow me, children," the younger Brenner says. Were all the kids named numbers? Then the camera switches from inside the room to the hall just outside the door, where all the kids file out.

Owens comes back into the control room. "How's she doing?"

Brenner watches the tank calmly. "Very well. She's swimming now."

"Good." Owens stands next to him. "Because I just got off the phone with Stinson. We don't have much time."

"Well then, she'll just have to swim faster."

Go on to the next page.

You go up to Owens. "What do you mean, you don't have much time? What's going on?"

"It's a long story, kid."

"You have something better to do?" You can tell you've got him. He leads you out of the room and down the hall to another office.

"Have a seat." He points to a chair as he closes the door and sits behind a desk. "What exactly do you know about Eleven?"

"Considering I just found out her name is Eleven, not much. I met Jane—I mean, Eleven—the day before I met you." You lean back. "You're stalling. What's going on?"

"So you heard me say earlier that Eleven was powerful. But her powers are gone now. We're trying to get them back."

"Why?" Normally you would question the idea of a person having superpowers, but this lab wouldn't be here if it was a hoax.

He shows you a picture of a girl in a cheerleading uniform. "A few days ago this girl in Hawkins, Indiana, was murdered. Her name was Chrissy Cunningham. Then a boy was killed in a similar way the next day. His name was Fred Benson."

Turn to the next page.

You can't believe it. "Wait, Fred is dead?"

"How do you know him?" Owens can't hide his look of shock.

"I—I don't. I mean, I've never met him in person. He was supposed to host me when I got to Hawkins for a student journalist conference I was going to attend."

"I'm sorry you had to find out this way." Owens looks at you, concerned. "But you should be very glad you are not in Hawkins right now."

"What do you mean?"

Owens pinches the bridge of his nose as he sighs. "Chrissy and Fred weren't killed by—the—the usual ways. They were killed by someone with powers, powers like El used to have."

"So you need her to get her powers to find who killed them?"

"Not exactly." Owens leans back, his chair squeaking beneath him. "We know who killed them, but Eleven doesn't know it yet. She's the only one who can beat him, but—"

"But she needs her powers to be able to do it."

"That's right. We don't have much time. When Chrissy was killed, a gate opened."

"A gate?"

"A gate between our world and one we call the Upside Down, another dimension where the killer is. We believe that he's trying to open multiple gates, but we don't know why and we can't do anything about it without El."

Go on to the next page.

Owens runs his hand over his head. "But that's not the only reason we're short on time."

"What do you mean?"

"There are some in our government who think El is the danger, and they're looking for her. Remember when I told you that if you didn't come with us, you'd have to stay with the Byerses?" You nod. "Some government agents just attacked the Byerses' house. Jonathan, Mike, and Will are missing, along with two of the agents we posted to protect them. We know the kids haven't been captured, but other than that, we have no idea where they are. If they found the Byerses' house, it's only a matter of time before they find us."

"So Jane needs to get her powers and defeat this superpowered murderer before the government catches her?"

"I see you understand the dilemma we're in."

"So why show her some old memories? How does that help her get her powers back?"

"I have no idea. That would be Dr. Brenner's area of expertise. If I could have done this without him, trust me, I would have." It's clear there's no love lost between Owens and Brenner. Jane seemed terrified of him too.

A woman bursts into the office. "Dr. Owens, we need you."

Owens runs out the door, and you follow.

Turn to the next page.

In the control room, people are running about. The machine you saw earlier is scribbling frantically.

"What's going on?" Owens looks at Brenner.

The woman answers, "She's going into cardiac arrest."

"Okay, that's enough. Pull her out," Owens says firmly. Brenner ignores Owens. "Pull her out!" The others in the room heed Owens's command. The tank is opened and Jane is carried to a table. A doctor picks up a pair of defibrillators.

"Clear!" She presses the paddles onto Jane's chest and shocks her. There's no response. "Again!" The second shock wakes her. She sputters and coughs, blood trailing down from her nose.

"It's okay. It will take time to adjust," Brenner says soothingly to Jane. "But you're safe now." Jane suddenly grabs one of the paddles and smashes it against Brenner's face. She jumps off the table, then sprints down the hall. You chase after her. She's heading to the elevator!

"Jane! Wait!" you call out. Three security guards cut you off and surround Jane. They grab her and push her down to her knees.

You try to pull one of the guards off Jane. She screams. An overhead light bursts in a cascade of sparks as you are thrown back. Your head hits something as chaos erupts around you.

If you try to help her, turn to page 22.

If you choose to stay out of the way, turn to page 23.

In the darkness and confusion you are carried into a small room. Slowly you get up, your head throbbing. You try to think back—the last thing you remember was . . . Jane used her powers! It worked! She had them back. You swing your legs over the side of the bed and feel cold metal hit your ankle. Looking down, you see a chain hooking your right foot to the bed. "Hello? Is anyone out there? Jane? Owens?"

"They can't hear you." A voice you recognize comes over a speaker.

"Dr. Brenner, where am I? Where's Jane and Owens?"

"They are back in the other part of the lab, still working on the NINA Project, and in mourning."

"Mourning?" Your spine prickles. "Did . . . did someone else in Hawkins die?"

"Oh, no, not Hawkins. Right here." Brenner's voice is eerily calm. "Poor Eleven didn't mean to hurt her new friend, but her powers—she couldn't control them. And now she thinks you're dead. Eleven needs me now, to help her control her powers, to make sure this never happens again. She's finally home with her papa. That means you'll be staying here indefinitely."

"You can't do this!" you yell. "Aren't you her father? Don't you care about her?"

"I do care about her. I care about *all* my children."

The End

Jane screams, and the room explodes! The lightbulbs burst, sparks fall from the ceiling, and the three guards fall back. Owens catches up to you and pulls you back.

"These are her powers?"

"Some of them," he answers. "The more explosive ones."

"She has more?" Just then Jane stands and turns toward you and Owens, the shock evident on her face.

"My—my powers . . ." She looks at her hands. You remember the look on her face when she screamed at Angela at school. Was this what she was trying to do?

"Now you see it is working. Come on, Eleven." Brenner reaches out his hand. "Let's go back. You need to see one more memory. The truth."

"What I saw . . ." Jane hesitates. "The blood, so much blood. What if . . . what if I don't want to remember?" There was no blood on the surveillance tape. What is she talking about?

"You must, Eleven," Brenner says firmly. Jane takes Brenner's hand and enters the tank once more. Brenner retrieves a videotape labeled September 8, 1979, puts it into the VCR, and presses play.

"Are you sure about this?" Owens asks Brenner.

"You wanted results," Brenner says. The tension between them is palpable. Something has everyone in the room scared. When the tape plays, you see it. You glimpse a tattoo on the blond orderly's wrist and realize he is actually One, Brenner's first psychic kid. He removes something from his neck and he regains his powers. Then he kills everyone until Jane stops him, reducing him to dust.

Turn to the next page.

"Their bones . . . their eyes . . . ," you gasp.

"Same thing that happened to Chrissy and Fred." Now you know who the murderer is; it's been One all along. Jane comes out of the tank shaking, then raises her arms, and the tank begins to lift off the floor. Everyone is too stunned to speak. Then she drops the tank, shaking the ground.

"You did it, Jane." Your voice is hushed in awe. Then Jane turns and runs. You follow her into another room. She turns on the sink, sits on her bed, and covers her eyes. You try to speak to her, but she shushes you. Then she opens her eyes. "My friends are in danger! We need to go to Hawkins right now!" Brenner bursts into the room and injects Jane in the neck, and she loses consciousness.

"What are you doing?" you scream. Brenner pushes you aside and carries Jane out of the room. Just then an alarm sounds. You hear gunshots. The secret base has been found! Brenner runs out the door with Jane. You chase him up a set of stairs that leads to the surface, where a helicopter hovers over you. You duck down as bullets whizz past your head.

A bullet catches Brenner, and he falls. You try to crawl over to Jane, but the chaos around you makes it difficult. Jane slowly stands up and raises her hands. She screams and uses her powers to send the helicopter crashing to the ground in a fiery blaze. You run toward her. "Jane, we need to run!" Suddenly, you see a Surfer Boy Pizza truck speeding toward you.

Mike, Will, and Jonathan are on board with a familiar delivery guy named Argyle. As you and Jane climb in, they say their friend Max is in serious trouble.

Turn to page 45.

You find yourself in the Byerses' house with Jonathan, Will, and Mike late at night. Stinson, the woman who brought you back after the meeting with Owens, is sitting across from you, explaining the situation. A student, Chrissy Cunningham, has been murdered in Hawkins, and the town is in danger.

"I'm sorry. I guess I'm having trouble understanding any of this." Jonathan cannot hide the frustration in his voice. "I mean, what exactly is going on in Hawkins? What is responsible for these killings?"

"That's what we're trying to ascertain," Stinson answers.

"Where is El?" Mike repeats his question.

"With Owens," you answer. Mike looks at you. "I was with them. But I chose to come back here."

"Okay, so where is El, like, right now?"

"For her safety it's best you don't know; she's working on getting her powers back to help your friends in Hawkins," Stinson explains. Mike gets up in frustration.

"How long will that take?" Jonathan tries to move the conversation along.

"We don't know. It could be weeks, months?"

"Months!" Will clenches his fist. "Our friends live in Hawkins!"

"My family lives in Hawkins!" Mike slams his hands on the couch.

"And I'll work to contain the situation until Eleven is ready. In the meantime, it is vitally important that you do not speak to anyone about this." Mike tries to say something, but she cuts him off.

Turn to the next page.

"There are factions in our government who are working directly against Eleven, who are, in fact, searching for her as we speak. We can't risk contact. If Eleven is jeopardized, so are your friends, and so is your family. Eleven trusted us; now we're asking the same of you." Stinson looks at Mike. She takes a breath. "Agents Harmon and Wallace will be here to protect you. This is for you." She pulls a letter out of her jacket pocket and hands it to Mike. He immediately goes upstairs to read it. Stinson leaves, and you are now stuck under house arrest.

The morning passes quickly into afternoon. Harmon and Wallace sit in front of the TV watching golf for most of the day. You head upstairs and knock on Will's door. "Come in," he calls. Inside Will is tossing a ball while Mike sits on the bed.

"I just don't think they thought this through." Will says as he paces. "If this goes on for months and people can't get ahold of us, they're gonna totally freak out."

"Yeah, my mom's going to wonder where I am when I don't come back from spring break," you say as you sit on the floor and lean against a wall.

"Yeah," Mike mumbles, staring at the letter he received from Jane last night.

Will looks at him sadly. "You can keep staring at it, but it's not going to change, right?"

Jonathan comes into the room. "We can't stay here." He closes the door behind him.

Go on to the next page.

"Listen." He grabs Will's desk chair and sits. "Let's assume Owens's friends are telling the truth. We can't contact Hawkins without alerting the military and putting El in danger. Fine. Then we'll just go to them."

"Go to Hawkins?" Mike leans in closer.

"How?" Will asks. "We don't have a car or money."

"We'll hail ourselves a ride." He holds up a coupon for Surfer Boy Pizza. Mike and Will nod in agreement, then go down to arrange a pizza delivery.

"Look, if you want to stay here, that's fine. We need to get to Hawkins to help our friends," Jonathan says, looking at you. You're not sure what to do. Part of you knows that staying here is safer than leaving, and you don't owe anything to Jane or the rest of them. Then again, did Jane's stunt at Rink-O-Mania save you from a worse fate in Hawkins? According to the Surfer Boy Pizza advertisements, you've got thirty minutes or less to make your decision.

Turn to the next page.

28

The doorbell rings. Pizza's here. You still haven't made up your mind. The boys are itching to get out of the house and on their way to Hawkins. *Bang!* You hear a gunshot.

"What the hell was that?" Jonathan runs toward the bedroom door. "Stay here!" He runs into the hall, and more gunshots follow. "We gotta go!" he yells. The window breaks, and you see someone pushing their way in. Jonathan grabs Will and pulls him into the hall. You and Mike follow. "Move! Move!"

Harmon gestures to you to run toward him as he gives you cover. "Follow me!" Harmon yells over the gunfire. He moves toward the back door, but it bursts open. More soldiers come through, guns blazing. Harmon is limping as he grabs you and shoves a pen in your hand. "Don't lose this! Call NINA!"

"The pizza truck!" Jonathan yells. He runs toward it and bangs on the driver's window. "Stop the car!"

It's Argyle in the driver's seat. "The hell is going on? Is that real blood?" You all jump into the truck. Jonathan gets in and slams the side door.

"Drive!" you yell at Argyle. He speeds off.

Go on to the next page.

You look up to see a car chasing you. The others see it too. "Argyle, you need to get off the road now!" Jonathan yells.

"Get off the road!" you yell. He jerks the wheel to the side, into the desert night.

After losing the attackers, you stop in a junkyard. Argyle stays in the truck. Mike and Will sit on a broken car talking, holding the pen Harmon gave you. No one knows who Nina is. Jonathan looks sick, staring at nothing.

"I'm going for a walk," you tell him. He nods. You get up to the road, pick a direction, and start moving. Somehow a fluff piece for the school paper turned into you getting arrested, then being abducted by some agents, put under house arrest, and escaping a gunfight. You want to throw up. How did things go so wrong? In the bright sun, something glints in the distance. You hold your hand up to shade your eyes. It's a phone booth. You dig in your pockets and find some coins, enough to make one call. If only you could get in touch with Stinson. You slap your side. Of course! Somehow Stinson knew about the transport to the jail for you and Jane. Maybe she knows someone at the jail? It's a long shot, but it could be worth it. You think of your mom; she's probably waiting to hear from you, thinking you're in Hawkins.

If you choose to call the jail, turn to the next page.

If you choose to call your mom, turn to page 64.

As much as you want to reassure your mom that you're okay, there's something bigger at stake. It's worth a shot. You go into the phone booth and find a copy of the Yellow Pages. You look up the number for the jail, insert the coins, and dial. Someone picks up!

"Please give the identification number for the person you wish to call," the voice on the other end says in a bored drawl.

"I don't have an identification number, but her name is Stinson."

"First name?"

"I—I don't know. Just Stinson. She's a friend of Owens."

"There's no record of a Stinson or Owens being held here."

"No, no, she's not a prisoner!"

"We don't allow calls to guards on this line. Please hang up and—"

"No, she's not a guard either. She's an agent. I need to talk to her—"

"No crank calls, kid." The line goes dead. You slam the phone on the receiver. Dead end. You rip the page out of the phone book and are about to tear it into pieces, then stop yourself and put it in your pocket instead. You take a deep breath and return to the others. When you get back, the boys are jumping around with smiles on their faces.

"What happened?" You run up to them.

"We got it! The number for NINA! We had it the whole time! It was in the pen!" Mike holds up a slip of paper with a number on it. Maybe your walk wasn't a waste of time!

"There's a phone just a short walk from here!" Everyone gets in the truck to drive to the phone booth. You all surround the booth as Will reads the number to Mike, who dials.

Go on to the next page.

"Is it ringing?" Will asks.

Mike shakes his head. "No, it's just making weird sounds." He hands the phone to Will. "Does this sound familiar?"

Will listens. "War games . . . We're not calling a person. We're calling a computer."

Mike runs to the passenger side of the truck and grabs a map from the glove compartment. "If it's a computer, we need a hacker to find it. And the only hacker I know lives in Utah."

"Utah?" you and Jonathan both ask.

"Salt Lake City, to be precise," Mike continues.

"Oh my god." Will smiles. Everyone gets in the car, and you're off to Utah!

"So now that we have time," you say, sitting with Mike and Will in the back, "tell me everything." They both look at you, unsure. "After everything that's happened in the last twenty-four hours, I think I deserve to know what's going on."

"Right now I wish Dustin was here to tell it," Mike mumbled. "He's one of our friends; actually, the person we're going to see is his girlfriend, Suzie. It was me, El, Dustin, and our other friend Lucas who found Will when he went missing."

"You went missing?" You look at him, recalling the day you met Jane, when she mentioned Will had been bullied. The name Zombie Boy comes back to you. "Okay, start from there."

Turn to the next page.

32

If it weren't for what you just went through, you would think this story was made up. You can't deny the truth now. Will went missing; that was when Mike and his friends found Jane, who escaped from a lab in Hawkins after accidentally opening a gate to another dimension, the Upside Down. Right now, you feel upside down. The creatures on the other side scare you. Is this what was waiting for you in Hawkins?

"If the gate the Russians made was closed by Jane or El, then what's going on in Hawkins now?"

"Your guess is as good as ours," Will says.

"You said the Upside Down had an alternate Hawkins. Do you think there's an alternate Lenora there?" You wonder how far this danger can spread.

"I don't know. I've only been in the Upside Down in Hawkins." Will gives you a sympathetic look.

Jonathan stops the truck and switches places with Argyle so he can drive for the next few hours. You lie down in the back and fall asleep instantly.

Go on to the next page.

You wake up as Jonathan is parking in front of a large house. You can hear the chaos inside. You step out of the truck and stretch your legs; the hours of sitting have been rough. You've made it to Salt Lake City, Utah, and are presumably at Suzie's house.

"I can't feel my butt," Argyle says as he gets out of the truck. "Can you guys feel your butts?"

"Everyone needs to be on their best behavior," Jonathan says as you walk to the front door.

"Why'd you look at me when you said that?" Argyle catches up to Jonathan.

"They're really religious," Mike explains.

"Yeah, and I'm like super spiritual, dude," Argyle insists.

"Yeah, I think they're spiritual too, just in a different way." Mike knocks on the door. It swings open, and you see a small child dressed only in shorts and covered in paint, holding a toy bow and arrow. "Oh, hey. Is Suzie here?" The kid shrieks and shoots an arrow, hitting Mike right between the eyes. You walk in and see an army of kids wreaking havoc; the entire house is a mess. The small archer runs toward a circuit breaker and flips a power switch.

"Cornelius!" An older girl runs to the breaker and flips it back. "I told you this is not a toy!" She locks eyes with Argyle. "Who the hell are you?"

"We're looking for Suzie," you cut in before Argyle introduces himself.

"Third floor, second door on your left." It takes Argyle a bit to pull himself away from her.

Turn to the next page.

"Okay," Suzie says after hearing the cover story, "that is a lot to process. I mean, that might be seriously the craziest thing I've ever heard." You choke down a laugh; if only she knew. "So I dial into this computer and find a location to something called NINA Project, and the NINA Project is a code for a video game console."

"And it's for Dustin," Will adds.

"I would do anything for my Dustybun." She sighs. "But I'm afraid there's been an unfortunate development. I'm grounded and don't have my computer anymore."

"Where is it?" you ask. Did you really come all this way for nothing?

"Father has it in his study." Suzie wrings her hands. The power dims and then comes back, and you can hear the oldest sister yelling at Cornelius again. "Actually, I might have an idea."

You hide with the others, waiting for the plan to start. Cornelius hits the breaker, shutting the power off. The study door opens, and Suzie's father comes out and goes down the stairs. The others slip into the study, but the power comes back too quickly! You run down the stairs and see that he has already made it to the breaker and is about to go back to his study. You need to think quickly. You see some cooking oil near you, and some skates left out.

If you choose to start a fire, go on to the next page.

If you choose to try to trip him, turn to page 47.

You grab the cooking oil, a trash can, and a match, then run back to the foot of the stairs. Pouring some cooking oil into the partially full trash can, you light a match and then drop it in. The entire thing ignites, and then you run up the stairs.

You pound on the door. "You guys need to hurry! We're running out of time!" You hear yelling downstairs. The fire has caught their attention. Suzie's father screams at the kids to get away from the fire. It won't be long before he grabs the extinguisher to put it out. "Come on! Come on!"

The door to the study flies open, and they rush out just as her father comes up the stairs. You race out of the house with the others. Suzie hands you a printout, smiling. You look at it and see the coordinates. "It worked!"

"Thanks to you," she says. "You bought us enough time. Now, if you'll excuse me, I have to deal with Cornelius." Her jaw drops. You turn to see Argyle appear out of the truck, with Suzie's sister looking disheveled. You quickly turn back to Suzie. "Thank you, Suzie. How do we get in touch with you if we need more help?"

She writes her number on the printed paper and smiles again. "Say hi to my Dustybun for me."

Before long you're on the road again, this time heading to Nevada with the coordinates Suzie obtained.

"We're going to do it," you say excitedly. "We're going to find the NINA Project!"

Turn to the next page.

After hours of driving, you've finally hit the border between Nevada and Utah. Jonathan pulls up to a gas station to fill the tank, and you take the chance to stretch. You walk into the convenience store, looking around for snacks. You grab a few bags of chips, some Airheads, Mars Men, Nerds, and Razzles, along with a few Cokes to help keep Jonathan and Argyle awake for the drive, and a couple of extra gas canisters for the road. You go up to the counter and pay for it all. "Pretty far for a pizza delivery . . . ," the clerk says.

You are about to exit the store when you notice another car. The car is suspiciously nondescript, but what catches your eyes is the person in the passenger seat holding binoculars pointed at the truck. Are you being followed? You hold up your snacks to block your face as you struggle to walk calmly to the truck. Jonathan has just finished filling the tank.

"Jonathan," you whisper, throwing the snacks and gas canisters into the back, "I think we're being watched."

"Watched?" He looks exhausted, like he could fall asleep on his feet at any second.

You tilt your head toward the other car, and he takes a peek. "Yeah, I don't think those are friends of Stinson. They're probably trying to follow us to NINA." Jonathan turns to the others. "We need to leave now."

Go on to the next page.

Argyle gets in the driver's seat and starts the truck. The other car starts its engine too.

"Argyle, when you get back on the road, go left," you tell him. He looks confused.

"I'm pretty sure Nevada is the other way, my dude."

"We can't let them know what direction we're going in." You give the same subtle nod toward the other car you gave Jonathan. Argyle turns to look. "Don't look at them! Jeez! We're being followed."

"Oh, right." Argyle nods. "Wait, are those the bad government dudes?" His eyes widen.

"Just go left, okay? And drive normally," Jonathan tells him.

Argyle pulls out of the gas station and turns. After a few seconds, the other car follows, maintaining distance.

"Guys . . . ," Will calls out, looking out the back of the truck. "There's another car now."

You turn to see the other lane taken up by a car matching the speed of the first one. Behind them you spot another. Three cars, all following you away from NINA.

"We can't keep going in this direction. We're losing time to get to El." Mike grabs your shoulder. He's right. If they are just following, then they'll keep at it until they realize you're taking them for a ride. "We need to lose them."

"Won't they know that we know that they know that we know we're being followed?" Argyle looks in the rearview mirror.

"What?" the rest of you ask in unison.

Argyle tilts his head. "I'm saying that if we try to run, won't the bad government dudes try to catch us?" It's a good point. So far the other cars aren't trying to overtake the truck because they don't believe you know you're being followed.

Turn to the next page.

38

The cars have been following you for fifteen minutes, and there is no sign of them letting up. Mike is frustrated as the truck gets farther and farther away from El. If they know that Argyle is leading them away from Jane, they haven't made any move yet.

"So we know they're determined to keep following us until we take them to El, right?" You sneak a glance at the three black cars still following from a distance.

"Yeah, so?" Jonathan turns to look at you. "Are you saying you have an idea?"

"Not exactly. But as Sherlock Holmes would say, 'The world is full of obvious things which nobody by any chance ever observes.'"

"So what's obvious?"

"They need to follow us. That means they have no idea where El is, which is a good thing. That means there's more pressure on us to not get caught. If they do catch us, who knows how they might try to get that information out of us."

"Okay, these things are all obvious, but how does it help now?"

"I think we risk it. I think we try to lose them. This weird equilibrium isn't helping us or them. We need to play our hand and deal with the consequences." You see Argyle's lighter lying on the ground, then look at the gas canisters you bought. "We need a way to make sure that once we run, they can't follow."

"We're on a highway with nothing around." Will points out the window. "What's going to stop them from just following us?"

"What about that?" Argyle nods toward a sign for a nearby city.

Go on to the next page.

"A city could provide more cover," you agree.

"You don't think they'd risk chasing us in the city? Remember what they did at the house. I don't think they care if they hurt anyone else."

"But Will's right. There's nothing out here to help us lose them," Mike counters.

You look back at the gas canister and lighter.

"A little pyrotechnics could help," you say.

The others catch your meaning. "And what if you blow us up in the process?" Will taps the gas canister. "Also, how do we know they won't just drive through the fire like in movies?"

It's clear the choice is being left up to you. A city does offer more places to hide, but that's only if you can get away.

"You sure you can lose them, Argyle?"

"No worries, I can do it. I've had to drive away from the cops in Lenora a bunch. And I've only been caught a few times."

If you choose to let Argyle try to lose them, turn to page 41.

If you choose to set the gas canister on fire, turn to page 44.

"Hold on, brochachos!" Argyle floors the pedal, and the speed knocks you back. You twist and get onto your hands and knees to look out the rear window. The other cars speed up. The chase is on!

Argyle swerves the truck through the exit, not bothering to obey the stop signs. The government cars continue giving chase. "They're still on us, Argyle!"

Argyle doesn't respond, too busy concentrating on the road ahead. You are now in the city, and other cars honk and swerve off the road as Argyle pushes his way through, running red lights and making sharp turns that lift the truck at times. It's a cacophony of screams as Argyle maneuvers the truck through the streets. A siren blares.

"Cops!" You kick yourself for forgetting that local law enforcement exists. Argyle's driving like a maniac attracts them, and they give chase along with the bad government dudes. "Argyle, cops!"

"I know! I know!" He swerves the truck to the right, hopping onto the sidewalk and crashing the truck into a lamppost. Your head hits the seat in front of you, and you black out.

Turn to the next page.

The chair you are cuffed to is hard and cold. You twist to try to make yourself more comfortable as you sit alone in the interrogation room. You are the last one to be interviewed by Colonel Sullivan, an intimidating man hell-bent on getting El. Your stomach drops as the door opens and he steps in.

"I could make this easy on you." He sits down. "I know you just happened to be in the wrong place at the wrong time. You only just met these people, and I'm sure they've misled you. The girl is dangerous and a threat to national security."

"I don't believe you." You sit up straight. "How can she be a threat when she doesn't even have her powers anymore?"

"Who told you that?" The colonel looks skeptical, but you can tell he's already heard this bit of information. Not even a hint of surprise shows on his face.

"I saw her trying to use her powers at school, and it didn't work. If she had her powers, she wouldn't have had to hit that girl in the face with a skate."

"You don't know what she's capable of, what she has done in the past." Just then the door opens, and a uniformed man steps in. He leans toward the colonel and whispers something. "It seems I have no need to talk to you anymore. We've found your map."

"Wh-what map?" You try to sound convincing, but the shock overcomes you. He knows where El is.

Go on to the next page.

Sitting in your cell across from Jane's, you see her trying to claw at the shock collar around her neck as it pulses her with pain. It's no use. She can't get it off. Mike is in the cell next to hers, begging her to stop. You crane your neck to see the hall of cells. Argyle, Jonathan, Will, Mike, Jane, Dr. Owens, and another man you've learned is Jane's "Papa," Dr. Brenner, are all in individual cells.

Owens had begged the colonel to spare Jane at least for a few more days, to prove she is innocent of the murders in Hawkins. You have no communication with the outside world, so none of you know what is happening in Hawkins. Jane has tried to use her powers to see her old freinds, but it's impossible now. You don't understand it, but somehow they were able to implant something into her to stop her powers.

Footsteps echo as a row of guards comes in. One by one they open the cell doors and walk each of you out. You are the last to exit your cell and be taken to another room. You brace yourself for the end. When you walk in, you see everyone is seated in front of a television, showing what looks like the aftermath of an earthquake. Tears are streaming down their faces. Your cuffs are unlocked, and you notice Jane's shock collar is off. "What happened?"

"Gone." Jane's voice is barely audible.

"Gone? What do you mean, gone?"

"Hawkins . . . everyone." Will's voice breaks. "They lost."

The End

"Just trust me!" you yell. "Take the next exit when I tell you!" You open the back of the pizza truck, dragging the gas tank with you. You unscrew the top and dump the contents onto the road, shaking it so it covers more space. "Ready? Now!" As Argyle turns onto the exit, you light the gas. The road explodes into flame, blocking the cars from following. Everyone yells in amazement! It worked! You're safe for now.

"It should be up on our right," Mike says, referring to the map. You've been on the road for hours.

"There's nothing out here," Jonathan answers. "You sure you got your measurements right?"

"Suzie's a genius, Jonathan," Will reminds him.

Jonathan hits the brakes, and Argyle wakes with a jolt. He jumps out of the truck and opens the side door, taking the map from Mike. They go over the coordinates as Argyle walks around the desert, yelling for "Nina," who he is convinced is a small woman.

"Argyle! Shut up!" You march over to him and trip, falling face-first into the dirt.

"Holy macaroni." Argyle helps you up. You both see it—tire tracks. You tell the others, and everyone jumps into the truck and follows the tracks. You hear a thrumming sound—up ahead is a helicopter! The military found El! Jonathan steps on it. You hear gunshots—they're shooting at El! You can see her raise her hands, and then the helicopter crashes down, exploding into a fiery ball. When you get closer, you see El kneeling next to a man taking his last breath. Mike jumps out of the truck and pulls her away. You found El just in time!

Go on to the next page.

"We need to get to Hawkins now!" Jane yells as the pizza truck speeds away.

"What?" Jonathan calls back. "It'll take days to drive there."

"We don't have days! Everyone is in danger!" You turn to see Jane looking at a sign advertising a scenic route. "A piggyback." She looks at you. You see the sign has a small girl riding on her mother's back. "I have a way." Jane turns to the others. "A way to protect Max from here. When One attacks, he'll be in Max's mind. She can carry me to Vecna. I can piggyback."

"Mind fight . . . righteous." Argyle nods.

"A bathtub would help," Jane continues.

"Yeah, gotta be clean to enter the mind," Argyle adds.

"What? No, no, it's a sensory deprivation tank," Mike corrects him.

"We'd need a lot of salt," Will answers. "How are we going to get that much salt?"

"Well, how much salt we talking, my dudes?" Argyle smiles. "I know of a magical place that has all your needs, my superpowered friend."

If someone told you the fate of the world would be decided in a pizza place, you wouldn't believe it. But here you are, stirring salt into an unplugged pizza dough freezer filled with water. Argyle was right—the Surfer Boy Pizza kitchens had more than enough salt. While you, Jonathan, and Will work on setting up the tank, Argyle makes a pizza. He hands each of you a slice.

"Eww, pineapple?" you groan.

"Try before you deny." He smiles and walks away. Behind you, you can hear Will and Jonathan whispering. You turn to see them hugging and look away before they see you.

Turn to the next page.

"Are we almost done?" you ask. Jonathan has been meticulous about the amount of salt needed. He nods. You call out to Mike and Jane: "It's time."

Jane puts on the glasses Mike made for her out of a pizza box and she gets into the tank, salty enough to let her float in the small space. The radio is tuned to static. After a few seconds, the lights in the pizza place begin to flicker. "Wild," Argyle gasps.

"I found them," Jane says. "Max, I'm coming. I'm coming, just hold on a little longer." The lights are erratic.

"What's happening?" Mike asks.

"I think I am in a memory," she answers. "A Max memory. I don't see her, but she's here. She has to be here." You can barely breathe as you wait. "I found her, but she's young. She can't see me, can't hear me. There is something that doesn't fit. I think it is another memory . . . Max, are you okay?" The lights go wild; it seems like anything with electricity is buzzing. Jane convulses and gasps for air.

"El? El? Can you hear me?" Mike yells. "Help me! Help me!" You grab Jane and help to lift her out of the freezer and onto a table. "El? Can you hear me?"

"Don't stop, Mike," Will encourages him. "You're the heart!"

"El," he continues, "I don't know if you can hear this, but I want you to know that I'm here, and I love you! You're my superhero! You can do anything! But right now you just have to fight!" The lights flare more erratically. After what feels like years, the lights stop and Jane opens her eyes.

"I—I think we lost," she whispers, looking teary-eyed at Mike. No one has any words.

The End

You grab the skates and push them in his path as he walks out of the kitchen. He stumbles but grabs the doorway to catch himself. It didn't work! He goes back up the stairs. You yell, "Time's up!" hoping they can hear you, but Suzie's squeal and her father's yelling signal your defeat.

"Now what?" Mike puts his head in his hands. Outside, you sit with the others on the sidewalk. Suzie will probably be banned from computers until she moves out, and without another genius hacker available, it's impossible to get the address.

"What if we went straight to Hawkins?" Will suggests.

"Without El?" Mike looks at him crossly. "When the government is trying to find her?"

"I don't know. We can't go back to Lenora. I'm just trying to come up with something." Will's eyes water slightly, but Mike doesn't seem to notice.

"No! We need to find El!"

"Well, the only person who knows where she is is Owens, and we can't contact him."

You pull out the ripped yellow page from your pocket. You are desperate. "Get me to a pay phone. I have an idea." You explain what you're thinking.

"What if they track our location?" Mike says.

"They didn't last time," you insist. "Anyway, do you have any better ideas?" That ends the debate quickly. Argyle drives around until he finds a pay phone outside a gas station. He parks and you get out; the others follow you. You slip in some coins and dial the number. After a few rings, someone picks up.

Turn to the next page.

"Please give the identification number for the person you wish to call." The voice on the line is different.

"I'd like to speak to Agent Stinson, please." You hold your breath.

"Please hold while I connect you." Your heart pounds as the phone rings once, twice, a third time.

"This is Stinson." You hear the familiar voice. "I'm glad you called back; we hoped you would."

"Prove this is you," you say, not wanting to be caught.

"I was about to ask you the same question." She sounds slightly amused.

"You first."

"I met you at a diner when Dr. Owens and I intercepted your transport. You were given the choice to go with Eleven or return to Lenora. You chose the latter. Now it's your turn. When I was at the Byerses' house, I gave Mike Wheeler a note from Eleven. The note had one sentence in it."

You turn to Mike. "What was in the letter Eleven gave you?"

"What? Why do you need to know that? It's private."

"She needs us to prove we're really us," you say, trying to hurry him along.

"It said, 'Dear Mike, I have gone to become a superhero again. From, El.'" You quickly repeat the words to Stinson. "We need a pickup right now. The Byerses' house was attacked."

"Where are you?" You give her a location and hang up. Now you wait.

Go on to the next page.

After waiting nervously for two hours in the outlet mall parking lot, you see a fleet of cars swerve into the gas station. A door opens and Stinson emerges. It worked! Stinson looks around for you, only seeing Argyle's pizza truck. You step out and wave. She sees you. The others come out, and you cross the street together.

Stinson informs you that she has made arrangements to get you to NINA, but you will need to leave the truck behind. Argyle is not too happy about it.

"What if we, like, hang the truck from the helicopter?" Argyle tries to negotiate with Stinson to bring the Surfer Boy pizza truck. "We could carry it to this Nina lady."

"Again . . ." Stinson is losing her patience. None of you intervene, instead choosing to enjoy the show. "We cannot carry the truck with us. We can, however, make sure that the truck gets back to Lenora safely."

Jonathan steps up. "Argyle, I think you just need to relax, okay?"

Argyle nods. "Purple palm tree delight?"

Jonathan nods too. "Yes, purple palm tree delight! Go! Go! Go!" Argyle runs to the truck. "Give him ten minutes," Jonathan says to Stinson, who rolls her eyes. With that taken care of, you all get in the car and drive to an airfield, transferring to a helicopter. It's happening! You're finally getting to NINA.

Turn to the next page.

Mike jumps out of the helicopter as soon as it touches down, running to the people there to greet you. You recognize Owens. "Where's El?" you hear Mike shout over the thrum of the helicopter. As soon as you all disembark, it takes off. You're in the middle of the desert. The only sign of human presence is something that looks like a concrete shed. Owens opens the door.

"I'll answer all your questions, but we need to get inside." You follow Owens down the stairs and into an elevator. The elevator takes you deep underground. When the elevator doors open, you stare into a series of tunnels. Owens leads the way. "Welcome to Project NINA," he says. You stare in amazement at the number of armed personnel and scientists. "All these people are here to help Eleven," Owens explains. Most people greet you as you pass, but you see someone pull back. At the end of the hall you see a room with a large metal capsule in it.

"Is that a sensory deprivation tank?" Mike asks.

"Good eye, kid. It's a little more than that, but yes, Eleven does float around in it." He smiles. You hear footsteps behind you and turn. "Mike, you may remember Dr. Brenner."

"What is he doing here?" Mike steps toward the man. "He's supposed to be dead!" Mike's reaction is shared by Jonathan and Will. You and Argyle are clueless.

"Dr. Brenner is the expert in this field. We need him to help Eleven."

"No!" Mike yells. "He hurt El! He tortured her, experimented on her, tried to keep her imprisoned. He shouldn't be here!"

"I see this is not the time for introductions." Dr. Brenner bows his head and leaves the room.

Go on to the next page.

"Where's El? I need to see her now."

"Mike?" You hear a quiet voice behind you. Mike turns and embraces El. She holds him tightly. Then she embraces Will and Jonathan, and even Argyle. She comes up to you and says, "Thank you." You nod, unsure what to do.

Mike takes her hand. "Brenner's here."

"I know," El says. You turn to see Dr. Brenner still moving down the hall. You slip out of the room while El, Mike, and the others swap stories about what has happened since leaving Lenora. You follow Brenner around a corner and catch him speaking to a guard.

"We need to move Eleven out of here, now," he whispers. The guard nods and walks away. You duck behind the corner before Brenner sees you and run back to the others.

When you make it to the room with the tank, you push through the gang to Owens. "We need to talk. All of us. Somewhere private. Now." Owens is taken aback but leads you to an office elsewhere in the bunker, and the others follow. "I overheard Brenner speaking to a guard. He wants to move El somewhere."

"But I don't have my powers back yet." El looks at Mike, whose worry shows.

"He can't be trusted," Mike reiterates.

"Hold on," Owens says. "He's not going to move Eleven without finishing this project. He needs her to have her powers back just like the rest of us."

"So what do you want us to do? Wait like sitting ducks for him to make a move?" Mike balls his fist. That's exactly what Owens's plan is.

Turn to the next page.

52

The next morning, El is up and ready for another round in the tank. The rest of you sit in the control room with Owens and Brenner. You watch Brenner like a hawk, tensing at his every movement.

"Are you sure this is necessary?" Owens says to him.

"You wanted results," Brenner says casually. There are monitors around the room, recording Jane inside the tank. Brenner takes a VHS tape and puts it in a VCR connected to a small television. "These children shouldn't be here."

"We're not leaving El," Mike says firmly. Owens leaves the room momentarily, and Brenner presses play on the VCR.

It's surveillance footage of a lab. A tall man dressed in white walks down the hall. He attacks everyone in his way. It's a bloodbath—screams reach a fever pitch until it gets eerily quiet. He spares no one. The last room he enters is filled with children of different ages, all in hospital gowns. He makes quick work of them, splitting their bones, blood pouring from their sunken eyes. You feel sick. He has one of the older boys spread out like he's on a crucifix. That's when you see someone come in the doors. It is a small child with a shaved head.

"Is that El?" Will whispers. Owens nods. The boy is killed like the others, and then the man turns to El.

"What is this?" you ask in a hushed voice.

"Eleven's past," Brenner answers coldly. You can't take your eyes off the television.

Go on to the next page.

El turns and tries to run out the doors, but they won't budge. He gets closer to her and touches her chin. "Why do you cry for them, Eleven? After everything they did to you? You think you need them, but you don't. Oh, but I know you're just scared. I was scared once too. I know what it's like to be different. To be alone in this world." He wipes a tear from Eleven's face, and she flinches.

"Like you, I didn't fit in with the other children. Something was wrong with me. All the teachers and the doctors said I was broken." Eleven trembles as he speaks. "My parents thought a change of scenery, a fresh start in Hawkins, might just cure me. It was absurd. As if the world would be any different here." He walks toward the mirror. "But then, to my surprise, our new home provided a discovery, and a sense of purpose. I uncovered a nest of black widows living inside a vent. They were endlessly fascinating. More than that, I found a great comfort in them. A kinship. Like me, they are solitary creatures. And deeply misunderstood. They are gods of our world. The most important of all predators."

Turn to the next page.

54

The tape continues: "Where others saw order, I saw a straitjacket. A cruel, oppressive world, dictated by made-up rules. Seconds, minutes, hours, days, weeks, months, years, decades. Each life a faded, lesser copy of the one before. Wake up, eat, work, sleep, reproduce, and die. Everyone is just waiting for it all to be over. I could not do that. I could not close off my mind and join in the madness. I could not pretend. And I realized I didn't have to. I could make my own rules. I showed my parents who they really were. I held up a mirror. My mother somehow knew it was I who was holding up that mirror, and she despised me for it. She called a doctor, an expert. She wanted him to lock me away, to fix me, even though it wasn't I who was broken. It was them. And so she left me with no choice but to act. To break free. I killed her first. With each life I took, I grew stronger. More powerful. They were becoming a part of me. But I was still a child. I did not yet know my limits, and it nearly killed me."

Go on to the next page.

"I woke up from my coma only to find myself placed in the care of a doctor, the very doctor I had hoped to escape, Dr. Martin Brenner. He began a program, and soon others were born. You were born. And I am so glad you were, Eleven." Jane turns away from him and looks at the corpses around her. "They're not gone, Eleven. They're still with me. In here." He points to his mind. "If you come with me, for the first time in your life, you will be free. Join me."

"No." El flings the man back. He hits the mirror and falls to the ground. He gets up. They both use their powers, holding their hands up as the lights flicker all around them. El starts to slide back, then finds her footing. She is thrown back, hitting the door and then falling to the ground. El is dragged across the floor, then lifted into the air, screaming. He turns her to face him. "It wasn't supposed to end like this!" El screams. He has her pinned with his powers. El manages to move her head to look directly at him, then raises her arms. With a scream, she pushes him back through the mirror into a room behind it. You turn away from the television to see the lights all around you flickering. It's happening in the real world! You turn back to the screen to see the man pinned up against the wall by El. She steps closer and screams, reaching an arm out. The man cries out in pain, a light emanates from his torso, and you watch him slowly disintegrate. A fleshy, pulsing hole opens in the wall behind them.

"A gate," Jonathan whispers. "She sent him to the Upside Down."

Turn to the next page.

56

Just then a younger Brenner enters the room. "What have you done?" El collapses. The tape ends. A machine whirrs, beeping sounds all around you.

"Get her out of there!" Owens yells.

"What's happening?" Mike rushes to the observation window. The tank is opened and El is pulled out and placed on a table. Defibrillators are readied. Mike rushes to her side. You watch the woman count down and then shock El. She opens her eyes.

"Eleven, can you hear us?" Owens asks. She sits up and turns to Mike. He helps her down from the table, and she faces the tank. She raises an arm and closes her eyes, and the lights begin to flicker. You hear screeching and metal breaking. She lifts the tank in the air, all the way to the ceiling, holds it there, then returns it gently back in its place.

"Man, that was super cool." Argyle's voice booms in the silence. El runs from the room. You all follow, but she enters another room and shuts the door. You hear water running.

"She's looking for our friends in Hawkins," Will explains.

"What did you see?" Jonathan takes her hands when she comes out the room.

"They—they are going to fight him. They are going to go to the Upside Down." Jonathan curses loudly.

"They were at Max's," El says.

Will grabs a phone and dials. "Hello? Max? . . . It's Will. Whatever you're planning, stop! We're on our way. No, listen, don't do anything until we get there!"

"You can't take her. She's not ready," Brenner protests.

Owens turns to Brenner. "And exactly where were you planning to take her? Or did you think we didn't know?" Brenner is shocked as guards loyal to Owens take him away.

Go on to the next page.

During the flight over to Hawkins, El fills you all in on the plan she overheard. Stinson says it's a good one, but they will need more muscle. She says she'll have agents join. Mike has fallen asleep in his seat. El gets up and sits next to you.

"Thank you," she says quietly. "Mike told me about how you helped." You nod.

"I have a question," you say. "It's probably stupid—"

"What is it?"

"What do you want me to call you? I met you as Jane, but everyone here calls you Eleven."

"We're friends. Call me El."

It takes four hours to get to Hawkins by private plane. When you get off the plane, you are greeted on the tarmac by faces you don't know. There are tears and hugs. You and Argyle stand off to the side, then introductions are made. A brunette named Nancy goes over the plan and divides up the teams. Stinson brings in some agents who pack a heavy arsenal of weapons. Nancy assigns you to the attack team.

El pulls you aside, and then Will. Each of them has a request. El wants you to look out for Max as part of the bait team, since she'll be One's target. Will wants you to look out for Mike as part of the distract team, because he worries Mike might do something rash. You go to Nancy and tell her your decision.

If you choose to go with the bait team to the Creel house, turn to the next page.

If you choose to stick with the distract team in the Upside Down, turn to page 59.

If you choose to go with the attack team, turn to page 63.

58

You choose to go with the bait team, staying in the real world. Your job is to keep Max safe while she lures One to her, leaving his body vulnerable. You don't completely understand, but you know that the main thing is that if Max doesn't come out of her trance, you need to play a particular Kate Bush song to wake her up. You are at One's childhood home with Will, Lucas, and his younger sister Erica, as well as two agents who are armed. This is where One killed his family and framed his father. Erica finds you and holds up a notepad: *Found Vecna.* You nod and follow her. The battle is about to begin.

One month later.
"Hello? Hello? Is anyone there? This is the Lenora party, over." It took you a while, but you've invested in a large radio tower to be able to reach your friends in Hawkins.

"This is the Hawkins party. We read you loud and clear. Over." You hear Dustin's voice. This has become a part of your life since returning to Lenora. Argyle shifts in his seat, a haze clinging to him. One—or Vecna, as the Hawkins gang calls him—was beaten. Each team was successful with their part, but Vecna is still out there plotting his next move. You meet with the others over the radio to figure out how to defeat him. You plan on visiting Hawkins this summer.

"Who's there with you? Over."

"Everyone," Dustin says.

"Awesome," you respond. "I've got Argyle. We're ready. Over."

The End

You are holding on to the bedsheets that the Hawkins gang has been using as a rope in and out of the gate to the Upside Down in Eddie's trailer. The others are waiting for you. You jump up and pull yourself through, feeling gravity shift, dropping you into a fall. You land on a mattress. "That. Was. Incredible."

Jonathan helps you up. The Upside Down version of Eddie's trailer is freezing and covered in vines. "Remember the hive mind," Jonathan reminds you. Dustin falls through after you. The team is complete.

"Everyone remember the plan?" Nancy looks at team distract—Mike, Dustin, Eddie, Argyle, and yourself, as well as two agents from Stinson's crew. You nod.

Turn to page 61.

"Cause a distraction, then get out of here," Mike responds. He can't hide his anger. El takes his hand. She is part of the attack team, along with Stinson, Nancy, Jonathan, Steve, Robin, and one other agent. Mike wanted to go with her but was overruled. Everyone says their goodbyes, and the attack team heads to the Upside Down Creel house.

"So," you say, turning to Eddie, "how did you want to distract these bats?"

"Demobats," Dustin corrects you again.

Eddie's face breaks into a wide grin. "Are you ready for the most metal concert ever?"

Over his radio, Dustin hears from Robin that it is time to initiate phase three of the plan. Eddie, standing on the roof of the trailer, holds his guitar. You plug in the amp, and he plays. You smile. It's Metallica. When the demobats close in, you retreat into the trailer.

Turn to the next page.

"We need to keep going!" Mike yells. You are all standing back-to-back in the trailer, listening to the demobats crawl along the roof. The plan was to keep them busy for a minute or two, but without knowing what was happening elsewhere, it was hard to gauge if you gave the attack team enough time.

"What do you want? An encore?" you snap. The demobats push through a vent and get into the trailer. The agents with you start shooting, but they keep coming. The agents stop to reload. Eddie screams and runs up to the vent, smashing his nail-covered trash-can lid shield into the roof, closing the vent.

"I'm not letting El get hurt!" Mike runs for the door, but you block him. The trailer begins to rock, knocking you to the ground. It's time for team distract to leave. Dustin goes up first, then Argyle. You try to get Mike to go, but he refuses, so you grab him by the shirt.

"Mike, I promised Will I'd keep you safe! You need to go now!" you yell. He doesn't listen, pulling away from you. "Mike! Stop!" Before he can get away, an agent knocks Mike out and hoists him through the gate. "Eddie, go!"

"Don't need to tell me twice!" He pulls himself out. You follow, and the last agent pulls himself through. Your part is over. Now you just wait for the attack team to return. You meet with the others at the rendezvous point. Mike is still knocked unconscious. Will runs up to you.

You turn to Will and take his hand. "Mike is lucky to have a friend who knows him so well. Thankfully an agent was there to get him out before he could do something stupid."

The End

You stick with the attack team. Leaving team distract at the Upside Down version of Eddie's trailer, you follow Nancy, Jonathan, Steve, Robin, El, and Stinson to the Creel house. When you get there, you see a glowing light in the park. It's Erica and Will from team bait.

"Okay, initiating phase three." You hear Erica's voice. Will's voice follows. "I feel him. He's got Max." Robin relays the message to team distract to start phase three. Dustin copies. Minutes later, you see the demobats rise into the sky and head for the trailer park. The distraction is working.

"Let's go." Nancy leads the way. It's time for phase four: the attack.

A few days later, you're back in Lenora, but your mind is still stuck in Hawkins. Vecna got away, and Hawkins has been ripped apart. You will just have to wait and see what the future holds in Hawkins.

The End

With the news of the murders in Hawkins, your mom is probably worried sick. You put in the coins and dial the number. The answering machine picks up.

"Hey, Mom, it's me." You try to sound casual. "Everything is great. My host family is . . . good. I love you. I'll see you soon." You hang up.

"We got the number!" Mike shouts, banging on the phone booth. "It was in the pen the whole time!" You move out of the way so that Mike can dial as Will tells him the number.

"Listen." Mike hands the phone to Will. Will holds it up to his ear. "War games."

"Nina's not a person; it's a computer!"

"Great, so how does that help us?" You hope there is an answer, because you have none.

"We need a hacker, and I know a good one who lives in Salt Lake City," Mike says.

Will smiles. "Oh my god." He turns to Jonathan and sings, "Turn around. Look at what you see!"

"You can't be serious," Jonathan groans.

"What does *The NeverEnding Story* have to do with this? Aside from accurately describing this trip . . ."

Go on to the next page.

Only an hour passes on your trip to meet Suzie, their friend Dustin's super-genius girlfriend, before you hear a loud whirring sound.

"Guys," Will calls out warily. He pulls Mike's sleeve and points up. In the distance, a large helicopter comes closer. "Jonathan, drive!"

Jonathan slams on the gas pedal, and the truck lurches forward. "How did they find us?" he yells.

"I don't know! I don't know! Just drive!" Mike yells. The helicopter is right on top of you "Oh no—"

You see a blockade on the road up ahead. "This is the United States military. Stop your vehicle, or we will open fire."

Stopping seems like the right idea.

Colonel Sullivan is an unforgiving man. The interrogations started with Argyle, followed by Jonathan, Will, and Mike—who is sporting new bruises—and it is now your turn. You know no one else has given anything up, and you don't plan to either. You sit across from him, scared out of your wits but comforted by the fact that you don't know much. The armed guards there don't help, though.

"Like I told the other guy," you start, "I barely know these people. I only met them a few days ago. I was just unlucky—"

"Wrong place, wrong time?" Sullivan asks, raising an eyebrow.

"Exactly," you say. "If I wasn't at the Byerses' house the day you guys attacked, I wouldn't even be here." The colonel just frowns.

Turn to the next page.

"I already know you are lying to me." Colonel Sullivan leans forward.

"I'm not, I swear! You can ask the editor in chief of my school paper. I was just with Jane and all of them at Rink-O-Mania for an article I was working on."

"Interesting." Sullivan taps his fingers on the table between you. "And what did you learn about Jane while working on this article?"

"Just that she was from Hawkins and had a long-distance boyfriend. We didn't even get to the main interview before she had that fight—"

"You mean before she assaulted a teenage girl?"

"I know it looked bad, but the circumstances—"

He interrupts you. "So how did you get to be at the Byerses' house after being arrested with Jane?"

You freeze. Does he know about your meeting with Owens? "I—I was let go after my name was cleared, and I—"

"Lying again, I see."

"What? No, I'm—"

"You were in the Byerses' house with two armed agents, and you expect me to believe you had no idea what was going on? Why were you there? How did you get there?"

You can feel the sweat building on your brow. You resist the urge to wipe it away in front of the colonel. He knows about Owens.

"Think carefully before you lie to me again." Sullivan crosses his arms. "You are not the only person we have access to."

Go on to the next page.

"You see I have eyes and ears everywhere. Everywhere." His stare intensifies. You struggle to breathe under his gaze. The speakers blare, and you hear—your own voice! *Hey, Mom, it's me. Everything is great. My host family is . . . good. I love you. I'll see you soon.*

"How did you—"

"Don't worry." His voice is unnervingly calm. "Your mother is fine. For now."

"Please, I'm telling you, I don't know—"

"I wouldn't lie again if I were you." It is a thinly veiled threat. Your home has been under surveillance. If they wanted to hurt your mom, they could do so at any time. "It's too bad only your parents could be found. Where is Joyce Byers?"

"I—I don't—" Joyce Byers must be Will and Jonathan's mom, but you haven't met her.

"This isn't a game, child. Lie to me again, and I will have a team descend on your home in seconds." He's got you.

"I can't tell you exactly where Mrs. Byers is, but I—" You think of your mother, home alone after a long day of work. "I can tell you where she was headed. But you have to promise me she and my mom will be safe."

"That depends on how valuable the information you give me is." He has the upper hand and he knows it. He's letting you know that your attempts to negotiate are futile.

"She was going to some business conference in Alaska." You're hurrying. "That's all I know, I swear!" Colonel Sullivan gestures for one of the guards to come forward. He whispers something to him. The guard nods and exits the room. "Please, that's all I know."

"You still haven't told me how you got to the Byerses' house. Who helped you?"

Turn to the next page.

He's already proven he knows more than he lets on. Your stomach is churning. It's clear what he wants. He wants you to reveal who has been helping Jane, as well as where she might be. You need to give him something.

"I met a man, with Jane. He was some kind of doctor. He told me I could go with them or go back to Lenora and stay with the Byerses. I really had no idea what was going on. Please, you have to believe me." Your voice catches and tears well up in your eyes as you imagine the danger your mother is in.

"Is this the man?" He slides a photo of Dr. Owens across the table. You nod. He already knew all this. "I'm going to make you a deal." Colonel Sullivan looks you straight in the eye. "You tell me what you know about Jane's whereabouts, and I will spare your mother. Do we have a deal?"

If you choose to tell Sullivan everything,
go on to the next page.

If you choose not to cooperate, turn to page 72.

With your interview done, you are walked back to your cell. You turn to see Mike running up to the bars.

"What happened?" he yells.

You turn to him. "I'm sorry. I'm so sorry. They were going to hurt my mom." Guards open his cell and go in. You walk away, hearing Mike yell out in pain. When it gets quiet, you hear footsteps moving away. They have the pen with the number. They will find Jane.

Turn to the next page.

"I thought the threat was contained," Sullivan says. "I was wrong."

It's been a few days since Jane and Owens were apprehended and brought to the military prison. With the help of some technology you don't quite understand, they've been able to suppress her newly regained powers. Now you are all gathered together for some reason. You sit in the back away from the others, who refuse to even look at you after your betrayal.

"No." Mike hisses. His voice grows louder. "I don't want your stupid apology! It's too late! My sisters, my parents, they're all gone! Dustin, Lucas, Max, Steve, Robin, Erica, everyone we knew and cared about are gone! Hawkins is gone!"

"And I am sorry for that," Sullivan continues. "We should have—"

"Don't tell us what you should have done." Mike stops him. "We know what you should have done. What are you going to do now?"

"He's out there." Will touches his neck. "I can feel him stronger than I ever have before. He won't stop with Hawkins. He'll—"

"That's why we need your help," Sullivan continues. "We need you." He looks directly at Jane. "We cannot win this fight without you."

"My powers—" Jane starts.

"Will be returned to you. The inhibitor inside you will be removed, and you'll regain your power."

"Like One."

Go on to the next page.

"And how is it you came into possession of this inhibitor, exactly? As far as we know, the only one created was used on One by Dr. Brenner. With him deceased, how could you have gotten—" Owens gets up from his seat.

"I can't give you the details, but we have access to Dr. Brenner's past work." Sullivan notes the frown on Owens's face. "I understand that given my past mistakes, you are not inclined to trust me. Tell me what I have to do to earn that trust and it will be done. We must work together to combat this threat." Sullivan continues after the room calms down. "I need your help to save the world."

"I have a condition," Mike says, his face turning red. "Send that person back to Lenora and out of our sight." He's pointing at you. The others agree. Owens is silent, but you can tell he doesn't want you here either.

"Consider it done," Sullivan says. You are immediately escorted out from the room. The fate of the world will be decided without you.

The End

"I'm sorry. I don't know anything." A tear streams down your face. Inside you ache for your mom, but you know that if Sullivan reaches Jane, everyone is doomed, not just in Hawkins but maybe everywhere.

"Is that your final answer?"

You remain silent. When you are taken back to your cell, you see Mike and give him a nod. You can see his body relax a little. They know you haven't said anything. Mike mouths "Thank you" as you pass. You've held firm. Now you just hope Jane is able to get her powers in time to save Hawkins and the world.

It takes only a day for Sullivan to make good on his threat. He brings you into a room where you see your mother under arrest and imprisoned. She sees you, but before either of you can say anything, you are pulled out of the room.

Go on to the next page.

"Where are we?" You look down from the helicopter, sitting next to your mother, facing Mike and Will. Jonathan and Argyle sit farther away. Sullivan has let you all go and you are being transported, but you don't recognize the area. Most of it looks destroyed.

"It's . . . Hawkins," Jonathan says. This is Hawkins? The earth is ripped apart, and something like ash falls over the city. When you land, you are driven to another location. Getting out of the car, you all are greeted by Dr. Owens.

"We couldn't get to Hawkins in time." Owens ushers you all into his new office. People are working urgently. "Colonel Sullivan found us."

Owens tells you what they've been able to piece together: their friends were able to figure out how to get to the Upside Down dimension and faced an enemy of Jane's named One. They did not survive. The bodies of Nancy Wheeler, Steve Harrington, Robin Buckley, Dustin Henderson, and Eddie Munson were not found, so it is believed they perished in the Upside Down. The remains of Max Mayfield and Lucas Sinclair were found in an abandoned house along with another teenager. The only survivor among their friends was Lucas's younger sister, Erica Sinclair, who was found knocked out in the park across the street from the abandoned house. Despite Erica's report of what happened, Colonel Sullivan is still convinced of Jane's involvement.

"Where's El?" Mike asks through tears.

Owens takes a deep breath. "We don't know. When Sullivan attacked, El was taken by Dr. Brenner."

"Brenner is alive? And he has El?" The panic in Mike's voice is overwhelming. You can tell that wherever Jane is, she is not safe.

The End

She probably wouldn't want to talk right now anyway, judging by the tears in her eyes. You decide to leave it alone and head home. In two days, you'll be flying to Hawkins for the conference, getting there a few days early because it is the cheapest flight you could get.

You unlock the door to your home to let yourself in. The living room is how you left it this morning after your mom got up early to go to her shift; she won't be back for another couple of hours. The phone in the kitchen rings.

"Hello?" you answer while twirling the cord between your fingers.

"I said I needed a name by the end of the day!" the editor's nasal voice screeches from the other end. You roll your eyes; of course, this was coming.

"I didn't find anyone interesting enough," you answer blandly. You are not in the mood for his tantrums, but you try to keep your cool. You know he wants to get under your skin.

"I don't care! When I tell you to do something, you do it or you're off the paper!"

"Fine, then I'm off the paper. I don't need it." Your cheeks begin to heat up. "It's a stupid paper that writes about nothing, and only your mom reads it anyway. I quit!" You slam the phone down and take a few deep breaths. You'll be out of here soon and doing real journalism, you just know it. You look at the clock; it's time to call your host family in Indiana. You dial the area code for Hawkins and then the number. After a few rings, the call is picked up. "Hello, Fred?" You speak to the student hosting you for the first time. He seems distracted, but he assures you everything is ready for your arrival. You can't wait!

Go on to the next page.

You feel sick; the flight is turbulent, and the smells of cigarettes and stale coffee permeate everything. With a strong thud, the plane lands in Hawkins. You grip the headrest of the seat in front of you as the plane rolls to a stop.

At the arrivals area, you scan for your host family. Fred said he would be holding a sign with your name on it.

An hour passes, and no one has come to pick you up. You head to a pay phone, slip in some coins, and dial the number you have memorized at this point. The line is busy. Did they forget you were arriving today? Fred said everything was ready for you. How could they have forgotten? Thankfully, you have their address written down. You check your bag for cash and realize you don't have enough for a cab. You'll need to take a bus. You go to the information counter and ask for a map of the bus routes.

"You'll need to take Bus Thirteen to downtown Hawkins and transfer from there. It's the only bus that comes to the airport," she says as she hands you the map and points to the doors on her left. "Bus stop is out that way."

"Thank you." You head to the bus stop.

Turn to the next page.

It's early, and the streets are practically empty. The driver nods to you with his sleepy eyes and a cup of coffee in one hand. You are the only one riding at this hour in the sleepy town.

Hawkins is much smaller than you imagined. You wonder how this place could be the host of a national student conference—it's so quiet and, frankly, even more boring-looking than Lenora.

Sirens blare, making the bus driver jump, and a police car goes by at breakneck speed. Then you see the police cars turn into a lot, where you see the sign for a trailer park. Something is going on. Like any reporter, you're curious; of course, it could just be a robbery or a fight or something mundane. The bus is nearing the trailer park; you could pull the cord and get off to see what's happening. If it's nothing, you'll have to wait for the next bus, and waiting alone in a place you've never been doesn't sound pleasant.

If you choose to continue on the bus, go on to the next page.

If you choose to get off the bus, turn to page 170.

You get off at your next stop, which is only a couple of blocks away from Fred's home. You step up to the front door, hesitating before knocking.

A woman opens the door. "Can I help you?"

"I'm sorry to bother you, ma'am, but I'm the visiting student who was meant to stay here. I'm—"

"Oh! Did Fred not pick you up from the airport?" She ushers you inside. "I'm Mrs. Benson, his mother. Fred was supposed to be at school this morning preparing the latest school paper, and then was going to pick you up. Let me just call the school and see what happened. Also, in the garage we have Fred's old bike. He doesn't use it much anymore, but a lot of the kids get around town on bikes, so I thought you'd like to use one to explore."

She leads you to a guest room and leaves you to unpack. You let your suitcase just lie there. You can hear her voice in the hall on the phone. "He's not there? Well, do you know . . . Oh, he left with Nancy? . . . Thank you for letting me know." Mrs. Benson knocks on your door.

"I'm sorry my son wasn't there to pick you up. He was at school and then apparently left with a friend from the school paper. I'm sure he has a reason for not being there. I was out this morning and only got back shortly before you got here."

"It's no problem!"

"Well, while you wait, would you like something to drink? I was just about to sit down with some hot chocolate in the living room before I head out for an appointment." You accept the offer. Mrs. Benson turns on the TV, and the news is on.

Turn to the next page.

"The deceased person has been identified as a Hawkins High School student," the reporter is saying into the microphone. In the background you can see an ambulance and a number of trailer homes. Medics are rolling a gurney with a body bag. "Police have confirmed that this is a homicide."

"Oh my goodness!" Mrs. Benson gasps as she hands you a cup of hot chocolate. This must be why you saw police cars racing to that trailer park. Mrs. Benson leaves the room, and you turn to see her standing in the hall, picking up the phone and dialing frantically. "I just saw the news!" You listen in on the conversation while keeping an eye on the news. Maybe you should have gotten off the bus after all. Your ears perk up as Mrs. Benson's conversation continues. "No, Fred was home last night, thank goodness! He left this morning to meet with the other kids on the school paper, and you know he's been planning that conference. How about Andrew? . . . Oh, the celebration at Benny's Burgers? I suppose a lot of the kids would have been there last night. . . . Yes, I should be heading out now. I'll see you soon."

When Mrs. Benson comes back, she hands you a key to the house and says goodbye. You hear the car pull away. You're alone in the Bensons' house now. The news doesn't give any more details about the murder; instead, they cut to interviews with neighbors expressing their shock. You wonder if Fred might know who was killed. Hawkins seems like a pretty small place, after all. You do have a bike, and the Bensons have a phone book. You look up the address for Benny's Burgers and head over to talk to students there.

Go on to the next page.

Benny's Burgers looks like it might have once been a nice place, but not any longer. Trash litters the exterior, everything is boarded up, and there is a pungent smell coming from the place. You recognize that smell: sweaty jocks. A cop car is parked outside. If they are here, it must be about the murder, right? You find a side entrance that isn't boarded up and walk in. Inside it's even dirtier, and the smell is suffocating. The disposable cups littering the floor and sounds of puking in the distance tell a clear story: there was some party here last night. You see a group of jocks sitting near a TV, watching the news.

"Do you really think it was Chrissy?" one boy says.

"She never showed last night, and now the police are talking to Jason. It's got to be her," another boy answers.

"Why would Chrissy be at the trailer park?"

"Hey, what are you guys watching?" You turn to see a boy behind you rocking a flat top. The others finally notice you. You quickly introduce yourself and say you're visiting from out of town. They assume you were there last night for the party, and you don't correct them. The two boys sitting by the TV are Patrick and Andrew, and the boy with the flat top is named Lucas. The other two fill Lucas in on the news.

"Wait, the police are here?" Lucas asks.

"Yeah, they took Jason into another room a while ago."

You need to meet Jason. Just then Jason comes storming into the room. He takes a look at you and pauses. "Who the hell are you?"

Turn to the next page.

"What did the police want?" Patrick interjects before you can answer.

"It was Chrissy. . . . Chrissy's dead."

The entire room explodes with questions. Jason gets them to quiet down, his anger returning. "She's dead. But we know who did this to her!"

"We do?" You're surprised by this news. How would Jason know already? "Have the police caught the murderer?"

"No, the police haven't caught him yet, but it's clear they know it was him. It was that freak Eddie Munson!"

The name means nothing to you, but the reaction in the room tells you what you need to know: Eddie Munson is public enemy number one.

"Eddie Munson is a part of that freak devil cult Hellfire." Jason pounds the table. The entire team of lettermen has gathered to get more information.

"Hellfire isn't a cult," Lucas says.

"You say something, Sinclair?" Jason thunders.

"It's just a D&D club." It's clear the rest of the room doesn't understand what he's saying.

"D&D is Dungeons and Dragons. It's a roleplaying game," you clarify.

Lucas nods gratefully for your support.

"And how exactly do you know all that, Sinclair?" Andrew asks.

Go on to the next page.

"Well . . . it's my—it's my sister. Yeah, she's like, a total nerd." There's fear in Lucas's eyes. You wonder if he knows more than he is letting on. "She plays sometimes—"

"I'm sure your sister isn't killing people, right?" Jason almost sounds tender. "But I've read that if the wrong person plays this game, it can warp their mind. They confuse fantasy and reality, and innocent people die." The room gets louder; you can see that Jason is galvanizing the team.

"Then let's go hunt some freak!" Jason yells. The room explodes into a frenzy. You look around and notice everyone cheering, except for Lucas. Maybe you were right; maybe he knows more than he's letting on.

Turn to the next page.

It's early the next morning. You crashed at Benny's Burgers for a night of restless sleep. The student, Chrissy, was possibly murdered by a D&D cult?

Jason is outside, packing things into his car. Patrick is with him, and so is Andrew. You go up to Jason. "I'd like to help."

"Sure. The more the better." Jason's stare is icy and unwavering. It makes you nervous.

Lucas comes out of Benny's Burgers. "What are you guys doing?" The look of fear is still on his face.

"We're gearing up," Patrick says.

"Preparing for the hunt," Andrew adds. Lucas joins you, and you all get into the car.

Driving around mostly leads to dead ends. Jason has one more place to check. You can hear the music coming from the garage as he pulls up. You all get out of the car and walk over to a band practicing. One of the band members says, "You're a little early, fellas. Show's not till next week."

"We're looking for Eddie Munson," Jason says. The bandmate eyes Jason, then turns to Lucas, looking confused. "Lucas? What are you doing with these losers?"

Before Lucas can answer, Jason punches the band member. "Where's Eddie?" The bandmate screams out a name—Dustin Henderson. Lucas looks like he's about to vomit. He knows something. "Now, where do we find this Dustin?"

Go on to the next page.

It doesn't take too long to drive to Dustin's house. Jason, Patrick, and Andrew get out of the car and pound on the door. It looks like no one is home. As Jason continues to try to get someone's attention, you see Lucas going around back. You follow; you're sure something's up with that kid.

He proves you right.

He climbs into the house through a small window. You inch closer to see what he is doing. He is on a radio, speaking to someone. "Just listen! Are you guys looking for Eddie?"

"Yeah, and we found him, no thanks to you," a lisping voice answers. This is big—Eddie has been found! You're still unsure how Lucas is connected to all this. "He's at a boathouse on Coal Mill Road. Don't worry, he's safe."

"You guys know he killed Chrissy, right?"

Another voice answers, "Lucas, you're so behind, it's ridiculous. Just meet us at the school, okay? We'll explain later." You hear footsteps and hide. It's Jason. He looks through the window and yells at Lucas.

"What the hell are you doing?"

As Lucas jumps out the window, you take the opportunity to get behind the boys. "I was looking for clues. I found one. He's in a cabin—I can show you where." The address he describes is not Coal Mill Road. He's lying, but why?

If you choose to reveal Lucas's lie, turn to the next page.

If you choose to keep what you know a secret, turn to page 129.

"Wait!" you yell. They stop and look at you. You look over at Lucas, fear radiating off of him. He can't be trusted. "He's lying to you."

"What?" Jason takes a step closer to you. Before you can answer, Lucas bolts. Andrew chases him and tackles him to the ground. Patrick helps hold him down. You turn to Jason. "I heard him. He was on the radio, I think talking to that Dustin guy. They found Eddie." Jason's blue eyes widen, then he abruptly turns and jumps on Lucas, pummeling him. Lucas's nose starts to bleed, then his mouth. Andrew and Patrick just watch.

"Jason, Eddie didn't do this! You have to believe me," Lucas tries to explain. Is he just trying to save himself, or does he really believe Eddie—the guy the cops are looking for—had nothing to do with it?

"Stop! Stop!" You run over to them. "You'll kill him!" You grab Jason's arm. "We don't know where Eddie is! We need him!" Jason stops, then shakes you off.

"Boys, grab him," Jason says to the other two. Lucas is dragged to the car.

"What are you doing?" You step in front of Andrew and Patrick to block them.

"We're going to get some answers," Jason says nonchalantly. He gets in the car. "If you're not with us, you're against us." His cold glare makes your skin crawl. It's a clear threat. You get in the car.

Go on to the next page.

You feel sick. Each member of the team takes turns punching Lucas, who is tied to a chair, but he refuses to give any answers. You know you can stop this by revealing everything you heard at Dustin's house, but Lucas's refusal to save himself makes you question whether you should say anything. Is he really that dedicated to a cult, or is something else going on?

Jason comes into the room. "Anything?"

Andrew shakes his head. "He hasn't said anything."

Jason turns to you. "You sure you didn't hear anything else?"

You look over at Lucas, his eyes pleading with you. He knows you know. You shake your head. "No, sorry. I just know they found Eddie."

"Dustin Henderson, right?" another teammate says. "I know him. He used to hang out with our old captain, Steve Harrington."

"Harrington? This kid is friends with Harrington? So I guess we need to go talk to him. He works at the video store, right?" Jason turns back to Lucas. "Watch him. We can't let him warn the freaks."

Then he turns to you and whispers, "You're coming with us. I need someone I can trust."

Turn to the next page.

Andrew cups his hands around his face, trying to see inside the video store more clearly. "Closed? How can it be closed?"

"Stand back." Jason grabs a rock and smashes the glass door. Reaching in, he turns the latch and the door opens. "Search everywhere."

You step carefully over the shattered glass. You notice the computer was left on. You jump behind the counter to get a closer look. On the screen you see an account pulled up for someone named Rick, and an address is shown: Coal Mill Road. Bingo. You write down the address on a slip of paper and pocket it, then exit the search.

"Find anything?"

You jump. You didn't even feel Jason get closer. How much did he see? "Not sure. Still looking."

Jason nods and goes to check in with the others. You absentmindedly touch your pocket. You could just give the address to Jason now; it would cover up your lie about not knowing where Eddie is after spying on Lucas. Something nags at you: Lucas seemed adamant that Eddie couldn't have done this. He's already proven he knows more than he's let on.

"All right." Jason stands at the broken door. "Nothing's here. Let's head back to Benny's." You try to keep your hands away from your pocket as Jason drives to the makeshift headquarters.

Go on to the next page.

Lucas's face is swollen. The rest of the team is with Jason, trying to figure out what their next move is, so you have some privacy.

"Lucas," you whisper.

"I'm not going to say anything to them. Jason is a raging lunatic."

"I agree." You pause, taking in Lucas's skeptical look. "I know where Eddie is. That boathouse on Coal Mill Road? I've got the address for it."

"Then why aren't you giving it to Jason?"

"Because . . ." You pause, remembering the look on Jason's face when he attacked that band member and then Lucas. "I'm not sure he's thinking straight."

"So you believe me."

"I didn't say that." You pull up a chair. "But I'm willing to hear you out."

"All I know is that Eddie isn't a bad guy, and this cult stuff isn't real. It's just a D&D club."

"How do you know? Because of your sister? What if she's lying about it too? What if she's part of the cult?"

"I know because . . . because I'm in the Hellfire Club, not my sister." Lucas looks you in the eye. "If you get me out of here, I can prove that Jason is wrong." You look around. If there was any time to escape, it would be now. Do you trust Lucas or Jason? Do you trust neither and go it alone?

If you choose to tell Jason, turn to the next page.

If you choose to help Lucas escape, turn to page 112.

*If you choose to head to Coal Mill Road yourself,
turn to page 261.*

"I can't do it." You shake your head. "You may think Eddie is innocent, but you don't have any proof. If he was innocent, why not go to the police? Why would he run and hide?"

"I know he must have his reasons. Please, you have to believe me."

"I'm sorry." You get up and head to Jason. "I think I'm going to turn in early." You decide not to tell him immediately. You'll give him the address tomorrow after Chrissy's funeral. For now, you'll hang out at Benny's. Jason is having a get-together at his house for friends who knew and loved Chrissy, a small farewell before the funeral. He asks if you would like to go.

Go on to the next page.

After the funeral ends, you are back on the hunt for Eddie. You get in the car. Jason drives to the address on Coal Mill Road. He pulls up to a cabin. Closer to the lake, you see the boathouse.

"He should be in there," you inform Jason. Everyone gets out of the car and runs toward the boathouse. You hear a splash and see someone trying to swim away; that must be Eddie Munson! Jason and Patrick dive in and quickly subdue him. You reach them just as Jason pulls Eddie back to shore. "Okay, we have him. We need to call the cops!" you yell.

Jason drags Eddie by the hair farther up the shore and then jumps on him. Straddling Eddie, he throws punch after punch, blood spraying in all directions. "Jason, stop! We need to call the cops!" You turn to Patrick and push him back toward the house. "Call the police!"

Patrick turns and runs back to the house, but in the blink of an eye he vanishes from your sight. You look up and see him floating in the air. "Patrick!" you scream. Jason stops hitting Eddie and looks your way. You scream again to Patrick, but he doesn't answer.

Then you hear a bloodcurdling snap. Patrick's limbs start to twist and break. You are frozen as you watch Patrick drop. Jason runs toward him, and you follow. "Patrick! Patrick! Come on, wake up!" Jason shakes Patrick. As you get closer, you see a gruesome sight. Patrick's jaw is broken and hanging open, and his eyes are sunken in. There is blood all over his face. Jason keeps trying to wake Patrick, screaming at the top of his lungs, but you know he is dead. You rush to the cabin and dial 911. When you come back out, you see Jason sobbing over Patrick's body. Eddie has disappeared.

Turn to the next page.

It is dark out. The police lights reflect off the water. Light flashes around Patrick's body as investigators take pictures of the crime scene. You are shaken to your core. The image of Patrick being raised into the air and then broken replays over and over in your mind. A yell brings you back to your senses.

"I'm telling you, it was Eddie Munson! He made a deal with the devil and killed Patrick!" Jason races toward you and grabs your arm, screaming in your face. "Tell them! Tell them what you saw! Tell them that Eddie did this!" The cops pull him off you. The chief of police takes you aside to be interviewed. You feel sick to your stomach.

"I need you to describe what you saw with as much detail as possible," Chief Powell says to you gently. You look into his eyes, with no idea how to start.

"Jason says this was Eddie Munson's doing. Do you agree with him?"

What do you say? Yes, Eddie was there, just like he was present for Chrissy's murder. But if Eddie had such power, why did he let Jason beat the crap out of him? Why didn't he use his powers to save himself? Could his compulsion to kill really be that strong, or was he particular about his victims? You run it through in your head.

Turn to page 92.

"It has to be him," you tell the chief. "He was trying to get away, and when he couldn't, Patrick was— He was—" You can't finish the sentence.

"Do you know where Eddie is now?"

You shake your head. "When Patrick— When it happened, I didn't— I wasn't looking at Eddie. And when it was over, he was gone."

"Jason says you were the one who figured out where Eddie was hiding. How did you manage that?" You tell the chief about Lucas's betrayal, the communication with someone named Dustin who is helping Eddie, and how you managed to get the address from the video rental store. "Where is Dustin now?"

"I—I don't know. But Lucas is at Benny's. Jason had him tied up. He might know." Powell radios to have Lucas picked up. He tells you to go home.

Jason brings you to his house and sets up a sleeping bag for you. "I can't be alone." You nod. He seems like a good person to stick with for now.

Go on to the next page.

In the morning, you wake up feeling sore all over. The Carvers are watching the news. You see Chief Powell on the television. Chief Powell announces the deaths of Patrick McKinney and Fred Benson and names Eddie Munson as a suspect.

You're shocked to hear the name Fred Benson. You think of his mom, who was so welcoming to you. That feels like weeks ago now.

"They're not going to tell the truth." Jason's voice makes you jump. He looks as though he spent the whole night crying. "We've got to tell Hawkins the truth about Eddie, about Lucas, about Hellfire." He rushes up the stairs and comes back down holding a book, and runs out the door to his car. You follow him and get in.

"Where are we going?"

"We need to get ready for the town hall."

Turn to the next page.

94

It is after two o'clock, and the town hall has already started. Jason has gathered the entire team and hands out stacks of flyers. "Make sure everyone leaves with a flyer." He pushes through the doors into the meeting. You and the others follow closely.

Powell is standing at a podium answering questions. "I understand that you're all upset, but I promise you we will find him."

"No!" Jason yells from the back of the room. The crowd turns toward him.

"Jason." Powell keeps his voice calm, but even from the back of the room, you can see the panic on his face. "Son, why don't we talk about this in private?"

"Why? So you can keep me quiet? So you can keep the truth from coming out? Look, I don't know about the rest of you, but I can't bear to listen to any more excuses and lies."

"That's enough." Powell raises his voice.

Go on to the next page.

Jason pushes his way to the stage. People in the crowd yell their support for him. "I think we've all had enough." The room bursts into applause as he grabs a microphone. "Last night, I saw things. Things I can't explain. Things the police don't want to believe. And things that I don't want to believe myself. But I know what I saw. I know." The crowd is absolutely silent. "These murders are ritualistic sacrifices." The crowd gasps at this revelation. You feel sick to your stomach. "We've all heard about how satanic cults are spreading through our country like some disease. And Eddie Munson is the leader of one of these cults. A cult that operates right here in Hawkins."

You tune out Jason's voice as you scan the crowd. They are enraptured by him, clinging to every word he says. "They call themselves Hellfire—"

Turn to page 97.

"That's wrong!" A young girl stands up. "The Hellfire isn't a cult. It's a club for nerds."

"Erica!" The woman next to her pulls her back down.

"Just the facts!" she responds. Andrew tells you she's Lucas's sister, Erica.

"A club. A harmless club, That's what they want you to think," Jason continues. "But it's a lie." The team starts handing out flyers. "Last night I remembered Romans 12:21. 'Do not be overcome by evil, but overcome evil with good.' And God knows there's good in this town. So much good! It's in this room!" Members of the crowd applaud. "So I came here today, humbly, to ask you to join me in this fight. Let us cast out this evil and save Hawkins together."

A man in a hat and jean jacket gets up and turns to face the crowd. "What are y'all just sitting around for? You heard the kid." He leaves the room. Others follow.

Powell tries to get their attention. "I want to be clear: anyone interfering with this investigation will be arrested."

No one pays him any attention as they leave.

Turn to the next page.

You stay with the team at Benny's. You assume Lucas has long since been picked up by the police. The phone rings constantly with tips from the vigilante mobs roaming the streets well past the curfew Powell imposed. You log every tip that comes in. Another call comes in and you answer the phone. It's a tip from someone with a police scanner.

"There were three of them at Lover's Lake, two boys and a girl. One of them is that kid that shot the winning basket at the championship game, Lucas Sinclair." After thanking the caller, you hang up the phone. If Lucas isn't under arrest, does that mean he was cleared by the police? You can't go to Jason with this information, not after what you saw him do to Lucas. Still, what would he be doing at the scene of Patrick's murder? Was he there when it happened? You open the phone book and look up the Sinclairs. Luckily, there's only one family with that name, and their address is listed.

If you choose to stay at Benny's, go on to the next page.

If you choose to head to the Sinclair residence,
turn to page 104.

You decide to leave it alone. If Lucas was released by the cops, there is no need for you to do anything more. You stay by the phones, continuing to log tips.

After some hours, you get up to take a break. Andrew takes over your post. So far every tip has been useless, and Jason is only getting more frustrated. You hear Andrew slam down the phone and run out the door. You follow and see him approach Jason. If he was bothering Jason with the tip, it must be important. Jason and Andrew immediately head for his car. "Jason!" you yell. "What is it?"

"Something strange is going on at the Creel house. Sinclair's sister is there. Come on!" You run to the car and get in. Jason speeds off.

As you swerve through the dark streets, you learn that you're going to a creepy place where some murders happened years ago. People think the house is haunted.

When you arrive, you see lights coming from inside and from the park. You recognize the girl in the playground rocket structure from the town hall. Jason swerves to a stop. Andrew gets out and runs after the girl. You follow Jason into the house. He runs up the stairs, all the way to an attic. When you catch up, you see a sight beyond words. Jason is kneeling next to a redheaded girl sitting on the ground. Her body is shaking, but she doesn't respond to his calls.

Lucas turns to you for help. "Don't let him do this. If I wake her up too early, we all die."

Turn to the next page.

Jason pulls out his gun and points it at Lucas. "No. If you don't wake her up right now, you die." You try to shake the girl out of her trance.

"Just listen!" Lucas pleads. "The thing that killed Chrissy, Fred, and Patrick, we call him Vecna. He lives in another dimension. That's why you can't see him."

"You expect me to believe that?"

"It's the truth." Lucas holds his ground. "Chrissy, she was seeing things, terrible things. Things Vecna forced her to see. She was scared. She needed help."

"See, that's how I know you're lying." Jason looks menacing. "If Chrissy wanted help, she would've come to me! Not Eddie! Not that freak!"

You remember your phone calls with Fred before you flew out to Hawkins. He seemed fine. But so did Chrissy, according to Jason, and now they're both dead.

"You have five seconds to wake her up," Jason threatens. He counts down, but Lucas tackles him. The gun goes off, and then falls out of Jason's hands.

If you choose help Jason, go on to the next page.

If you choose to help Lucas, turn to page 102.

You tackle Lucas, helping Jason get the upper hand. Lucas pushes you off, but Jason gets on top of him and starts punching until Lucas's already swollen face starts to bleed. He grabs Lucas's neck and squeezes. You hear something clatter and turn to see the redheaded girl rising off the floor.

You jump up and grab her leg, but you can't pull her down. She is up to the ceiling now. Your grip slips and you fall flat on your back, hitting your head hard. You can't move. You are directly below the girl watching as her limbs break like Patrick's did the night before. Her blood drips onto your face.

"Max!" Lucas yells as he pushes you out of the way.

Max drops. Lucas catches her in his arms.

"Lucas? Lucas, I can't feel or see anything!" Somehow Max is alive.

"I know. I know. It's okay. We're going to get you some help, okay? Just . . . just hold on!"

"Lucas, I'm scared. I'm so scared. I'm so scared. I don't want to die! I'm not ready! I don't want to go! I'm not ready," she begs. You hear Lucas trying to comfort her.

"Max. Max. Stay with me. Stay with me, Max! Don't go, Max! Stay with me!" You hear the girl take her last gasp of breath. Lucas screams her name in agony. The ground beneath you starts to shake. You turn to see a gaping red hole open up, spreading toward you. It burns! It burns!

The End

You kick the gun away and try to jump into the fight to help Lucas, but he yells at you to stop.

"You need to protect Max!" He sounds desperate. "If the trance goes on for too long, you need to get her out of it!" He yells and charges at Jason, smashing his head into a window. You turn to see the girl, Max, start to lift off the floor like Patrick did.

"She's floating! She's floating! What do I do?" you yell.

"Walkman! Put the headphones on her and press play! Do it now!"

You do as he says. Then you run to where you kicked the gun and pick it up, turning back to Lucas and Jason. "Jason, stop or I'll shoot!"

He freezes. "How could you? How could you side with those freaks? They killed Chrissy! They killed your friend Fred!" Jason falls to his knees, powerless.

"Get to Max," you yell at Lucas. The girl from the rocket comes up the stairs. "Are you a friend of Lucas's?" you yell, never taking your eyes off Jason.

"I'm his sister, not his friend. Just the facts." She runs toward Lucas. You hear a thud; something has dropped.

"Lucas?" another voice says.

"Max! You're okay! I've got you!"

Go on to the next page.

It's been two days since you helped Lucas fend off Jason. Max is safe—at least physically. Lucas gives you the full story of what has been happening in Hawkins. Eddie was innocent. You learn he sacrificed himself to help save the town that still considers him a criminal. Jason was sent to a psychiatric ward for a severe mental breakdown. He maintains that Eddie was a cult leader and Lucas was one of his acolytes. Lucas is not implicated in any of the murders, having alibis for all of them thanks to being locked up in Benny's Burgers.

You arrive at the airport. Lucas is there to see you off.

"Thank you," he says.

"Don't thank me," you say. "I could have ruined everything." You are ready to go home and put Hawkins behind you.

The End

You get to Lucas's house and see the lights are all off. The house next door has cop cars parked out front. You get closer, peering in through the windows. Lucas is there, along with his sister, Erica, from the town hall, and a curly-haired boy. The light above them begins to flicker. It continues in a consistent pattern. The girl notices as well, informing the others. The curly-haired boy pulls the others aside. They run out of your sight. The light stops flickering. You step back and look at the whole house. In an upstairs window, you see lights flickering again. Was this how they contacted the devil? Was Jason right the whole time? You run back to Lucas's house, grab your bike, and wait.

You see Lucas open a window and climb out. His sister comes out after him, and then the curly-haired boy. They jump down from the roof onto some trash cans and grab bikes. Another head pops out the window; it's a police officer!

"Hey!" the officer yells. "Excuse me! No, get back here!"

"Do it!" the curly-haired boy yells.

Erica gets down next to the cop car. "I guess it's just a minor misdemeanor." She stabs the tire, deflating it. Then they get on their bikes and ride away. You follow them to the trailer park.

Go on to the next page.

You recognize it from the news reports as Eddie's trailer—where Chrissy was murdered by Eddie. You look through a window. The curly-haired boy is tying bedsheets together. Lucas drops a mattress on the floor. You look up and see a big tear in the ceiling. Water damage? Blood? The curly-haired boy throws the bedsheets up and they somehow stay there; they must be caught on the roof. Then you see a short-haired girl come out of the hole and fall down onto the mattress. The others around her are giddy. You take a few steps back to look at the roof, but you can't see anyone up there. Back at the window you see Eddie being helped up from the mattress. They all look up expectantly, but something changes. They start to panic. Some of them run farther into the trailer. A few minutes pass and then you see another boy coming down from the ceiling, carrying the limp body of a girl. Did you just witness another sacrifice? The boy lays the girl down on the mattress. She looks unresponsive. You run back to your bike and speed away. You need to get Jason! Eddie has killed again.

Turn to the next page.

"Jason!" You're out of breath by the time you reach Benny's. "Where's Jason? I need to talk to him now!" Andrew sees you first and leads you to Jason.

"What happened to you?"

"It's Eddie! I saw him! He's killed again! Others were helping him, Lucas and his sister. We need to go now!"

"Where was this?"

"Back at Eddie's trailer. I followed Lucas there and then I saw— This girl, she was lying there. She looked dead!"

"Let's move!" You jump in Jason's car, and he speeds off.

When you arrive at the trailer park, Jason narrowly misses a trailer that's exiting. At Eddie's, you see the cultists are long gone. "I was standing right here! That hole in the ceiling, Eddie came out of that, down onto that mattress. That's where I saw the girl. There were about six or seven of them." You turn to Jason, feeling insane. "You've got to believe me! I swear I saw it!"

"I believe you," Jason says. He looks back into the window. "They're not here, and it looks like they took the body this time."

"What do we do?"

"If it's more than just Eddie involved, like I always believed, then we need to be armed. Who knows how many cultists are out there?" You get back in the car, and Jason drives back to the town.

Go on to the next page.

It seems like the whole town is buying out the inventory at War Zone, a store that boasts the largest stock of firearms in Hawkins. You walk through the aisles staring at knives, guns, camo, and other gear and clothing. It's a whole new world. You see someone at the counter and stop suddenly, looking around for Jason. When you find him, you're in a daze. "Jason, the girl I saw get murdered . . . she's here."

"What?"

"That's her, right at the counter. Maybe she got away?"

"You sure that's her?"

"I'm positive." Jason leads the way to the counter.

"Nancy Wheeler," he says casually. "I'm surprised to see you here." You recognize the name; Fred had mentioned her in your correspondence before you flew out to Hawkins.

"Well, you know, scary times," she says. She's buying a gun.

"I saw you in Eddie's trailer," you say.

"I'm sorry—"

"Look, we know about the cult. I saw what they tried to do to you—Eddie Munson and his friends?"

She's frightened. "I don't know what you're talking about. And I haven't seen Eddie Munson since school got out."

"Is there a problem here?" A boy comes up to stand next to Nancy. He's the same boy you saw carrying her down from the ceiling in Eddie's trailer!

"You were there too." You turn to Jason. "He was there. I saw him!"

Turn to the next page.

"What are you talking about?" the boy asks. "I was where?"

Jason swings and punches him in the face. He yells for the others, who come running. You try to grab Nancy and pull her to safety, but she resists you, running out of the store with the shotgun she held. Jason is pummeling the boy. The clerk yells at him to stop. The boy doesn't stand a chance, not with the whole team surrounding him.

"I'm going to ask you one more time!" Jason yells at the boy. "Where is Eddie?"

The boy smiles and spits out some blood. "Babysitting." Jason punches him again.

"I'm calling the cops!" the clerk yells. The crowd surrounding you makes it hard to get away. Jason and the others run. You try to follow them, but the clerk leaps across the counter and grabs you. The boy, badly bloodied, is too weak to stand.

It doesn't take long for the cops to come and pick you and the boy up.

Go on to the next page.

You're in a holding cell with the boy from the War Zone, who you've learned is named Steve Harrington. You're surprised the cops keep you in the same cell, considering what happened.

"I know you're part of the cult." You try to sound threatening.

"What are you talking about?"

"I saw you and that girl in the trailer with Eddie and Lucas and others." The police seemed to get no information from him, so it's up to you.

"I'm not part of a cult," Steve says, holding an ice bag to his face. "You shouldn't listen to all the crap Jason says."

"Then what were you doing with Eddie in his trailer? And don't tell me you weren't there. I saw you with my own two eyes carrying that girl—" You're knocked to the ground by the sheer force of shaking around you. An earthquake? A cop opens the holding cell door and tells you to get out. Clearly they've never dealt with an earthquake before, but this is also the strongest one you've ever felt and you're far away from California. Steve bolts through the gate and out into the streets. You chase after him.

Turn to the next page.

Your lungs are on fire, but you don't stop running as Steve gets farther away from downtown. He goes to an old house and races up the stairs, where you follow him to an attic. When you enter the attic, you are stunned.

Lucas is there, holding the redheaded girl you saw escape the cops with him. He's sobbing over her, begging her to stay with him. You see Jason lying unconscious on the ground by a smashed window. Steve is with Lucas and the girl. Lucas begs for an ambulance. The ground begins to shake again. Lucas and Steve drag the girl toward the door when a hole opens. It looks like lava. The hole spreads—you run to Jason and grab his legs, trying to drag him out of the way, but it's too late. He's burned alive.

You run out of the building as it collapses. Outside you see Steve, Lucas, Erica, and the girl, her eyes open. "Is she . . . ?"

Steve checks for her pulse. "She's alive. Oh god, she's alive."

Go on to the next page.

The earthquake is described as a gate to hell by the townspeople. You don't think they're wrong. It was a 7.9 magnitude that ripped the town in half. Federal agencies have arrived to help with the relief efforts, and a steady caravan of cars leaves the town, probably for good. The death count rises.

This is your last day in Hawkins, and you have one more stop to make. When you arrive at the hospital, you ask for the redheaded girl, who you now know is named Max Mayfield. The receptionist points you in the right direction. You carry flowers in one hand and chocolates in another—a small gift to help her recover from whatever the cult did to her. When you open the door, you're surprised to see Lucas and his sister.

"What are you doing here?" you and he both ask at the same time.

"I'm here for my friend—"

"Your friend? I saw you in that attic. I saw you in that trailer. You may have lucked out with this earthquake, but you and I both know that girl's injuries happened before the quake!" You're heated.

"I would never hurt Max! If it wasn't for you and Jason and his idiot followers, Max would be safe. She wouldn't be like— like this!" He gestures to her hospital bed. You see she's in a full body cast, her eyes closed. "I could have saved her, but you got in the way! You destroyed her life! You destroyed my life!" Lucas pushes you out the door and slams it in your face. When you try the door again, it is locked.

The End

"Okay, let's get you out of here. Don't move till I tell you to." The others are distracted, listening to another Jason pep talk. You untie Lucas's binds. He stays still.

"Did you come here with Jason?"

Lucas shakes his head. "I rode my bike. It should still be there." You look out the window; the path to your bikes is clear.

"Good. When I give the signal, I want you to run for your bike and start pedaling as fast as you can. If we lose the element of surprise, we won't be able to outride a car—"

"Not without superpowers, anyway . . . ," he mumbles.

"What?" You shake your head. "Never mind. Just get ready." You look around and see a gas stove. "Please, please work." Turning the dial, a blue flame ignites. You grab some nearby garbage and streamers and throw them on the fire. They light up, and the flames grow larger. Then the fire alarm goes off. "Run!"

You and Lucas run out the door to your bikes and pedal away. "That should buy us some time," you yell. "Now let's go talk to Eddie." You tell Lucas the address, and he leads the way.

"Eddie!" Lucas pounds on the door to the cabin on Coal Mill Road. By now Jason and the others will be looking for you and Lucas. "Eddie, it's me, Lucas. I'm here to help."

You hear rummaging inside, and then the door opens. A tall, long-haired boy answers the door. "Get in, quickly." You're face to face with an alleged murderer.

Go on to the next page.

"I already told Dustin and the others what happened with Chrissy."

"I want to hear it from you," you repeat. Empty cans of SpaghettiOs and junk food wrappers surround you. It's clear Eddie's been hiding out here for a while.

"Okay." Eddie stretches his back, and then crouches closer to you. "I didn't kill Chrissy. Something else, I don't know what, killed her."

"What?" You're in disbelief. "You can't be serious. You were there, but you don't know?"

"Look, Lucas, Dustin and your other friends believed me. They told me about the Mind Flayer and everything. Just talk to them."

"Wait, are you saying the Mind Flayer is back?" Lucas grabs Eddie's shoulders. "Are you sure?"

"I don't know. Dustin was going to look into it." Eddie pulls out of Lucas's hold. It's like you're no longer in the room.

"Where is he now?"

"I don't know, but I've got a way to contact him." Eddie hands Lucas a radio. Lucas grabs it and starts speaking.

"Dustin! Dustin, are you there? It's Lucas. I'm with Eddie."

"Lucas? You need to meet us at the school right now! It's Max!"

"Max? What about Max?" Without another word, Lucas drops the radio and runs out the door. You chase him as he bikes away. You jump onto your bike and follow.

"Lucas! Where are you going?"

"I have to get to Max!"

Turn to the next page.

114

You get off your bike and follow Lucas inside the school. "Lucas? What's going on?" You chase him down the empty hallway. When he turns the corner, you hear screams. Crap! Crap! Crap! Then you hear Lucas's voice.

"It's me! It's me."

"Jeez, what's wrong with you?" someone answers.

"I'm sorry, guys. I just biked eight miles. Give me a second." You round the corner—

"Watch out!" A boy with unusually nice hair lunges at you, but Lucas steps in the way.

"Wait! Wait! This is a friend."

"I'm with Lucas!" you call out at the same time.

Lucas looks at the others, catching the eye of a redhead. "I mean, not with me with me. I mean, with me, but not in that—"

"Seriously, Lucas?" the redhead responds. "Not the time."

Lucas approaches the redhead. "Max, are you okay? What happened?"

"Look, I don't know how things run around here," you say, "but where I'm from, kids breaking into the school doesn't look good with the authorities. Maybe we should go somewhere else?"

"Right," the guy with the nice hair says. "We should probably do that."

"Let's go to my place," another girl says. The others nod in agreement, and you're off.

Go on to the next page.

"Welcome to the Wheelers'," Dustin announces as he gets out of the car. You've been introduced to everyone you rode with.

"Wait, Wheeler, as in Nancy Wheeler?"

"Yeah." Nancy comes up behind you. "Have we met?"

"Yes. I mean no. I mean, I've heard your name. I am in town for the student journalism conference Fred Benson was organizing. Wait, have you seen Fred? He was supposed to pick me up from the airport yesterday and never showed."

Her face turns grim. "I'm sorry to have to tell you this, but . . ." She swallows. "Fred was found dead this morning." You are stunned into silence. "Let's get inside." She gently guides you to a side door that leads into the basement. Once everyone is settled, you and Lucas are filled in on what happened. When the story is finished, the room is silent with dread.

Turn to the next page.

"So you expect me to believe," you start slowly, "that there's some kind of demon thing in Hawkins—"

"We're calling him Vecna," Dustin chimes in. Everyone glares at him. "Okay, not the time, I see."

"Okay, so you're telling me this Vecna is behind all these murders?" Everyone looks grim. "You can't be serious."

A girl jumps up. "Believe what you want, but we're telling you we've all seen some crazy stuff here."

"Robin's right," Lucas says. "You're just going to have to trust us."

"So this vision you had." You turn to Max. "You think you're next on this Vecna's kill list?"

"Chrissy and Fred were both seeing the counselor, Miss Kelley, for headaches, nightmares, and visions. They both died within twenty-four hours of their first vision. I just had mine."

"And you're sure Eddie has nothing to do with this?"

"He wasn't anywhere near the second murder," Dustin exclaims. "We were with him at the boathouse."

"I was the last person with Fred," Nancy says quietly. "Robin and I may have a lead."

Go on to the next page.

At the house the next day, you wait with the others while Robin and Nancy follow their lead: a visit to an asylum to see a patient named Victor Creel. Nancy's orders were to stay in the basement and wait for them to return.

Max sits in a corner writing furiously. Lucas watches her closely, along with Steve and Dustin. You can tell they are worried for Max, and it seems genuine, but you still can't wrap your head around this Vecna stuff. Is this just a ruse? Is it a distraction to stop you from turning in Eddie? You're torn. No one is paying attention to you, so this could be a chance to break away. You can't find out the truth by sitting here and waiting. You're still not sure you can trust them.

You quietly slip out the side door and into the daylight. You haven't gotten any sleep; adrenaline and curiosity are the only things keeping you standing. You weigh your options. You could go back to the school and look through the files on Chrissy and Fred, as well as Max. You could also check out the trailer park, which you still haven't been to. Or was it time to go back to Jason? "Might as well do it all," you mutter to yourself as you get on Chrissy's bike.

Turn to the next page.

Luckily the school is still unlocked, and so is the counselor's office. You open the filing cabinet and look for Chrissy's, Fred's, and Max's files. Spreading them out on the table side by side, you scan them for similarities. Sure enough, what Max described was accurate. All three of them were dealing with headaches, nightmares, and then visions. The reasons they were seeing the counselor were different, though: Chrissy was having trouble at home; Fred survived a horrific car accident in which someone died; Max was seeing the counselor for the death of her older brother in a mall fire that she survived. You know that Nancy and Fred were friends, and Max is part of the group of ghostbusters, but Chrissy doesn't seem connected at all, except through the basketball team. It was clear that Lucas didn't really know Chrissy. Then there's always the Eddie connection; everyone is linked to him except for Fred, as far as you know.

"What's the connection?" you mumble to yourself as you flip through their files some more. You read the handwritten notes: *Struggles with feelings of guilt.* Guilt shows up in the notes for all three of them. You go back to the files and pull them out one by one, reading for other students who had the same symptoms and also feelings of guilt, writing down their names just in case. You recognize the picture in one of the files. It's Patrick from the basketball team. You compile your list of names and put the files back as well as you can, then head to your next stop: Eddie's trailer.

Go on to the next page.

It doesn't take you long to find the right trailer, with all the bright yellow police tape around it. No one is around, thankfully. You pass under the police tape and go up to the trailer door, taking another look around to make sure you're not seen, then turn the handle and go in.

A large, fleshy hole pulsates on the ceiling. You walk toward it and look up. It looks like it leads somewhere, but you can't reach. You find a chair, then drag it under the hole and get on. Close enough. You close your eyes, take a deep breath and hold it, then stick your head in the hole. The stringy, wet feeling of the hole makes you want to gag, but you control yourself. Then you open your eyes.

It's the trailer. You're looking down into the trailer from the ceiling somehow. You pull your head out and see that you're still on the chair, on the table, under the hole. You stick your head back in and you see the trailer again, but you realize it's different. The air is filled with floating dust particles, and everything feels cold. You pull your head back out and jump down from your makeshift ladder and burst out of the trailer. What is going on?!

Turn to the next page.

120

Grabbing your borrowed bike, you pedal for your life as panic begins to take hold. You try to calm yourself down, try to think rationally, but what you just saw defies everything you thought you knew about the world. If you were keeping score, that hole would definitely put some points on the board for the Vecna theory. Your legs begin to tire, so you stop pedaling.

"Crap! Crap! Crap!" you hiss. As impossible as it seems, they were telling the truth. You were going to check in with Jason and see what he's found, but now you know he's on the wrong path, and so are the cops. So is everyone except for a bunch of kids! "Crap!"

You have to move, so you ride to Benny's Burgers. Jason needs to know the truth.

When you get to Benny's Burgers, you see Jason's car out front. You try to steel yourself as you enter the building. It's quiet except for the TV blaring in the back.

"Where have you been?" You jump at Jason's voice.

"I—I was following some leads."

"Sinclair's escaped. You wouldn't happen to know anything about it, would you?"

"What?" You feign surprise, hoping it's convincing enough. "When I left, he was still tied up. What happened?"

"He broke free from his ties and started a fire in the kitchen." Jason shakes his head. "Forget about it. Anyway, I'm glad you're back. I really need someone I can trust. Did you find anything?" You brace yourself.

Go on to the next page.

You watch him carefully. "Did you know that Chrissy was seeing the school counselor?"

"What?" Jason's surprise looks genuine. "Why would she be seeing the counselor?"

"I don't know. I was hoping you did."

"No, there's some mistake. If something was wrong, she would have come to me."

"So she never said anything to you about headaches, nightmares, anything like that?"

"No." Jason is vehement. "She was fine. Everything was fine. Why are you asking? Why were you even in the counselor's office?"

"I—" You glance at the TV and see that the news is still on. "I heard about what happened to Fred, and before he—before that happened, he told me he was seeing the counselor."

"Yeah, but that has nothing to do with Chrissy." Jason's eyes go wide. "It's Eddie. Eddie is the connection. He's doing something to people. It's part of his cult." Your heart sinks. It's clear there is no getting through to Jason at this point.

"R-right," you stammer. "I guess I was just hoping to find anything that could help."

"I appreciate it," Jason says kindly, "but we know who did this."

"Do—do you know where he is?"

"Not yet," he answers. You try not to let the relief show on your face. "But we'll find him. Are you crashing here tonight?"

"Umm, no, I—I think I'll go check in on Fred's parents. I'm staying with them, so I should be there . . ."

"Right," he says. "You should be there with them. We'll start the search again tomorrow." You nod and get on your bike to head back to the Wheeler house.

Turn to the next page.

"Where have you been?" Dustin opens the side door and practically pulls you into the basement. "You missed a lot!"

"What happened?" Everyone is gathered around Max, who is listening to a Walkman. The music is blasting loud enough that you can hear it on the other side of the room.

"First, where have you been?" Nancy moves Dustin aside.

"I went to follow some of my own leads."

Nancy looks at you skeptically. "And?"

"I believe you." You shake your head. "I went to Eddie's trailer, and I saw—I don't even know how to describe it—I saw this hole in the ceiling. When I poked my head through, I saw the trailer on the other side, but it was different."

"Was there some floating dust everywhere?"

"Yes—"

"Oh crap! Oh crap!" Dustin begins to hyperventilate.

"A gate," Nancy answers.

"You've seen these before?" You grab Nancy and turn her to face you.

"It's a doorway. It leads to the Upside Down. That's where the Mind Flayer and the Demogorgon came from."

"Yeah, but I thought Hopper closed the gate." Lucas looks around for confirmation. "The one at the mall with the Russians." Your mind is spinning. *Russians? What?*

"He did." Nancy looks dazed. "But I guess there's a new one now in Eddie's trailer."

Go on to the next page.

You wake up early the next morning to find everyone asleep. Looking around the room, you can't help but wonder how this weird group got together in the first place; this is the strangest sleepover ever. You watch Max get up and walk up the stairs. You follow. Upstairs, Mrs. Wheeler makes breakfast while Max sits at the table with Nancy's younger sister. You say good morning to Mrs. Wheeler and take a seat next to Max, who is furiously drawing. "Can't sleep?"

"Kind of hard to, with everything going on." Max continues drawing. You're not sure what to say. After the gang told you about Max's latest vision and how she needs to listen to music to keep Vecna out of her head or she'll be killed, everything has felt more real, more urgent. "Just thought I'd draw things I remember from my last vision. I got to a place that I don't think Vecna wanted me to see. Of course, I'm no artist like Will."

"Will?" You pick up some of the scattered drawings, but nothing makes sense to you.

"Yeah, Will was a friend of ours who got lost in the Upside Down. His older brother, Jonathan, is Nancy's boyfriend, and our friend El lives with them. After Hopp— El's dad died when we were fighting the Mind Flayer last year, they moved to this place in California called Lenora."

"Wait, seriously?" You put down the pictures. "I'm from Lenora."

"Holy—" She drops a crayon. "Wait, do you know the Byerses? Jonathan and Will?" You shrug. "Well, El told Mike in a letter that she gets to school in a pizza truck since Jonathan's car broke down. If you ever see people getting a ride in a pizza truck, you'll know it's them." You smile, because you know exactly who drives a pizza truck to school. It's strange to think of home.

Turn to the next page.

"A pizza truck?"

"Yeah, one of Jonathan's friends works for some pizza place and gives them rides since Jonathan's car broke down."

"Actually," you say, thinking about your school for the first time in a long, long time, "I do know someone who uses a pizza truck to get to school. . . . We're not friends, but he's delivered pizza to my house a bunch."

"Well, unless there's more than one pizza truck at your school, it's probably him."

"Small world."

"Yeah." The conversation dies down. You watch Max continue to draw, still unable to make sense of the pictures. "I wish El was here."

"The superpowered friend of yours?"

"In Lenora she goes by Jane Hopper." You shrug at the name.

"There you guys are," Nancy says, standing behind you. "What are you doing?"

"I couldn't sleep, so I was drawing what I remembered from my vision."

"Wait." Nancy pauses over one picture. "Is this a door?"

"Yeah, how did you know?"

"Well, it helps that I've seen it before." Nancy collects the drawings and begins arranging them. When she steps back, you see that she's formed a larger picture of a house out of the different parts. "It's the Creel house." Nancy gathers the others to go to the abandoned home.

Go on to the next page.

You expect the house to be empty, but all the furniture, fixtures, artwork, it's all there. The grandfather clock that is stuck at 9:50 is the same one Max has been seeing in her visions. Everyone is searching the house. You are in the foyer again after coming up empty. You're not sure what you are even looking for.

A voice suddenly crackles over the walkie-talkie in Dustin's backpack. "Hey, Dustin? You there? It's Eddie. You remember me, right?" You run to the backpack.

"Eddie? What's wrong?"

"It's Jason and his goons. They found me. You guys need to get here quick!" You curse and run up the stairs, yelling.

"What's wrong?" Dustin looks down from the railing.

"It's Eddie! We need to go now!"

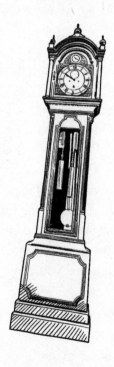

Turn to the next page.

Nancy screeches to a halt near the cabin. You see a car parked outside and hear noises coming from inside the cabin.

"They haven't found Eddie yet." You point to the boathouse, where a curtain moves. "We need to get him out of there."

"Okay, and what about those guys?" Dustin asks, pointing at the cabin. You duck down as some jocks come out the front door.

"Dustin, Lucas, and Eddie can't be seen." Steve pushes Dustin farther down. "Just leave it to me. I'll—I'll distract them. You guys get Eddie and get out of here."

"No, Steve," Dustin protests, but Steve is already on the move.

"I'll stay with Steve," Nancy says, following close behind. Robin pulls you toward the boathouse.

"What are we going to do? Walk over there and then walk him back?" Max says.

"You got a better idea?" Robin says, handing some of Max's sass back to her. Just then you hear a yell. You see Steve fighting Jason. "Oh—Steve—oh . . ."

"This is it! Get in the car!" Max yells, jumping into the driver's seat. The keys are still in the ignition. She starts the engine.

"What are you doing?" Robin yells. She's the last one in the car.

"I'm the zoomer," Max says, and then floors it. She drives straight for the boathouse. Dustin yells for Eddie to get in the car. He jumps in, and Max swerves the car back up toward the cabin, aiming for the crowd gathered around Steve and Jason.

"Max! Max! Max! What are you doing!" Robin yells. The crowd breaks for cover.

Go on to the next page.

Nancy drags a bleeding Steve into the car, and Max takes off. You look behind to see the jocks in their car. It's a chase.

"Hold on." Max switches gears and swerves the car onto another road.

"No! No! No! Not again!" Steve yells in the back. You hold on for dear life as Max tries to lose the jocks, but they are hot on her trail, driving as recklessly as she is. You hear a siren blare.

"Great! Cops!" Steve is exasperated. "Max! Slow down."

"Quiet, Mom!" she snaps. She makes another turn. "You guys remember the way to that secret Russian base, right?"

"You can't be serious!" Dustin exclaims.

Max swerves to a halt in front of the ruins of a mall. Everyone gets out, and Robin leads the way inside. You run up the broken escalators to the second floor and into an ice cream store. Robin opens a back door into a series of hallways that leads to a loading dock.

"Oh, please, please, please—" Robin mutters as she pulls on the door. It opens, leading to a storage room.

"Stop right there!"

You turn to see the police, guns pointing straight at you. You've been caught.

Turn to the next page.

There is a raging mob outside the police station. Since word got out about Eddie's capture, the town has exploded in a frenzy of vigilantism, like the lynch mobs you learned about in history class. You take calming breaths. The mob is out there, and the police have put up a perimeter to make sure no one gets through. You're all in a holding cell, waiting for news about your fates.

Chief Powell comes in and unlocks the cell. "Eddie Munson, come with me." Eddie gets up and follows Powell out.

"What's going on?" you ask the others, who are also alarmed. "They already interviewed us all?" After twenty minutes, Powell comes out with Eddie. He unlocks the cell again, but instead of guiding Eddie in, he releases the rest of you.

"What happened?" Dustin asks Eddie.

"They believed me," he says, shocked.

"What? How?"

"There was another murder while we were in custody. Witnesses saw the same thing I saw happen to Chrissy."

"So they know you're innocent?" Dustin smiles. "This is great!"

"Have you forgotten the crowd out there?" you say, pointing to the door. "Even if the police believe Eddie is innocent, there's no telling what that mob might do."

"So what, we just stay here while Vecna goes on killing more people?"

"I think he's only got one kill left," Max says quietly, her headphones still playing music.

"And now we're trapped here . . ." You bury your head in your hands. Game over.

The End

Lucas leads the way deeper into the woods. You don't know where Coal Mill Road is, but you do remember the mention of a boathouse. You go up to Jason to get more information.

"Is there a lake or river nearby?"

Jason looks at you quizzically. "A lake or river? No. Why?"

"No real reason . . . I just wanted to know if we'd need to swim after Eddie when we find him."

So Lucas is not leading you to a boathouse at all, which means he is leading everyone the wrong way. Lucas stops at a small clearing in front of a cabin that looks abandoned and says this is the place. There's something familiar about it, but you can't place it yet. Lucas doesn't search with the others, further confirming to you that he is lying. You pretend to search while keeping an eye on him. Someone used to live here, but it must have been a long time ago. You remember the last day of school, the girl with the weird yell and her broken diorama. How odd that it looks like this place. You notice Lucas slowly backing away from the cabin. You can't let him go, not without getting some answers.

Turn to the next page.

You take care not to be overheard by others. "Did a girl around your age live here?"

He looks shocked. "How did you know that?"

"I met her in Lenora," you lie.

"You're from Lenora? Look, I don't have time to explain, but I can't stay with Jason."

"Where are you going?"

"The school." He looks at the cabin to make sure no one is watching. "My friends said to meet there."

"So you lied to Jason."

"Come with me," he implores you. "Jason's . . . Something's not right with him. You saw what he did to Eddie's band. I can't let him get to Dustin or Eddie. If you know my friends in Lenora, then you know that we're not the bad guys here."

Again, you can only fake understanding. It's clear Lucas is going to run. You look back at the cabin; all you would have to do is yell and you could stop Lucas. You could also just let him go and tell Jason about the boathouse on Coal Mill Road. You look back at Lucas; if you follow him now, you can always tell Jason later.

"Okay, lead the way." He turns and runs, and you follow, hoping you won't regret it.

Go on to the next page.

It's late at night by the time you and Lucas are able to get bikes and ride to the school. Two cars are parked outside the school, and three girls and two boys are waiting. Could this be a trap? Is a bloodthirsty cult waiting for you? Lucas turns to you. "These are my friends. We're leaving now." Great, a second location, or would this be the third?

"Took you long enough," the redheaded girl says. Her arms are crossed, and she's looking out the window. Lucas looks hurt but says nothing. The car stops in front of a house, and everyone gets out. You are led to a side door into a basement. Introductions are made.

"If you all are so sure Eddie didn't kill her, why don't you just tell the police?" you ask.

"We could if Hopper was still around," Nancy says. "But we know he is innocent."

"And what exactly do you know?"

"Lucky you," Max says. "I had to go through a whole thing with Lucas to get the full story. . . ."

Turn to the next page.

While Nancy and Robin are at Pennhurst, you assess your situation. Bottom line: you are suddenly part of a demon-fighting party? The "proof" was some newspaper clippings that had no mention of demons but did detail toxic lab experiments, corrupt mayors, and cover-ups. You attempt to piece together all that you've learned, but you're stuck. You look at the boys, evaluating them. You settle on Dustin; he likes to talk. "Hey, Dustin, I've got some questions about Vecman."

"Vecna," he corrects you, and gets up to sit with you. "What do you want to know?"

"Start from the beginning. How did you first find out about Vecna?"

"Well, when Eddie told us about how Chrissy died, I"—he emphasized the word I—"deduced it could only be someone like the Mind Flayer."

"The who? Maybe start earlier." You think back to the clippings. "What happened in '83?"

"Oh, you want to go that far back?" Dustin realizes. You have an urge to strangle him, and yet there is something endearing about him. "The day our friend Will disappeared, we met this girl—her name is Eleven, and we call her El. But yeah, we met El and she had all these cool powers. Turns out she opened a portal to another dimension. We call it the Upside Down. And a monster from the Upside Down, I named it the Demogorgon, took Will. It also killed Nancy's friend Barb. But with El's help, we killed it. But that wasn't the end. Oh no."

Go on to the next page.

Before you can get more information, Max interrupts. She hands letters to Dustin, Lucas, and Steve. "And give these to Mike, Will, and El, if you can ever get ahold of them. Don't read them now. It's a fail-safe, for after . . . if things don't work out."

"Wait, whoa. Max, things are going to work out," Lucas insists.

"No!" Max raises her voice. "No, I don't need you to reassure me right now and tell me it's all going to work out, because people have been telling me that my entire life and it's almost never true. It's never true. I mean, of course this jerk curses me. Should've seen that one coming."

The room is silent. Max turns and grabs the radio. "If we go to East Hawkins, will this reach Pennhurst?"

"Of course, yeah," Dustin confirms. The next thing you know, you are in Steve's car despite his protests, heading toward the trailer park. Max's trailer is right next door to Eddie's. She tells you all to wait for her, and then goes inside to deliver her letter.

You glance over at Eddie's trailer. No one is around; it would be so easy to go in, investigate the crime scene, and get some real clues to this mystery. The others aren't paying attention. You could slip away if you wanted, and then come right back without anyone being the wiser.

If you choose to go inside Eddie's trailer, turn to the next page.

If you choose to wait for Max, turn to page 150.

134

You take the chance to see the trailer. If this demon exists, maybe you can find definitive proof. Looking around to make sure you aren't seen, you carefully approach the trailer. You slip through the door and shut it quietly. The others told you Chrissy died in the main living room; you look around the floor carefully but see nothing. As you walk into the room, something sticky drips on your head. You look up and—

You run out of the trailer, nearly falling over as you get back to the others. You clutch Lucas's shirt. "There's—you need to see this—it's—"

"Hold on, hold on, I can't understand you."

"Just come with me." You start pulling him, and yell to the others, "Dustin! Steve! Grab Max and meet me in Eddie's trailer now!"

When you pull Lucas through the door, he immediately sees it. The others follow. "Oh my god oh my god oh my god." Dustin paces the room.

"What is that?" You point at the membrane on the ceiling.

"It's a gate," Lucas says. "But how can there be a gate? El closed the one in Hawkins Lab two years ago."

"Do you think part of the Mind Flayer is still alive? Or didn't Nancy and Jonathan say the Demogorgon was able to open small gates?" Max asks, taking another step closer to the gate.

"If there was a Demogorgon loose, Eddie would have seen it when it got Chrissy. He said that she just floated into the air, and then her bones were broken and her eyes sunken in."

"Maybe he ran away before it opened?" Lucas says.

"Shouldn't the police have noticed this?" you ask. "I mean, it's right there."

Turn to page 136.

136

"Let's maybe talk about this somewhere else?" Steve says, trying to usher everyone back out the door. "Come on, Max." He taps her shoulder, but she doesn't move. "Max?" He goes around her and grabs her shoulders, shaking her hard. "Guys, she's not waking up!"

"She's in another trance!" Lucas pushes Steve out the way, trying to get Max to wake up. "Max? Max! Wake up! Wake up now!" She begins to levitate as Lucas desperately tries to pull her back down.

"I'm calling Nance!" Dustin runs out of the trailer. Max gets higher, and Lucas loses his grip.

"Out of the way!" You pull a table beneath her; you and Lucas jump on and both try to pull Max down. Her head pushes through the membrane; she's being lifted into the gate. Dustin runs back into the room with the radio yelling it is a code red. Steve jumps up onto the table and tries to help you and Lucas pull her down. Then she drops. Lucas catches her in his arms.

"Max? Max? Are you okay?" She opens her eyes.

"Lucas?" She looks up at him, breathing heavily and in tears.

"I'm here. I'm here." He hugs her tightly.

Go on to the next page.

You get in the car with the others. Max is in shock, tears streaming down her face, as she describes what happened. "I saw the clock again, four chimes, then I heard a voice . . . He—he said my time was coming soon. The clock hands were turning backward, and I saw Billy, then I—I saw him dying again." She breaks down.

"Try them again," Steve says to Dustin. Dustin pulls out his radio and tries to get hold of Nancy and Robin.

"Dustin? What happened?" Robin answers.

"You guys need to come back right now!"

Back in the Wheelers' basement, you are all sitting around Max as she describes her vision to Nancy and Robin.

"And you guys say she was lifted into the air?" Nancy turns to you.

"Yeah, just like Eddie described Chrissy," Dustin answers.

"But Vecna lifted Chrissy when he wanted to kill her," Robin says. "And when Victor's wife, Virginia, was killed, she was also lifted into the air."

"How did you escape?" Nancy asked Max.

"I didn't," she whispered. "It was like he changed his mind. He showed me the cemetery like he knew—" She hesitates.

"Knew what?" Lucas takes her hand.

"Like he knew the next place I wanted to go was to see Billy. Like I was supposed to be there instead of in the trailer."

Turn to the next page.

"Where's your Walkman?" Robin asks Max.

"My Walkman?" Max looks at her in disbelief. "I think I left it in the car."

Robin turns to Steve. "Keys. Now." He tosses her his car keys and she runs—albeit weirdly—out the side door.

"Why would he change his mind?" you ask. "Why would it matter where she was killed?"

"The portal opened sometime after Chrissy was killed, right?" Nancy asks. "Maybe that's how it opens."

"Does that mean Vecna changed his mind because he already had a portal there?" Dustin asks.

"If that's the case, then there should be a portal where Fred was killed too," Nancy says. "When I was talking to Powell and Callahan, there wasn't a portal near Fred. I'm sure of it. We need to go back."

Robin bursts back into the basement holding the Walkman and a bunch of cassette tapes. "Music. That's how Victor escaped Vecna."

"Voice of an angel—" Nancy recites.

"Exactly. Quick." Robin tosses the Walkman and tapes to Max. "Pick a song, something that has meaning to you, something special. If you listen to the music, maybe you can block Vecna."

"It's only a temporary solution," Nancy says. "We need to find a way to stop Vecna if we want to keep Max safe." She gets up and grabs a map of Hawkins from a nearby shelf.

Go on to the next page.

"This is where Chrissy was killed." She marks the map. "And here's where Fred was killed. Max had her first vision at the school. You said he kept showing you the cemetery?" Max nods, listening to a song. You can just barely make it out: "Running Up That Hill," by Kate Bush. "So the cemetery is here on the map. We know there was a gate at Hawkins Lab, but that should be closed. And the key under Starcourt Mall was also destroyed."

"What about the tunnels?" Dustin asks. "They snaked underground."

"Yeah, actually, what happened to those?" Steve looks at Dustin.

"Hopper said that all the farms around the lab were affected by the tunnels, but as far as we know they never reached the town, and they should have been stopped when El closed the gate in the lab." Nancy marks the different farms on the map. "The trailer park is closer to those farms, though. And when I went through the gate the Demogorgon made, that was in the same area between Steve's house and where Will disappeared. But that gate closed pretty quickly; it didn't stay like this one."

"What exactly does this all mean?" You look at the different marks on the map. Aside from the farms circling the lab, there doesn't seem to be a pattern.

"I don't know, but if Vecna needs his portals open in different places, there has to be a reason. I think we should go to the place where Fred died, at least to confirm this theory."

Turn to the next page.

The spot where Fred died looks like a regular road. You don't see any portal. "Are you sure this is where he died?" you ask Nancy.

"I'm positive. It was right here, in the middle of the road."

"So I guess there goes that theory?" You look for guidance from the others. Nancy seems unconvinced. "Can you cover a gate?"

"Jonathan said Mrs. Byers saw Will through the wall, but when she broke it apart with her axe, the wall just opened to the outside, and that was back when we knew the smaller gates were temporary." Nancy stares at the spot where Fred died. She gets on her hands and knees, her head an inch off the ground. "There's a crack, right here!"

"I don't know about Hawkins, but cracks in the road are pretty common where I'm from." Nancy is not amused by your quip.

"If I could make the crack bigger, then maybe we can see it better," Nancy says, trying to pry the crack open with her fingers.

"I don't suppose you have a jackhammer in your trunk?"

"I've got a hammer," Steve says. He goes to his car and returns with the aforementioned hammer. Nancy grabs it from him and uses the thin edges of the back to get into the crack. Small chunks of cheaply laid asphalt break off. She stands back up, pointing down with the hammer. You see it too, the red glow of a gate shining through the larger crack.

Go on to the next page.

"So Vecna's trying to open small gates around town, but why?" Robin asks as she gets on the ground to look closer at the gate. "And if he can open gates, why hasn't he or something else come through yet?"

"We know there are two gates, right?" Max says, rewinding her tape. "If I was at the cemetery or any other place, then there would be a third . . ." She trails off, and her eyes widen. "Four chimes. In both visions I had, the clock chimed exactly four times. It was the same clock both times too."

"You think Vecna's trying to make four gates?" you ask Max as you help Robin back up to her feet.

"I don't know, but it could be. Not sure I want to have another vision to check."

"If that's the case," you say, "then why is he giving us hints, like it's some sort of game?"

"And why is this wizard obsessed with clocks? Maybe he's like a clockmaker or something?" Steve says.

"I think you cracked the case, Steve." Dustin gets a dirty look from Steve for his sarcasm.

"Well, whatever his game is, we're not going to get any more clues from staring at that gate," you say, eager to get away from it. "Also, maybe we should all share our special song, just in case . . ."

As Steve drives back, Nancy stares at the map intensely. Aside from the low din of Max's Walkman, the car is silent. "So," you say, "if we're all staying in the Wheelers' basement, I was wondering if I could get a ride to the Bensons' place to pick up my stuff . . ."

Turn to the next page.

Once Steve drops the others off, you get in the front seat and he drives you to Fred's house. The ride is awkwardly silent. You realize you haven't had a true conversation with Steve—he's always just around.

"So were you a part of the D&D club when you were in high school?" You try to make small talk.

"Nah, I was too cool in high school for that nerdy stuff." His smile is slightly rueful.

"Oh, then how do you— I mean, how did you get into . . ."

"All this?" he finishes for you. "You know how it goes—boy likes girl, girl meets Demogorgon, boy is in the right place at the right time to help girl fight Demogorgon, boy is an idiot and loses girl. I didn't really know about any of this stuff until I saw it at the Byerses' house. Nancy had a bat with some nails in it that I used. I still have it in the back. It comes in handy."

"You beat a demon with a bat? I can't tell if that's really brave or really stupid."

"It was a Demogorgon, not a demon. But, yeah, that's Harrington genes for you—brave but not too bright." There's sadness in his voice. "Anyway, after that, I met Dustin, and now I'm kind of the designated babysitter. Here we are."

It's late, but the lights are on inside the Bensons' house. You knock on the door, and Mrs. Benson answers. You quickly explain to her that you've made other arrangements so they can have privacy in their grief. Mrs. Benson is gracious about it. You drag your suitcase down the stairs and load it into Steve's car.

"Well, well, well, look who we have here." It's Jason! "And Steve Harrington, too."

Go on to the next page.

"What are you doing here, Jason?" You drop your hand from the trunk door.

"Looking for you . . . and Sinclair," he says. "I asked around and found out you were staying here."

"Well, as you can see, Lucas is not here." Steve steps forward.

Jason ignores him. "So where have you been? I haven't seen you since we went to the cabin." His pupils are dilated. He stalks you like prey.

"I—I got lost. After that, I was exploring Hawkins, trying to find a place to stay so the Bensons don't have me to bother them."

"Lost? Really? Because a couple of my boys are pretty sure they saw you running off with Sinclair." He clenches his fist. "Where is he?"

"Okay, dude, maybe back off. He's not here."

"Actually, I'm glad you're here, Harrington. Aren't you friends with that kid Dustin Henderson?"

"What about it?"

"Nothing, just that I heard he's been looking for Eddie Munson." Jason leans against Steve's car, blocking the driver's door. "Have you seen him? I went by his house, but he hasn't been there in a while, it seems."

"No, sorry." Steve tries to look nonchalant. "I've been busy."

"See, I don't believe you. I think you're lying to me." Jason narrows his eyes. "And I have to wonder why you would lie to me. Maybe it's because you're part of Eddie's little cult?"

"I don't know what you're talking about. I didn't know Eddie in high school. Why would I be friends with him now?"

Turn to the next page.

144

"Look, I know a lot more than you think, Harrington." Jason slams his fist on the roof of the car. "So don't lie to me. Where is Eddie? Is he with that freak Henderson?"

"Get off my car, Carver."

"Or what? You going to fight me like you did Byers?"

This is getting ugly fast. Jason has seen you with Steve. If he was waiting here for you to come back, he might have his car parked somewhere nearby. He could easily follow you and Steve back to the Wheeler house. You need to keep him away from the others. Judging by Jason's taunt, you're not sure how Steve might do in a fight, but maybe with your help he could take Jason? But a fight is only a temporary solution if Jason starts searching for you after. You need to make a decision and end this quickly. Jason doesn't know where Lucas is. You could tell him anything.

If you choose to fight Jason, go on to the next page.

If you choose to lie to Jason, turn to page 148.

"Off. My. Car. Carver." Steve grits his teeth. Jason doesn't even bother looking at him. He's glaring at you.

"Not until I find out some things—"

Steve swings, catching Jason in the mouth. Jason recovers quickly and punches back. They exchange more blows, Jason slowly pushing Steve back. You run to the trunk of Steve's car. You see it behind your suitcase—the Demogorgon fighting bat! You pull it out and yell, "Back off, Jason!" He is on top of Steve, whose face is bleeding. "I said back off!"

Jason puts his hands up. "I knew it! I knew you were working with that freak!"

"Get off him, or I swear I'll aim for your head." You get into a batting stance, holding your ground. Jason gets off of Steve. When he's away from Steve, you get closer. "You okay?"

"Never better," Steve says, picking himself up.

You turn to Jason. "Keys. Now."

"What?"

"Give me your car keys now!" you yell, tightening your grip on the bat. Jason fumbles in his pockets and then tosses the keys toward you. Steve picks them up off the ground. "We're leaving. I'll toss your keys out the window when we're far enough. If you move, say goodbye to your keys. Got it?" Jason nods, his fury thinly veiled.

You slam the trunk shut and get in. Steve starts the car and drives off. When you are about to round the corner out of the cul-de-sac, you toss the keys out the window. Now Jason won't be able to follow.

"For the record, last year I beat a Russian spy," Steve says, wiping blood from his brow.

Turn to the next page.

146

You pull up to the Wheeler house just as Nancy's car does. You get out and run toward them. "What happened?"

"You guys took too long. We went to the Creel house." Nancy looks over your shoulder. "Oh my god, Steve. What happened?"

Dustin gets out of the car. "Did you lose another fight?"

"Shut up, Henderson," Steve mutters.

When everyone is inside, you tell the others what happened with Jason. After Dustin's reaction, you leave out the part with the bat, for Steve's sake. "Did you find anything at the Creel house?" you ask when you are done telling your story.

"We found Vecna," Dustin answers. "He's at the Creel house, but—"

"But in the Upside Down," Lucas finishes.

"So what does that mean for us?"

"It means that we're one step closer to defeating Vecna," Nancy answers. "At least that's what we'll need to tell Eddie when we see him tomorrow."

The side door bursts open, and a throng of boys all sporting the same letterman jackets break into Nancy's house wielding crowbars, bats, and other weapons. You were followed! Nancy tries to lead you up the stairs, but you're surrounded.

Jason walks in, breathing deeply. "I told you, I know more than you think."

Go on to the next page.

Jason and his goons round you all up and drive you to jail. He and his "eyewitnesses" claim they saw all of you with Eddie Munson, that you were aiding and abetting his crimes. With that many people testifying to the same story, Chief Powell has no choice but to hold you while he contacts everyone's family except yours. Dustin has his head buried in his hands, while Lucas holds Max quietly, desperately singing "Running Up That Hill" in her ear. The Walkman was confiscated, despite everyone's protests. There are tears in their eyes. You see Nancy watching them; then she puts her head on Robin's shoulder. Steve puts his arm around her, holding a bag of ice to his face with his other hand. Eddie is somewhere out there with the whole town hunting him. Vecna is still at large. And Max doesn't have her protection.

"It's you and me . . . it's you and me, you won't be unhappy . . . ," Lucas sings in her ear.

The End

"Wait." You step between Jason and Steve. "I don't know where Lucas is now, but I can tell you where I lost him."

"Good. My car's nearby." He steps away from Steve.

"I said I would tell you. I've got to go—"

"No!" Jason thunders. "I'm not letting you out of my sight again . . . friend." Steve looks like he's about to throw down, so you quickly accept the ride.

"Okay, sure. I'll take you there." You turn to Steve. "I'll see you later. Thanks for the ride." He tries to object, but you glare at him and mouth *Be quiet.* Steve looks at you and then Jason, then back at you. He sighs and nods.

"Yeah, no problem." He backs off. You wait until Steve has gotten in his car and driven out of sight before you turn to Jason. You hope your gamble will pay off. "The last I saw, he broke into the school."

"The school? Show me." You get into Jason's car, and he drives to Hawkins High. You turn back to see other cars following. He wasn't alone.

When you get to the school, the door is still unlocked. You lead Jason through the halls. Then you remember what Max said she found right before her first vision. "Where's the counselor's office?"

"Why do you want—"

"Maybe we can find more information about Eddie." You swallow your disgust. "I mean, he is a freak, right? Isn't that what shrinks are for?" Jason looks desperate. This could be an advantage.

Go on to the next page.

Jason leads you to the counselor's office. It's still unlocked as well. You go inside and open the file cabinets, looking for Chrissy's and Fred's files. You toss Chrissy's file to Jason. He catches it and looks at the cover. "What's this?"

"Chrissy's file. She was seeing the counselor for some problems."

"Chrissy's? Chrissy didn't need a shrink. She was fine." He tosses the file on the floor.

"I really think you should read it, Jason."

"No. I don't know what kind of game you're playing here—"

"Jason, she was scared!" you yell, trying to get through to him. "She was having nightmares, trouble sleeping, headaches, and then visions. She went to Eddie's that night because she was buying—"

"Stop lying! You didn't even know her!" Jason screams at you. "She didn't go with Eddie. She'd never go with that freak anywhere, not when she had me." He grabs you by your throat and pushes you against the wall. "Where is he? Where is Eddie?" he screams, slamming your head against the wall.

"I don't know! I've never even seen him."

"You're lying!" He punches you, and everything goes black.

When you wake up, you're back at Benny's Burgers, tied up in a booth. You head is ringing, and your neck is sore. "Hello?" you call out. There's no answer. "Hello!" Your panic starts to rise. Did they just leave you here? You try to get out of the ropes, but it's no use. You've been captured. You just hope that the others can solve this mystery before Jason gets hold of Eddie.

The End

"Hey, that was longer than twenty seconds," Steve says as Max comes back to the car. Max is flustered. "Hey, whoa, whoa, whoa, are you all right?"

"I'm fine. Just drive." She slams the door shut.

"Did something happen?" Dustin asks.

"Can we please just go?" She looks out the window and tells Steve where to go next: the Roane Hill Cemetery. Everyone is quiet on the ride up. Steve parks at the bottom of a hill. Max gets out, and Lucas tries to follow her. "Lucas, please just wait in the car."

"Max, wait. Max, please." He stops her from going farther. You watch them from the car. "Just listen to me. Just, please . . . I know something happened there with your mother. Was it Vecna?"

"I told you, I'm fine. Okay?" She looks away from him. "I mean, as fine as someone who's hurtling toward a gruesome death can be."

"Max, you know you can talk to me, right?"

She hesitates. "Yeah, I know that."

"Okay, then why do you keep pushing me away?" Lucas pulls out the letter Max gave him from his pocket. "I don't need a letter. I don't want a letter! Just talk to me. To your friends. We're right here. I'm right here. Okay?"

"Just wait in the car. This won't take long." She runs up the hill. Lucas stares after her a moment, then turns back to the car.

Go on to the next page.

"Who is here?" you ask the others as Lucas gets in the car. "I mean, who is she visiting?"

"Her brother, Billy," Lucas says, staring out the window up the hill, where you see Max sitting in front of a tombstone. "He was killed last year by the Mind Flayer."

"Dustin mentioned the Mind Flayer earlier, but I don't understand. Was he another invisible demon like Vecna?"

"No, he took over people's minds. He took over Billy's, made him do horrible things. But . . . at the last minute, somehow, Billy broke free and helped save us all."

"The government covered it up, saying it was a mall fire that killed all the people the Mind Flayer took," Dustin adds.

"Were Billy and Max very close?"

"No," they all answer at once. Then Steve says, "He wasn't the nicest person, especially not to her. But in the end, he did the right thing, so you could say it's complicated."

The car is quiet after that. The minutes pass; Max sits incredibly still. "All right." Steve looks at his watch. "It's been long enough." He gets out of the car.

"Steve, just give her some time," Lucas protests.

"I have, all right, Lucas? I'm calling it. She wants to get a lawyer, she can." You watch him walk up the hill to Max. She doesn't even look at him. He kneels down and touches her shoulder. Still no reaction.

"Something's wrong!" You push the car door open and run up the hill. Lucas and Dustin follow.

Turn to the next page.

Steve is shaking Max and calling her name, but she is unresponsive. Vecna has her! You all start trying to wake her from the trance, but nothing seems to work. You don't think she can hear you. Steve grabs Dustin by the shirt.

"Call Nancy and Robin! Go get 'em! Go!" He thrusts Dustin back. Dustin scrambles to his feet and runs down the hill. You are still shaking Max.

"Do either of you have water? Maybe if we splash her?" you say, trying to come up with anything that might help.

"No, no, we didn't bring any!" Steve continues yelling at Max to wake up.

"I've got it!" Dustin runs back up the hill clutching something to his chest. "I've got it!" He drops a Walkman and some cassette tapes on the grass. "What's her favorite song?"

"Why?" Lucas yells.

"Robin said if she listens . . . It's too much to explain right now. What's her favorite song?"

Lucas scrambles through the tapes. You are all yelling at this point, urging him to go faster, repeatedly asking what her favorite song is. You turn to look at Max.

"I don't think she's breathing right! Hurry!"

"It's here! It's here!" Lucas hands Steve a Kate Bush tape. He puts it in the Walkman as Dustin places the headphones on Max. Steve hits play. You hold your breath. The music blares loudly in her ears, but it seems to have no effect. She rises into the air, still in her trance. You all get up and watch her. She's so high up! Lucas is screaming. She drops to the ground, breathing, eyes open, out of her trance!

"I'm still . . . I'm still here," Max cries, gasping for breath.

Turn to page 154.

You are back at the Wheelers' house, gathering information with the others. Max tells you about her vision and starts drawing images. Nancy picks up one of her drawings. "Is this a door you saw?"

"Yeah," Max answers. "How did you know that?"

"It helps that I've seen it before," Nancy says. "We need to go to the Creel house, now."

Go on to the next page.

The door to the Creel house is boarded up. Steve uses his hammer to pry the nails out, and the board falls back, kicking up dust. A beautiful window of stained glass marks the door. He tries the doorknob; it's locked.

"Oh, look, I found a key." Robin holds up a brick. She throws the brick through the stained glass, and Steve reaches in carefully to unlock the door. The door creaks open. You step warily past the threshold, your skin crawling at the thought that a whole family died in this house.

"Okay, I promise I'm going to stop asking this, but you guys see that, right?" Max is frozen in front of a grandfather clock.

"Is that what you saw in your visions?" you ask. She nods. Robin wipes the clockface. It stopped at 9:50. You open the glass case and swing the clapper, and the clock chimes. "Does it sound the same?"

"No, it was more . . . distorted."

"The answers have to be here. It can't be a coincidence that this is the clock Max saw," Nancy says. "We should split up, look for clues."

"Okay, Nancy Drew," you joke.

"Don't call me that!" she snaps. She shakes her head. "Sorry, I just . . . Someone I really didn't like used to call me that." She heads upstairs with Robin. You follow.

"Hey, wait up!" You jump the stairs two at a time. "You never really said anything about what you learned from Creel."

Turn to the next page.

As you look through the different rooms with Nancy and Robin, they fill you in on what they learned. "It started small, finding dead, mangled animals. Then they started having visions. At dinner the day his family was killed, everything electric in the house was turned on. His wife died the same way Chrissy did; then he was in a vision. He followed music out of the vision and saw his daughter was dead and his son was in a coma. His son died a week later."

"Did Creel ever see or hear from Vecna again?"

"No. As far as we know, Chrissy's was the first murder since then." The rooms are covered in dust and webs. "They just left everything . . ."

"I guess a triple homicide isn't good for resale value." Robin scans the old furniture with her flashlight.

"Why do you think Vecna waited so long to kill them?" You look around for anything that might look like a portal.

"What do you mean?"

"I mean, he's some kind of magical wizard that can kill without being seen, right? Why toy with his victims? It seems . . . almost too human."

"You call that human?" Robin quips.

"I— Have you read anything about serial killers?" you ask. They both look at you oddly. "I'll take that as a no. Anyway, I've been reading some books about them, and a lot of experts say that as children they may torture animals and stuff. And a lot of the time they have a pattern to how they kill. Like how Jack the Ripper left the bodies of his victims in a certain pose . . ."

"Where are you going with this?" Robin asks. You hear glass break!

Go on to the next page.

You run out into the hall to find Steve running backward out a room into the hall.

"Whoa, whoa." Nancy stops him. "What's wrong?"

"There was a spider. It's a black widow." He shuts the door to the room. "Don't go in there." When he turns, you see spiderwebs in his hair. Nancy helps him pick them out.

"If there's a spider nesting in there, you're never going to find it till it lays eggs and all the babies spill out," Robin teases as she passes through the hall. You follow her.

"What's wrong with you?" Steve asks. Robin just laughs at him. "Robin, seriously?" You hear him talking to Nancy but don't pay any attention.

"Platonic with a capital P," Robin calls out, pulling you back to their conversation. Robin nudges you as you walk up the stairs to the attic together. "So tell me more about your serial killer obsession."

You roll your eyes. "It's not an obsession. I read a story about the Zodiac Killer some months ago, and I was curious. It's just weird that this magical wizard would follow the same pattern. If Creel was right and the demon was the one tormenting dead animals, then moved on to people, that's just odd to me. Also, showing the victims visions before killing them, it's like a game. The Zodiac Killer would leave messages for the police and codes and stuff."

"So Vecna behaves like a serial killer?"

"I guess. But if he is a serial killer, why stop after the Creels? Why wait twenty-seven years? I mean, the Zodiac Killer just stopped, but for all we know he could be dead. This Vecna is clearly still around. . . . Robin?" You turn to see you're alone in the room. Then you hear the chimes. Then you hear music—it's Kate Bush! You're in Vecna's trance!

Turn to the next page.

You run toward the music as fast as you can, down the stairs and to the front door of the house, past the grandfather clock, its hands spinning backward as it chimes four times. "Human? I am a god," a deep voice echoes. *Vecna?* You burst through the door and see your body in the distance. Robin is shaking you. Max is holding her headphones around your head. You jump through and find yourself back in your body. You collapse. Robin helps you up and walks you out of the house. The rest follow.

"What happened?" Nancy asks as everyone loads into the car.

"I think I offended the demon." You lean on Max's shoulder as she plays the music loud enough for both of you to hear. "This is definitely my new favorite song."

"Focus," Nancy says as she drives away from the Creel house.

"Vecna just said he is a god. He was upset that I told Robin he seemed human. When I heard the music, I ran. I also heard the four chimes and saw the same clock."

"Great, a demon with thin skin," Lucas groans.

"What were you doing before you had the vision?" Nancy asks. Robin informs them of your conversation. "You guys saw what happened to the flashlights?"

"What happened?" You sit up.

"They started flickering just like when Will was in the Upside Down."

"So Vecna is somewhere on the other side." Lucas takes Max's hand.

Dustin scratches his chin. "Somehow he can make a psychic link with his victims from there. But why kill random teens?"

Go on to the next page.

"I think if we can figure out why he stopped killing between 1959 and now, we might be able to figure that out," you say. "That's a long time to stop and then suddenly start again. Also, why the Creels? Then Chrissy, Fred, and Max? As far as we know, none of them are connected to the Creels either, right?"

"What are we going to tell Eddie?" Robin asks.

"We'll just tell him that we're one step closer to finding Vecna," Nancy says, trying to convince herself as much as anyone.

"See, a positive spin," Steve says to Robin.

"Dustin? Wheeler? Anybody?" Eddie's voice comes over the radio.

"Eddie, this is Dustin."

"Jason is here! He's in Rick's cabin. He hasn't found me yet, but I need an extraction as soon as possible."

Nancy races to the boathouse. She parks farther away. You can see Jason's car out front. "How are we going to get Eddie past them?"

"I've got an idea," Max says. She runs into the woods, then starts screaming for help. The jocks take the bait, sprinting from the cabin in her direction. Steve gets up and runs to the car, followed by Dustin.

"What about Max?" Dustin asks.

"I got this. You guys get Eddie out of here. We'll meet you at the Wheelers'." Steve runs off. Nancy drives as fast as she can.

Turn to the next page.

"What a good mama bird you are." Robin laughs when Steve and Max show up.

"Shut up," Steve says, still out of breath. Max follows him into the basement, and they both flop down on the couch.

"Now what?" you ask the others. "We've got a wanted suspect in your basement, an ego-driven wizard, his next victim, and . . . nothing. That's it. We're nowhere close to figuring out what his plan is or even why he's doing this."

"He said he was a god in your vision, right?" Nancy asks.

"Yeah, but . . . don't tell me we really think he is one?"

"No, but he certainly has incredible powers. Who else do we know with power like that?"

"Eleven!" Steve answers. He's quite happy with himself for being right.

"So you're saying that this wizard might have superpowers like your friend?" you clarify. "In that case, why did he target the Creels and then stop, just to pick back up again now? And why is he in the Upside Down? Has he been there since the 1950s, or did he go through the gate your friend made?"

"I don't know. But if we're looking for information on superpowered people, I know where we can go . . ." The others seem to get her meaning.

"Hi. New here, remember? Where are we going?"

Go on to the next page.

Getting into the empty husk of the Hawkins Lab was easy, but searching the entire building is a whole other issue. You shine a flashlight on the directory mounted on the wall as Nancy and Dustin read through the different offices.

"There." Nancy points. "Dr. Owens's office."

"I thought you said the head doctor was named Brenner," you say as Nancy leads the way through the lab.

"Brenner was the head doctor, and the guy who experimented on El, but he died when the Demogorgon attacked. Owens took over after," Dustin says. "He was better, I guess. At least Will was coming here for treatment, but El still had to go into hiding until she saved his life from the demodogs."

"The demo-what-now?" Every time you think you have a handle on what is going on, you are thrown again. Lucas opens the door to Owens's office. All of the furniture is still there. "Are we sure there's anything left here? I mean, wouldn't the government take all of its records?"

"Hopper fought a Soviet spy here who was looking for information when they were building the Key. If they thought they could find something, maybe we can too."

"I'm sorry, did you say Soviet spy?" You pull Dustin to the side. "Okay, when we get out of here, I need you to tell me everything from the beginning, because . . . what the hell?"

"Sure, sure, no problem." You both continue searching. It seems like every inch of the room is covered by someone. You sit at the desk and open the drawers. They are all empty.

"Maybe I can tell you the story now." Dustin jumps up to sit on the desk. You feel something hit your lap.

Turn to the next page.

"What the . . . ?" You look down to see a piece of the desk has fallen into your lap. You push back the chair and climb under the desk. There's a hidden compartment! "I think I found something!" You pull open the compartment and retrieve a trove of documents. You get up and place them on the desk, shoving Dustin aside.

"These papers must belong to Brenner!" you said. "Owens surely wouldn't have left these here if he knew about them."

The others gather around as you read through the different documents. You pull out a file with a picture on it.

"That's Henry Creel!" Nancy says. "We saw a picture of his family in the newspaper. Why would Brenner have a picture of him?" She takes the file from you.

"Maybe he was trying to find Vecna too?" Dustin says. "If he was in Hawkins when the murders happened, maybe—"

"No." Nancy lays the file out open. "Look." You scan through the page. "Henry Creel didn't die in 1959. He was taken by Brenner after killing his own family with his powers. He's listed as One."

"So he was here even before Eleven?" Max asks.

"Well, where is he now?" You pick up the file and turn to the end. "The last date is from 1979." You hand the files to the others. "I can't make heads or tails of this."

"Oh my god," Nancy and Dustin say at the same time.

Go on to the next page.

"Henry Creel was One," you say. "Somehow Brenner was able to block his powers."

"That explains why there were no more murders after the Creels." Robin turns the file to face her so she can read it.

"That's not all it says," Dustin adds. "It looks like El knew One."

"What?"

"From what Brenner could put together, One tricked El into setting him free. Then he went on a murderous rampage, until El stopped him by—"

"Sending him to the Upside Down," Nancy finishes.

"Did she ever mention this One guy to any of you?" you ask. The others shake their heads. Nancy picks up the file and flips through it again.

"This explains it. El lost her memories after she sent him there."

"So Vecna isn't a wizard at all. He's from our world?" Steve asks. "Does that mean he's been in the Upside Down this whole time? I mean, even when Will was there?"

"I guess so, but that doesn't explain why he's killing again. El sent him there in 1979. It's been seven years since and he's only just getting back to it?" You continue to look through the files to see if there's anything else.

"What if he couldn't break through? What if he didn't know how El sent him there and couldn't affect our world until El opened the first gate?"

"So you're saying the Demogorgon, the demodogs, the Mind Flayer, it was all him?" Dustin asks. "Wait, that means we know how his powers work."

Turn to the next page.

"What do you mean?"

"When El tries to reach someone's mind, she's in a meditative space. Vecna must do the same thing when he reaches into his victims."

"The lights were flickering in the attic of the Creel house when you had your vision," Nancy says. "That must be where he is on the other side, a place where he feels safe to leave his body vulnerable. So all we need to do is find a way to get into the Upside Down to get to him while he's in a trance . . ."

"Okay, forgetting that you said the gates are all closed now, we still don't have any idea what his plan is. Is he just going to kill random people one at a time until all of Hawkins is dead?" You gather the papers and close the file.

"Last year Billy told El that the Mind Flayer was building the monster for her," Max says. "What if Vecna isn't working for the Mind Flayer? What if the Mind Flayer was working for Vecna?"

"So when El closed the gate on him at the lab, Vecna realized she would still be in his way," Dustin adds. "When he built the monster and attacked El, it was to get rid of her so he could come through."

"We are positively sure there is no gate open now, right?" You look at the others. "Right?"

Dustin pulls out a compass. "Wrong."

Go on to the next page.

Dustin directs Steve as he drives. When the car can no longer follow the path, you get out and follow Dustin on foot. He leads you deeper into the dark woods. You can't help but wonder if these were the same woods the Demogorgon went hunting in at night.

"Wait," Steve says. "Max and I were just here when we ran from Jason."

"Yeah," Max confirms. "We were definitely here." As you walk, you start to hear noises.

"Why are the police here?" You walk closer and see photographers taking pictures, the flash illuminating everything around them. You see a white sheet covering something. "Oh no."

"The gate is in that direction." Dustin points.

"Right where someone was killed," you say. "We need to get out of here." You turn to go back the way you came. When you reach the car, everyone gets in and drives away.

Turn to the next page.

166

In the morning, you watch the press conference on television. Another Hawkins High student, Patrick McKinney, was found dead last night in the woods. They are linking the murder to Chrissy's and Fred's. Dustin leads you all back downstairs, where Eddie waits in hiding. "I think I know what Vecna's plan is." Eddie pulls out a map. "Here's where Chrissy died, here's where Fred died, and here's where Patrick died. Dustin's compass detected a gate where Patrick was killed. That must mean that there are other gates. Three gates."

"Four chimes!" Max stands up. "In my visions, the grandfather clock chimes four times exactly. Four chimes, four gates."

"But why does he need four gates? Can't he come through any of the ones he's already made?" you ask.

"I don't know, but I don't want to wait to find out," Nancy says. "We know how Vecna works, and we know where his body is. We also know how to get to him." She points to the spot where Chrissy died. "We've got one shot at this."

You spend the rest of the day preparing for the battle of your life.

Dustin and Eddie Munson climb to the roof of Eddie's trailer, only it isn't really his trailer. Going through the gate turned your whole world upside down. Everything you thought you knew was wrong. You check the makeshift spears and shields once more. Dustin gets the signal from the others over the radio. It's time to defeat a demon and his army of twisted creatures.

Go on to the next page.

"Chrissy, this one's for you!" Eddie yells, and then starts playing Metallica. You watch from the ground as Eddie plays his guitar in what he's calling "the most metal concert ever." Dustin watches for the demobats, giving Eddie a countdown. You see them getting closer. Eddie finishes his guitar solo and gets down from the roof. You all run into the trailer and barricade the door. "That was insane!"

"Dude, most metal ever!" Dustin yells, and they jump up and down together. You are too busy listening for danger. The trailer shakes slightly as something hits the roof with a thud. It's the demobats! You stand back-to-back with Dustin and Eddie, wielding hunting knives tied to sticks and shields made of trash cans spiked with nails.

"They're on the roof," Dustin says, following the sounds. "They can't get in through there, can they?" A demobat bursts through the vent, screeching. You run up and stab it with your spear. Its blood splashes you in the face with every hit. Eddie pushes you aside and slams his shield into the ceiling. It holds, closing the vent.

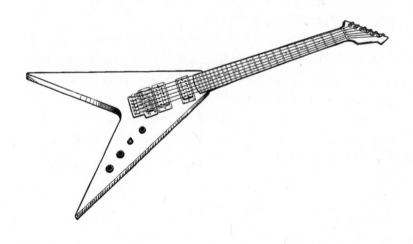

Turn to the next page.

"Are there any other vents?" Dustin asks. Eddie grabs his spear and runs to the back of the trailer into his bedroom. Demobats flood through the vent, getting into the room. Eddie slams the door.

"We gotta go!" Eddie yells. The door cracks and splits. Dustin climbs to the gate first and falls through. Eddie passes you the rope next; you climb, then fall through onto the mattress below.

"Eddie, come on! Hurry up!" Dustin yells. You get up and see Eddie climbing. He stops halfway.

"Eddie, you're so close! Eddie! C'mon!" Dustin yells. Eddie lets go of the rope and drops back down into the other dimension. "Eddie? Eddie, what are you doing? Eddie, no!" Eddie cuts the rope and pushes the mattress on his side out of the way. Dustin puts his hands on his head and yells, "Eddie, stop! Eddie, stop! Eddie, what are you doing?"

"Buying more time." Eddie runs out of sight as Dustin screams, begging him to come back. You push Dustin away and find a chair. Placing it under the gate, you get up and pull yourself through, landing back in the cursed trailer with a thud, twisting your leg beneath you. You limp across the room and pull the mattress back under the gate.

"Come on! We have to help him!" Dustin jumps up on the chair and falls through the gate, landing on the mattress. Dustin pushes out the door with his spear and you follow, despite the shooting pains in your leg.

"Eddie!" Dustin yells as he runs. You can see Eddie biking away from the horde of demobats chasing him. He stops and gets off the bike, then turns to face them. "What are you doing?"

Go on to the next page.

You reach him just as the demobats have him down on the ground, biting his sides and squeezing the life out of him. Dustin races ahead of you, wielding his spear. You limp as fast as you can and join him, cutting a demobat's tail off Eddie's neck. You're able to fend them off but can feel yourself growing weak. You see Dustin and Eddie still struggling. The demobats start screeching and dropping to the ground! This is your chance! You and Dustin grab Eddie and help him get back to the trailer and into the real world.

When Nancy, Steve, and Robin come back through the gate, you all get in the car and head to the Creel house. Everything is in chaos. The Creel house is destroyed, and in its place is a massive gate. You see Erica and Lucas outside. Lucas is on the ground, holding something.

"Where's Max?" Dustin yells.

When you get closer, you see her broken in Lucas's arms, eyes open, staring at nothing. Dustin jumps out of the car before it stops and runs to them. You follow. "Is she . . . ?"

"No," Lucas cries. "She was gone for a whole minute, but then her heart . . . it just started again."

"Four kills, four gates." Dustin looks around. "End of the world."

The End

Your curiosity gets the better of you. You pull the cord and exit. You wait for the bus to drive away before you stick the suitcase behind a bush at the trailer park entrance and then head in. Cop cars and an ambulance have pulled into the park. A small crowd is gathered, and you join them, trying to blend in.

"Make way!" a paramedic yells as he pulls a gurney with a closed black bag on top. Someone has died! There are gasps from the crowd, whispers about those "no-good Munsons." News crews start pulling up. This is huge! A reporter walks up to a police officer; you get closer to listen in.

"Have you identified the victim?" The reporter seems to know the officer.

"You know I can't tell you anything officially," he responds.

"Then unofficially? Off the record?"

"A kid from the high school." The man lights a cigarette. "Murdered."

"How are you so sure?"

"That I definitely can't tell you."

"Got a name?"

"Yeah," he sighs as he exhales. "Chrissy Cunningham."

You make a note to look into the victim's background. Just then a car pulls up.

Go on to the next page.

"Sorry, I have to deal with this." The officer turns away from the reporter and walks up to the car. You can see two teenagers in the front; they ask to be let in to see their friend, who lives here. While the officer is distracted, you quickly make your way to the trailer surrounded by police tape.

At this point, no police are going in or out of the trailer. You find a secluded spot, hang back, and wait. The two teenagers from the car appear—looks like they were able to get in after all. You watch them walk up to a trailer, probably the friend they were talking about. The preppy-dressed girl knocks on the door, and a woman answers.

"Hi, I'm Nancy Wheeler, and this is Fred Benson from the *Hawkins Tiger*—"

"I've talked to enough reporters." The woman slams the door closed. You look at the boy standing there. So this is where Fred was instead of picking you up from the airport? As a fellow journalist, you respect his hustle, though you're still a little peeved. You recognize the name Nancy Wheeler from past correspondence with Fred; she's Fred's boss, the editor of the paper.

Turn to the next page.

You watch as they move on to another trailer. So visiting a friend was a lie. . . . They're here for the story. You wonder if you should go up to them. A car engine revving pulls your attention away from them. A man in a suit gets out of a black car—you can tell he isn't police. FBI? Why would he be here for a simple murder, unless . . . the town is dealing with a serial killer? You watch the agent pass under the police tape. He flashes a badge at a police officer and heads into the trailer. You wait for more FBI to show up, but none do. The agent walks back out of the trailer and leaves quickly.

That was suspiciously quick. Were they really FBI agents?

"What about that one? With the flag?" You turn to see Nancy again.

"They were actually quite rude. I am not doing that again," Fred answers, hitting his notepad. "I'm telling you, we've talked to everyone."

"Nope. Not everyone!" She perks up and jogs to a fence. You look for someone there but don't see anyone. Then she kneels down next to . . . a dog. Really? "Hi there. Hi. Did you see something last night, huh? Oh, you want to tell us everything. . . ."

This is your chance to approach them. You make a beeline for Fred.

Go on to the next page.

"Um, hi." You approach them quickly.

"Ah!" Fred squeaks as he jumps.

"Oh, sorry, I didn't mean to—"

"What are you doing here?" Nancy comes over to you. Her perm looks new, and she's wearing a crisp white collared shirt and a gray sweater vest. Very, very preppy.

"I'm here for the conference," you blurt.

"What?" Nancy looks at you curiously.

Fred steps in. "Nancy, the conference? The one I've been planning for months?"

"Oh, right." Nancy turns back to you. "You're early by a couple days."

"Right . . ." You turn to the boy. "Fred Benson, right? You were supposed to be my host, but no one came to pick me up at the airport. I took the bus and then saw these cop cars. They're saying a student was murdered here."

"Yeah, it was on the news. That's why we came," Fred answers. "Sorry, I completely forgot about picking you up when we heard the news—I think we're going to have to cancel . . ."

"Forget the conference," you say, exasperated. "I want to help with the investigation."

"Who said we're investigating anything?" Nancy retorts.

"The dog told me," you joke. Nancy jerks back at that. You wonder if you've already blown it with her. "Look, I just approached you because I recognized you were fellow journalists, and I could use your help since I'm kind of stranded here right now."

Turn to the next page.

"I can help. I'm stuck here anyway until my return flight, since I can't afford to change it." You know you should be above pleading, but you are desperate.

"Look, I'm sure you're really good at what you do, but . . ." Something catches Nancy's eye behind you. "Fred, stay here and watch our guest." She walks off toward a man sitting alone on a picnic table. You're too far away to hear them. You can't help but feel your frustration rise—another editor dismissing you for no reason.

"Don't take it too personally. That's just how she is," Fred tries to reassure you. You nod but do not look away from Nancy speaking to the man. Your blood begins to boil.

Go on to the next page.

The minutes tick by, and you start to get impatient. "What's her problem, anyway?" you exclaim. The only response you get is the dog barking. "Hey, Fred, I'm talking to—"

You turn to find you are alone. You look for Fred and see him walking dazedly past some trees and then out of sight. Did he see something? A clue? You run toward where you last saw him. The trees are dense; you know if you go any farther, you'll get lost.

Nancy walks over to the dog as you return, looking pale as a ghost. "I just spoke to Wayne—have you heard the name Victor Creel? Wayne has this theory . . ." She pauses and shakes her head, like she's seeing you for the first time. "Hang on—where's Fred?"

"I saw him walk into those trees over there, then I lost him."

"What? Fred wouldn't do that—"

"Maybe he found something and was checking it out?"

She shakes her head. "That doesn't sound like Fred. Show me where you last saw him." You show her, and she starts calling out for Fred.

"I tried that, and he didn't answer," you tell her. You can see the fear growing in her eyes. "Is something wrong?"

She ignores you, calling out to Fred. You follow her.

Turn to the next page.

You've been searching for Fred so long it is dark now. You can barely see the trees in front of you.

"Look, we're wasting time looking by ourselves," you say. "We should tell the police."

She leads you back to the trailer park and walks up to the police officer who is guarding the entrance. "Hi, Officer. Officer!"

"What are you still doing here?" he answers.

"My . . . my friend from the car earlier, I . . . I can't find him."

"What do you mean, you can't find him?"

"He was here, and then he was just gone and . . . Did you maybe see him leave with somebody or . . . ?"

"I told you kids to go home. Jesus Christ." He turns away from Nancy and speaks into his radio. "This is Glenn. We might have a situation here."

"You need to look in the woods!" you call out after him. He curses under his breath.

Go on to the next page.

It's morning now. You hang back on the edge of a highway where Fred has been found. Nancy stands with the officers being interviewed; they've already finished talking to you. Behind her, you see the sheet covering Fred's body.

"And after you talked to Wayne, what happened?"

"I—I heard barking from the dog and then . . . he was just gone. My friend told me he walked off into the woods, so we went after him but couldn't find him."

"Did you see anyone lurking about? Who looks like they shouldn't be there?" the police ask her. She glances at you quickly, but then shakes her head.

"No. No, no, there was nobody there." She turns to Officer Glenn Daniels from the night before. "And I already told this to Officer Daniels. Did you look into Victor Creel?"

"Sorry, what was that?" the chief of police asks.

"Victor Creel," Officer Daniels answers. "Wayne got it in her head that the old nut did this."

The chief looks at Nancy reassuringly. "Victor's locked away tight, hun. You don't need to worry about him, all right?" He continues with his questioning as a car pulls up, catching Nancy's attention.

You turn to see a group of teens getting out of the car. She gives them a small wave, and a tall boy with nice hair waves back. Friends? You think so based on the look of relief on her face. You walk up to them and say hello.

"Hey," the boy says.

"I'm with Nancy."

Turn to the next page.

You find yourself sitting with Nancy and her friends, who you've now been introduced to, at a picnic table. You can't believe what you're hearing.

"So you're saying that this thing that killed Fred and Chrissy, it's from the Upside Down?" Nancy asks.

"Our working theory is that he attacks with a spell or a curse. Now, whether or not he's doing the bidding of the Mind Flayer or just loves killing teens, we don't know," the younger boy, Dustin, explains.

Max, a redheaded girl, adds, "All we know is this is something different."

"I don't understand," you jump in. "A curse? Mind Flayer? Two people are dead!"

Nancy turns to you. "Look, you have no idea what's going on. . . ."

"We've kind of been through this before," the short-haired girl, Robin, answers.

"Been through what?" you ask.

Nancy takes your hands and looks straight into your eyes. "Hawkins isn't like any other town. There's . . . a curse here."

"Yeah," Steve, the boy with nice hair, adds. "Though usually we rely on this girl with superpowers, but, uh, those are gone, so . . ."

"So when Eddie told you Chrissy was just in a trance and then was lifted into the air and killed, you all believe him?" While you and Nancy were looking for Fred, they found Eddie—the last person seen with Chrissy alive—and heard his side of the story.

Go on to the next page.

You can't believe what you are hearing, but they all seem so earnest. "Why should I believe you?"

"Are you kidding me—?" Dustin exclaims.

Nancy stops him. "Look, I get it's a lot to take in, but you said you're a journalist, right? Just keep an open mind and follow the story with us."

You nod. This is it, a big story. Even if what they are saying isn't true, you'll find out. "So why would this Mind Flayer—"

"Vecna," Dustin corrects you, "not the Mind Flayer."

"Okay." You try to hide your annoyance. "Why did this Vecna guy target Fred and Chrissy?"

"We should talk to Miss Kelley," Max answers. "I saw Chrissy leaving her office. Maybe she knows something?" The others agree with the plan.

Nancy nods. "You guys go with Steve. I'm going to look into another lead. I don't want to waste your time. It's a real shot in the dark."

"I'm coming with you," you chime in. It's clear Nancy has had something on her mind since before the incident with Fred, and you want to know what it is.

"So will I," says Robin. You go with Robin and Nancy, picking up your suitcase on the way out.

"Where are we going?" you ask.

"The library." Nancy turns the ignition and you're off.

Turn to the next page.

You've been in the basement of the library scanning microfilm of newspapers for anything related to Victor Creel. This was Nancy's shot in the dark. So far you've only found the basics of the case and its aftermath: Victor Creel moved to Hawkins with his family in the 1950s before murdering his wife, daughter, and son. He was declared insane. According to Nancy, the police say Victor is still locked up tight.

"We've been searching for a while, and you still haven't told us why," you say, breaking the silence.

"Wayne Munson told me that Victor Creel took their eyes out," says Nancy. "When he found Chrissy, her eyes were—"

"Like how they found Fred—" you finish. She nods.

"So you think that what happened to Victor's family could be the same thing that happened to Chrissy and Fred?" Robin continues. "How is this connected to the Upside Down?"

"It's just a hunch," Nancy says. "But what if Creel didn't do it? What if Vecna was behind it?"

"Or that guy just killed his family, and someone is copying him?" you mumble.

"Look, if you aren't going to take this seriously, why don't you just go?" Robin snaps.

"Where exactly? I'm stranded, remember?"

Nancy scribbles an address on a piece of paper and hands it to you. "There, that's my address. You can just go there." You feel your anger begin to rise from being dismissed. Maybe this is an opportunity to learn more about Nancy and her friends while she's not around?

If you choose to stay with Nancy and Robin,
go on to the next page.

If you choose to go to Nancy's house, turn to page 233.

"Okay, okay, I'll shut up." You don't want to give in, but you also don't want to leave this story. They seem to accept your answer, and the search continues.

"So, what are we looking for exactly?" Robin asks after a while. Nancy doesn't respond. "Nance? Any mention of dark wizards or alternate dimensions? Things in that vein?" You hold in a smirk.

"I don't know, okay?" Nancy answers, exasperated. "It's starting to seem like this was a big waste of time, and you're obviously bored. So why don't you just call Steve? I'm sure he'll come pick you up. And I mean, I'm not really in danger here, so . . ." She walks off.

Robin gives you a look and then goes after her. You shouldn't care, but knowing that Nancy is about to admit she's wrong is too tantalizing, so you follow.

"You do know that Steve and I are, like, totally not a thing, right?" you catch Robin saying. "Like, platonic with a capital P. Just in case that's adding any tension between us." She opens a drawer with more microfilm.

"Seriously—" you start, but Robin glares at you to shut up.

Nancy straightens; you think you see a slight blush on her cheeks. "It wasn't."

"Great," you say sarcastically. "Glad that's all cleared up."

"Weren't you supposed to be shutting up?" Robin asks. You roll your eyes. The three of you begin looking through drawers for more microfilm to check out.

Turn to the next page.

Robin looks through the drawer and pulls out a box. *"The Weekly Watcher?* I can't believe they have this."

"Don't they write about, like, Bigfoot and UFOs?" Nancy asks.

"May I remind you that we are looking for information on dark wizards? If someone's going to write about that, it's going to be these weirdos."

"Are you serious—?" you begin.

"Shutting up, remember?" Robin snaps. You sigh and roll your eyes. Heading back to the machine, Robin puts in the film and starts scanning. *"Victor Creel claims vengeful demon killed family. The murder that shocked a small community."*

Robin keeps reading: *"According to several insiders, Victor believed his house was haunted by an ancient demon. Victor allegedly hired a priest to exorcise the demon from his home. Pretty novel for the '50s. The Exorcist wasn't even out yet."*

"Part of the plea bargain sealed the records, so . . . ," Nancy adds.

"So you're saying"—you can hear your heart pounding in your head—"that this Vecna is the demon that killed his family?" You don't want to believe it, but there is a connection after all.

"Dustin, do you copy?" Robin calls into a radio as you exit the library. "So Nancy's a genius—Vecna's first victims date back all the way to 1959. Her shot in the dark was a bull's-eye."

"Okay, that's totally bonkers, but I can't really talk right now," Dustin answers. "You need to get to the school."

Go on to the next page.

"It was here. Right here!" Max shows you all a dead-end hallway at the school. While you, Nancy, and Robin were looking into Creel's connection to Vecna—which you're still not sure how you feel about—Max, Dustin, and Steve broke into the school to look through the counselor's files, after talking to her didn't give them anything useful.

"You saw a grandfather clock in the wall here?" you ask.

She nods. "It was so real. And then, when I got closer, suddenly I just . . . I woke up."

"It was like she was in a trance or something," Dustin explains. "Exactly what Eddie said happened to Chrissy."

"That's not even the bad part." Max leads you all into the counselor's office. "Fred and Chrissy, they both came to Miss Kelley for help. They were both having headaches, nightmares, trouble sleeping. And then they started seeing things from their past. And these visions, they kept on getting worse and worse, until eventually . . . everything ended. Chrissy's started a week ago, Fred's six days ago. I've been having them for five days. I don't know how long I have. All I know is that for Fred and Chrissy, they both died less than twenty-four hours after their first vision. And I just saw that goddamn clock, so . . . looks like I'm going to die tomorrow."

A loud clang erupts from the hall. Steven grabs a lamp and heads out. "Stay here."

You have no intention of doing so, and it looks like no one else does either. When you get into the hall, you hear footsteps coming closer. Steve gets ready to swing the lamp. A figure turns the corner, and everyone screams! "It's me! It's me!" yells a sweaty, out-of-breath boy.

Turn to the next page.

After the scare with Lucas at the school last night, you find yourself with Nancy and Robin this morning to go see Victor Creel at Pennhurst Mental Hospital, where he's been locked up since the murder of his family.

Pennhurst is not at all what you imagined an asylum would be like. You sit in the office of the head doctor, Dr. Hatch, with Nancy and Robin as he goes through the fake student profiles Nancy cooked up. "Three-point-nine GPAs, all of you. Impressive."

"We can only learn so much in a classroom." Nancy tries to smooth things over.

"And I'm sympathetic to your struggle, truly. But there is a protocol to visiting a patient like Victor," he answers. You have a sinking feeling in your stomach.

Go on to the next page.

"The fact of the matter is we did put in a request months ago and were denied," Robin lies. You glance over at Nancy, who keeps a poker face on. "Then we reapplied and were denied again. Coming here was a last-ditch effort to save our thesis. And I'm starting to think this whole thing is a colossal mistake, because nobody takes girls seriously in this field. They just don't! Other kids, they wanted to be astronauts, basketball players, rock stars, but I wanted to be you! Ten minutes with Victor, that's all I ask."

Silence hangs in the air. Dr. Hatch just nods. Holy crap, it worked! He leads you out the door on a small tour. You see people in white clothes milling about listening to calming music. "This is one of our more popular areas—the listening room. We found that music has a particularly calming effect on the broken mind. The right song, particularly one that holds some personal meaning, can prove a salient stimulus." He leads you out of the room and down some stairs.

"Dr. Hatch, do you think it might be possible for us to speak to Victor alone?" Nancy asks.

Robin jumps in. "We would love the challenge of speaking with Victor without the safety net of an expert such as yourself."

Surprisingly, he allows you to speak with Victor alone. As Nancy and Robin head toward the cells where Creel is kept, you look back to see a quizzical look on the doctor's face.

If you choose to talk to Creel, turn to the next page.

If you choose to spy on the doctor, turn to page 218.

If Dr. Hatch had any reservations, surely he wouldn't let you talk to Victor alone, right? A guard leads the way, and you follow Nancy and Robin toward Victor's cell. This looks more like how you pictured an asylum, cells and bars. A prison.

"Do not startle him. Do not touch him." The guard lists instructions as you get closer to the cell. "Stand five feet away from the bars at all times. Is that clear?" You nod. He pulls out his baton and runs it along the cell bars. "Victor, today's your lucky day! You got visitors. Real pretty ones." The guard leaves. Victor sits with his back to you. You can hear the screeching of his nails digging into a table.

"Victor? My name is Nancy Wheeler, and these are my friends." She steps closer to the bars. "We have some questions—"

"I don't talk to reporters," he answers gruffly. "Hatch knows that."

"We're not reporters. We're here because we believe you." Nancy is standing right up against the bars now. "And because we need your help."

"Whatever killed your family"—Robin stands next to Nancy—"we think it's back."

Victor turns to face you. His eyes are sewn shut! You all look at each other. Nancy presses on, explaining to him what has been happening in Hawkins. "Does any of this, anything we've told you, sound like what happened to your family?" He doesn't respond.

"We need to know how you survived that night." Robin puts a hand on a bar.

"Survived?" He laughs. "Is that what you call this? Did I survive?"

If you weren't sure he was insane before, you believe it now. Nancy and Robin seem to take in everything he says. *Be open to the possibilities,* you remind yourself.

Turn to page 188.

"No, I assure you," he continues, "I am still very much in hell. We had one month of peace in that house, and then it began. Dead animals, mutilated, tortured, began to appear near our home. Rabbits, squirrels, chickens, even dogs. The police chief blamed the attacks on a wildcat. This was no wildcat. This was a spawn of Satan. And it was even closer than I realized. My family began to have encounters conjured by this demon. Waking, living nightmares."

"Max," you whisper.

"This demon, it seemed to take pleasure in tormenting us," he continued. "My wife would see things, like hundreds of spiders that weren't there. Even poor, innocent Alice. She woke screaming in the night. It wasn't long before I began to have encounters of my own. Things from the war, things only I could know. I suppose all evil must have a home. And though I had no rational explanation for it, I could sense this demon always close. I became convinced it was hiding, nesting somewhere within the shadows of our home. It had cursed our town. It had cursed our home. It had cursed us."

"What happened the night your family died?" you ask, your voice hoarse, though you're sure you already know the answer.

Go on to the next page.

"We were having dinner, and the radio came on. Ella Fitzgerald, 'Dream a Little Dream of Me.' I got up to see what happened. Every light in the house started to flicker. Then . . . then Virginia was lifted into the air, her bones were broken in different directions, her eyes sunken in, and then she dropped onto the table. I tried to get the children out. I tried to save them! But . . ." You wince at the anguish in his voice. "I was back to France, back in the war. It was a memory. I had thought German soldiers were inside this house. I ordered its shelling. I was wrong. This demon, it was taunting me with my worst memories. And I was sure he would take me, just as he'd taken my Virginia. But then I heard another voice. At first I believed it was an angel, and I followed her, only to find myself in a nightmare far worse."

"You were back in your home," Robin continues.

"While I was away, the demon took my children. My daughter Alice was"—his voice chokes—"she was already dead. Henry slipped into a coma shortly after that. A week later, he died. I tried to join them. I tried! Hatch stopped the bleeding; he wouldn't let me join them."

"The angel you followed . . . who was she?" Nancy asks.

Victor doesn't answer. Instead, he starts humming "Dream a Little Dream of Me" and clutching his pillow. "Victor?"

"Something's not right," you say to the others.

"Yeah, no kidding." Robin scoffs.

"No, I mean the story," you continue. "It doesn't add up."

Just then Hatch bursts into the hall. "Was he everything you hoped he would be? I just had a very interesting conversation with Professor Brantley. Perhaps we should discuss in my office while we wait for the police."

Turn to the next page.

"You're not listening. Our friend is in danger." Nancy tries to reason with Dr. Hatch as he and some security escort you back to his office.

"Do you really expect me to believe anything you have to say at this point?" he retorts.

You block them out, your mind spinning from Victor's story. You go over the details in your mind again, mindlessly following the others.

"Music," you hear Robin saying. "The night of the murder, Victor said the radio went on. Then when we asked about the angel, he started humming."

"'Dream a Little Dream of Me,' by Ella Fitzgerald." You hurry to get closer to them.

"Voice of an angel," Nancy confirms.

"Hatch said that music can reach parts of the brain that words can't." Robin balls her hands into fists. "So maybe that's the key, a lifeline."

"A lifeline back to reality," Nancy elaborates. She pauses. "I think we can beat them." Without warning, she takes off.

You grab Robin's hand and pull her to start running. You all make it to the car, jump in, and speed away.

Go on to the next page.

"Robin, where the hell are you? This is a code red. I repeat, a code red!" Dustin's voice yells from the radio.

"Dustin, it's Robin. We copy," Robin answers.

"Finally! Please, please tell me you guys have figured this out! We can't wake up Max. Vecna's got her. We're at the cemetery."

"You need to play music! Play her favorite song loudly!" Robin yells into the radio. Nancy steps on it.

You're back at the Wheelers' house with the others. Max is plugged into a Walkman blaring Kate Bush. Everyone else is asleep, and the sun begins to rise. Try as you might, you can't sleep. Victor's story keeps turning in your mind. Something is bothering you about it, but you still can't figure it out. You turn to see Max getting up and going up the stairs. Dustin is supposed to be watching Max; each of you has been taking turns. When you look at him, you see he is fast asleep. You roll your eyes. "Might as well get up," you whisper as you follow Max.

Turn to the next page.

You find her sitting at the kitchen table. The Wheelers are up, and Mrs. Wheeler is preparing breakfast. You sit next to Max.

"Can't sleep?" you ask.

"No, you?"

"Me neither." You look at the table to see a pile of papers and crayons spread out. "What are you doing?"

"I'm just drawing what I remember from my vision."

"Is this a memory?" you ask, trying to make sense of the streaks of red across the page. Victor said his vision was from a memory.

"No." She keeps drawing. "This is something else. It's like I wasn't supposed to see this, like somehow I was in his mind."

"His mind?" You look at the pictures again, but it's useless. "I feel like Victor gave us a clue about this demon."

"You mean the music?" she asks.

"No." You shake your head. "I mean yes, he did give us that. But I think there was something else. If the demon that killed his family in 1959 is the same one today, why the long gap? It's 1986—that's twenty-seven years of no killings that we know of. He kills the same way each time, it seems, so if there were other murders, we would have found out about them, right?"

"I guess so." Max stops drawing. "What are you trying to say?"

"I'm not sure yet." You pause. Just then Nancy and Dustin come up the stairs.

Go on to the next page.

"What are you two doing?" Nancy asks as Dustin grabs a stack of pancakes from Mrs. Wheeler.

"Talking . . . Well, she's drawing." You point to Max.

Nancy picks up a drawing and freezes. "I know this door. It's the old Creel place."

You all get into Nancy's car, and she drives everyone to the Creel house. It's boarded up and covered in grime. You follow the others up the porch stairs to the door. Steve and Nancy remove the nails from the board covering the front door. When it drops, you see a stained-glass window in the door. Steve tries the handle. "It's locked."

Robin holds up a brick. "I found a key." She chucks the brick through the stained glass. Steve reaches through and opens the door. You all head in.

Lucas tries to turn on a lamp. "Looks like someone forgot to pay their electric bill." Dustin pulls out a flashlight and turns it on. The others do the same, except for Steve.

"Where did everyone get those?" he asks.

Dustin looks at him incredulously. "Do you need to be told everything? You're not a child."

You lean toward Steve. "I don't have one either."

"Thanks."

Dustin pulls off his backpack and hands it to Steve. "Back pocket." Steve pulls out two flashlights and hands you one, then drops the bag. Max stops in front of an old grandfather clock.

Turn to the next page.

"You guys are seeing this too, right?" she asks.

"Is this what you saw in your vision?" Nancy asks. Max nods. It's an ordinary clock. Robin wipes its dusty face and confirms.

"Okay, split into pairs and start searching," Nancy says. The others all split off, leaving you on your own. Guess they aren't used to odd numbers. You walk around the ground floor but don't see anything interesting, so you head upstairs. The floorboards creak and moan under you, adding to the ambience of the web- and dust-filled halls. You find another set of stairs behind a door that leads to an attic and go up.

The wood beams of the attic are covered in dust and cobwebs.

You scan the floor with your flashlight. In a corner, the light reflects off of something. You get closer, slowly, your breathing getting harder.

Jars. Old, dirty, sticky jars are what you find next to drawings of a giant creature. You pick one up and look inside to see webs and spiders. You think back to the past couple of days, and then it hits you: Virginia Creel had seen spiders in one of her visions from Vecna. You're not sure if it is connected, but it runs through your mind, reminding you of how Victor's story unsettled you—and not for the obvious reasons. You leave the attic.

Go on to the next page.

"Where have you been?" Robin hisses. Everyone else is back in the foyer.

"I was searching—"

"Never mind that. We found Vecna! Or at least we had him for a bit," Dustin interrupts.

"What?" You take a step back. "You saw him?"

"What? No!" Dustin looks frustrated. "Look!"

A dusty chandelier begins to glow overhead. The pale light is weak at first, but flickers and begins to brighten.

"It's like the Christmas lights," Nancy says.

"Christmas lights?" Robin asks before you can.

"Yeah, when Will was stuck in the Upside Down, the lights . . . came to life. That's how Joyce Byers was able to talk to him," Nancy explains. Will was the friend who was lost in the Upside Down all those years ago—their first adventure. Seems Robin wasn't there either.

"Vecna's here." Lucas stares at the lights. "In this house, just on the other side." The lights go out.

Turn to the next page.

"He's moving!" Steve leads the way, following Vecna's trail back to the attic, where you found the jars of spiders.

"Do you remember Victor's story?" You turn to Robin and Nancy. "Virginia saw spiders in her vision."

"What does that mean?" Lucas asks.

"I'm not sure yet," you answer.

In the attic, the single light flickers. Vecna. You all circle around it, and your flashlights begin to glow.

"Okay, what's happening?" Steve asks. No one answers.

"Is he just standing there?" you ask. The lights grow stronger, blaring in your faces until they explode. A shard of glass scratches your face. "Holy—! What was that?" you yell. It's clear from the looks on their faces that it's time to get out of there, quickly. You all race back to the car. Dustin grabs his backpack off the floor as he exits.

"What happened in there?" you ask as you squeeze into the back. The tires squeal as Nancy drives off toward her house.

"I have no idea," Dustin answers, followed by a string of curses.

Things only seem worse the next morning when you get to Eddie's hideout. Police are everywhere. "Do you think he was caught?" you ask the others. News crews are gathered around the chief of police. The chief informs the reporters of the murder of another student, Patrick McKinney.

Go on to the next page.

"We have also identified a person of interest, Eddie Munson." He holds up a picture of Eddie to the cameras. "We encourage anyone with information to please come forward."

"This is not good. This is really not good." Steve looks at Dustin.

Dustin's radio blares to life. "Dustin? Wheeler? Can you hear me?" Eddie's voice comes through the radio. "I'm at Skull Rock." Dustin pulls out a compass.

After walking for a long time following Dustin and his compass, you are nowhere near this Skull Rock place.

"You're going the wrong way," Steve says to Dustin.

"No, I'm not. My compass is pointing that way, so Skull Rock should be this way."

"No, man, Skull Rock is a super popular make-out spot," Steve explains. "Well, it wasn't popular until I made it popular. I practically invented it. We're heading in the wrong direction."

Steve leads you right to Skull Rock, where Eddie is waiting.

Turn to the next page.

"This doesn't make sense," Dustin protests. He continues to stare at his compass, walking in small circles. The others leave Dustin to his obsessing and gather around Eddie.

"What happened? Did you see the murder?" you ask.

Eddie nods. "I saw it, and I did the thing I apparently do now . . . I ran." The shame in his eyes sucks you in. It is devastating.

"Do you know what time the attack on Patrick happened?" Nancy asks.

Eddie takes off his watch and tosses it to her. "It was 9:27."

"Same time our flashlights went kablooey." Robin looks at Nancy.

"So that power we saw was Vecna attacking," you continue. "And somehow he's able to do this from the other side?"

"But how?" Nancy asks. "El closed the gates."

"Our superpowered friend, you know the one who lost her powers and moved away . . . ?" Steve explains.

"Yeah, you mentioned her," Eddie retorts.

"Boom!" Dustin yells, stopping his walking in circles. "I wasn't wrong. The compass was!" He points to his compass. "Lucas, do you remember what can affect a compass?"

"An electromagnetic field."

"Yep." Dustin smiles. "In the presence of a stronger electromagnetic field, the needle will deflect toward that power. The last time we saw that happen—"

"Was when there was a gate at Hawkins Lab!" Lucas finishes.

"So you're saying we have a way to Vecna," you finish. "Lead the way."

Turn to page 200.

200

You arrive back at Lover's Lake as it gets dark. "We were just here," you say.

"There's a gate in Lover's Lake?" Max asks.

"Only one way to find out." Steve points to a boat on the shore. Eddie and Steve push it into the water and then hold it. Robin gets in, then Eddie, then Nancy. Before anyone can say anything, you jump in too. Then Dustin follows but is stopped by Eddie.

"This boat holds four people max," he says.

"But it's my theory. I should get to go."

"You guys stay with Max and keep an eye out for trouble," Nancy says to the others, and takes the compass from Dustin. As you grab an oar and push off, Steve jumps into the boat.

"You said four max!" Dustin protests. Steve just shrugs. You row out to the center of the lake when Nancy says to slow down.

"So now what?" You look at the others. Steve takes off his shirt and shoes.

"Unless one of you guys can top being co-captain of the swim team and a certified lifeguard for three years, it's gotta be me that goes down there to check it out," Steve says. Eddie hands him a flashlight covered by a plastic bag.

"Be careful, Steve," Nancy says. You catch Robin giving them a look. There's some history here for sure. A love triangle? Steve dives off the boat. Nancy counts the time on her watch. After almost a minute, Steve surfaces.

"I found the gate. It's a small gate, but it's there." Just then Steve is pulled under! You look at the others. What happened? Without hesitation, Nancy jumps in after him, then Robin follows. You look over at Eddie, and then jump in too.

Go on to the next page.

You can see the gate glowing even in the dark water and swim toward it. When you push through, you find yourself out of the water and out of your world. The ground is covered in writhing vines, and the sky flashes with red lightning. It's the Upside Down. If you had any doubts at this point, there's no question now. You hear yelling and see Nancy and Robin fighting bat-like creatures that are attacking Steve. You help Eddie through the gate, then you both run toward the fight. The bats have Steve pinned to the ground, bleeding, and one is choking him with its tail. Nancy and Eddie get oars and swing at the bats. You and Robin stomp them. You grab one by the tail and step on its head and pull it apart. More appear. Searing pain hits your side as a bat knocks you to the ground and takes a bite out of you. Eddie hits it, crushing its skull, and you scramble back to your feet, bleeding. Steve is up, grabbing a bat by its tail and smashing it into the ground until it splits. The bats are dead.

"I already hate it here," you gasp. Eddie curses loudly as more bats appear, blocking the gate.

"We need to run for cover." Nancy dashes toward a line of trees in the direction of Skull Rock. You sprint as fast as you can. The cover of the rock allows you to catch your breath. "Don't touch the vines," Nancy warns you. "It's a hive mind."

"Now what?" you ask. "The only gate we know of is blocked by those . . . things."

"Demobats," Steve mumbles as Nancy dresses his wounds.

"What?"

"Dustin . . ." Steve winces as Nancy wraps something around him. "He would give them a name like Demogorgon, demodogs, Mind Flayer, you know?"

Turn to the next page.

"Okay, so what do we do with those demobats guarding the gate?" Eddie asks.

"I've got guns." Nancy scans the horizon. "If we can get to my place, we can use them to get through the demobats."

"Wait." You stop Nancy. "We can't just leave."

"I kinda think we should." Steve leans against the rock, pointing to his makeshift bandaging.

"No, think about it," you insist. "Where else are we going to find a way to defeat Vecna but here? We can't go through the gate now anyway, and it's the only one we know of."

"Not necessarily," Nancy interrupts. "If a gate is opened whenever Vecna makes a kill . . ."

"So you're saying there's a gate in my trailer?" Eddie finishes.

"Okay, so we have another way out," you continue. "But think about it: if there is a gate, why hasn't Vecna just come through?"

"Like the Demogorgon." Nancy looks at Steve. "When Will went missing into the Upside Down three years ago, the Demogorgon came out to our side."

"So why doesn't Vecna?" You take a step toward Nancy. "We're journalists, right? There's something here. I can feel it. Vecna is strong enough to go through the gate and wreak havoc on Hawkins, but he won't. There's got to be a reason."

"And it's not like we have El here with her powers to stop him." Nancy follows your line of thinking. "So what's stopping him?"

"This is crazy," Eddie hisses. "We need to get out of here!"

If you choose to go to the Creel house in the Upside Down, go on to the next page.

If you choose to head to Eddie's trailer, turn to page 215.

You manage to convince the others to go to the Creel house, despite Eddie's effusive disagreement. Steve leads the way, and you pull Nancy back to walk with you. It's time to tell her your suspicions.

"Do you remember when Victor told us about the different visions his family had?" She nods. "He mentioned that Virginia saw spiders, Alice found dead animals and had nightmares, and he saw things from the war."

"Right, so?"

"What did his son see?" You can tell Nancy is picking up your point. "Why was he the only one Victor didn't mention having visions? And then when Victor came out of his vision, Alice was already dead like Virginia, eyes sunken in, the whole nine yards, but Henry . . ."

"Henry was still alive and in a coma, no broken bones, no eyes sunken in."

"Exactly. I don't know what it means, but it's been bothering me this whole time. Why did Victor know about what everyone else saw but not mention Henry?"

"And why was Henry the only one who died differently?"

"If this demon is the same one from back then, then we know it can only kill one person at a time from the Upside Down: Chrissy, Fred, Patrick. Even Victor said Virginia was the first one to die. If it could, why wouldn't the demon kill them all at once?"

"What are you trying to say?"

"Alice was already dead when Victor escaped his vision. Why wasn't Henry?" You want to continue your point but are interrupted by Steve, who announces you are at the Creel house.

Turn to the next page.

The house is covered in demobats, hundreds of them. Getting closer would be a suicide mission. "You mean to tell me we came all this way for nothing?" Eddie hisses, then bites his fist.

"Maybe there's another way in?" you suggest. "If we can find a way to distract the bats, maybe we can get in?"

"Then what?" Eddie says. "Throw rocks at him? We're unarmed and could barely escape those demobats. How are we supposed to fight Vecna?"

"We're not going to fight him," you insist. "But maybe we can get some information?"

"We can't just walk in there unarmed!" Eddie says again.

"We won't be." Nancy looks at everyone. "I have weapons in my room. If we go to my house in the Upside Down, we should be able to get them and then come back to look around."

Nancy opens the door to her house and leads everyone up the stairs to her bedroom. She reaches into her closet and pulls out a shoebox. "Something's wrong," she says, looking inside the shoebox. "They're not here."

"Are you sure you're looking in the right place?"

"There's a six-year-old in the house. I know where I keep my guns." She drops the box and goes to her nightstand, pulling out a notebook from the drawer. She flips through the pages. "This diary should be full, but it's not. The last entry is November 6, 1983."

"The day Will disappeared." Steve and Nancy share a look.

Go on to the next page.

Nancy rushes out of the room, and you all follow. In the kitchen she finds a newspaper. The date reads November 6, 1983.

"Did we somehow go back in time, or is the Upside Down stuck in 1983?" you ask. No one has an answer.

"Wait." Steve looks around. "Do you guys hear that?" You listen and hear faint voices, a conversation. "Hello?" Steve starts to yell. "Henderson! Can you hear me?" With no answer, Steve looks at the rest of you. "It's Dustin. I can hear him."

"That means they are at my house but on the other side." She looks at a lamp nearby. "Does anyone know Morse code?"

"Does SOS count?" Eddie asks. Nancy nods, and Eddie taps out the code on the lightbulb. You hear Dustin's curse from the other side. He yells to meet you upstairs in Nancy's room. You all head back up and communicate with them using lights, saying that you'll rendezvous at Eddie's trailer. It's time to leave the Upside Down.

When you get to Eddie's trailer, you see Dustin, Lucas, Max, and a younger girl you don't know on the other side of the gate. They use a bedsheet as a rope and place a mattress on their end. Robin goes through first, then Eddie. You get ready to climb out.

"Nancy?" Steve shakes her. You turn to see Nancy is in a trance.

"Music!" you yell through the gate. "Find some music now!" You see the others disappear from the gate and hear them yelling about music. You turn back to Nancy and Steve. Just then Nancy is pulled out of her trance. You, Steve, and Nancy escape the Upside Down.

Turn to the next page.

Nancy is shivering on the couch in Max's living room, covered in a blanket, her eyes wide with fear. "Remember what you said about Henry's death?" You nod. "You were right—it was different. Because Henry didn't die. He was the demon." Nancy describes her vision. "He showed me how he killed his family and then was taken by Dr. Brenner, tattooed with the number one."

Dustin and Lucas stare at each other in shock. Nancy sees your confusion. "He was the scientist in charge of Hawkins Lab," she says. "He ran the experiments on El. He died when we were attacked by the Demogorgon back in 1983," Lucas explains.

"We keep coming back to that year," you mutter.

"That's not all he showed me," Nancy continued. "Henry, or Vecna, he knew El. His powers were somehow blocked all those years until El set him free. Then . . . then he killed everyone in the lab and El cast him into the Upside Down."

"So that explains why there were no more demon killings after the Creels were murdered." You try to fit the pieces of the puzzle together. You're convinced that you can find a way to defeat Vecna.

"He didn't just show me the past," Nancy says, covering herself more with the blanket. "He showed me things that haven't happened yet. I saw a dark cloud spreading over Hawkins, downtown on fire, dead soldiers, and a giant creature with a gaping mouth, and the creature wasn't alone. There were so many monsters. An army. And they were coming into Hawkins, into our neighborhoods, our homes. And then he showed me my mom, Holly, Mike, and . . . and they were all—" Her voice breaks. "He showed me four gates, spreading across Hawkins."

Go on to the next page.

"Four chimes," Max says. "Vecna's clock. It always chimes four times. Four exactly. He's been telling us his plan this whole time."

"Four kills," Lucas says, and turns to Max. "Four gates. End of the world."

"If that's true, he's only one kill away," Dustin says.

Steve looks at Max. "Try them again. Try them again." Max goes to the phone and dials.

"Who are you calling?"

"The Byerses," Dustin answers. "Will Byers—"

"Went missing in the Upside Down in 1983," you say, speeding him along.

"El, our superpowered friend, lives with them now in Lenora Hills, Cal—"

"California," you say, shocked. "Where I'm from."

Max hangs up the phone. "It rang a few times, then went to the busy signal."

"How is that possible?" Lucas asks. "It's been three days."

"You don't think there's something going on in Lenora, do you?" You wonder how far the Upside Down goes. Is there an alternate Lenora? Is your mom in danger?

"Last year, El said when she tried to get into Billy's mind, he told her the Mind Flayer was building all of this for her," Max says. You want to ask more about it, but Nancy speaks.

"It can't be just coincidence." Nancy gets up and goes to the window. "Whatever's happening in Lenora is connected to all of this. I'm sure of it. But Vecna can't hurt them, not if he's dead." She turns away from the window to look at everyone. "We have to go back in there. Back to the Upside Down."

Turn to the next page.

On paper, the plan seems simple enough. In practice, you feel sick to your stomach. You volunteer to stay with Lucas and Erica to help Max. It can also give you time to think more about all you've learned. You can't help but feel there's some missing piece, something more to know for defeating Vecna.

At a hunting store, you, Robin, Nancy, Erica, and Steve stock up on weapons. Eddie and the other known members of the Hellfire Club are staying out of sight after Erica described the mobs that were let loose by a basketball player named Jason Carver. Dustin gave you a list of things needed to make Molotov cocktails, and Nancy tells you what the creatures of the Upside Down hate. You scan the aisles, grabbing anything you think would be useful.

You see Nancy at the counter looking at guns. A boy in a letterman jacket comes up to her. Erica stops next to you. "That's Jason, the basketball player hunting Eddie." Your heart drops into your stomach. "I need to warn the others." She looks around, and you follow her gaze. The place is swarming with jocks. She races back down the aisle. You look back at Nancy. Should you intervene?

If you choose to let Nancy handle it, go on to the next page.

If you choose to intervene, turn to page 213.

You watch from afar as Jason gets closer to Nancy. He looks menacing, but she holds her ground. Eventually, he leaves her alone. You wait till the coast is clear and then go up to her.

"Are you okay?" She nods. The weapons you've all gathered are purchased and you run back to the car. Steve drives away swiftly. You see Jason standing outside the store as you pass.

"Remember," Nancy says, "no deviating from the plan, no matter what."

You, Max, Lucas, and Erica head into the house, carrying lanterns. Since everyone needs to stay silent, you also bring notepads to communicate. Erica finds Vecna and informs you all. It is time for phase one. You and Erica reach the park across from the house and wait in the rocket jungle gym for the signal from the others in the Upside Down. Your flashlight glows. They've made it to the other side. Erica speaks so the team in the Upside Down can hear: "Okay, the lovebirds have copied. Max is moving into phase two—distracting Vecna." You and Erica wait for the next sign. Finally it comes. When the light wanes, you know the team on the other side has moved into the Creel house.

Turn to the next page.

You and Erica stick close together, waiting for a signal that the plan is working. The suspense is terrible, but you remember Nancy's orders: do not deviate.

You hear a car engine revving; it's the jocks! You both jump down from the rocket. One of the vigilantes chases Erica while you sprint to the Creel house to warn Lucas.

Jason is faster and gets into the house first. Even worse, when you race into the dark house, you see Vecna. Something has gone wrong!

"Jason," you hear Lucas say, "you can't be here right now, man." You rush up the stairs to the attic and find the adversaries circling each other.

"Is this what you did to Chrissy?" Jason asks as he attempts to wake Max. Lucas tries to stop him. Jason pulls a gun from his jacket. You tackle him, and his gun goes off as it drops to the floor. You fumble blindly and grab it.

"Stay down!" you yell at Jason. He freezes. Max starts to lift off the ground. Lucas grabs the Walkman and blasts music in Max's ears. She wakes up.

Turn to page 212.

"Lucas, get Max out of here! Go find Erica!" you yell. Lucas grabs Max and leads her out of the attic, while you keep your eyes on Jason. "You are going to stay right there. If you move, if you follow us, you'll give me no choice. Nod if you understand." Jason nods.

You slowly back out of the attic. When you get to the stairs, you pause and pull out your flashlight. It's no longer glowing. You hope that means the team in the Upside Down was successful. You find Erica, Lucas, and Max, and you say, "We can't stay here, not with that maniac hunting us. We should get back to Eddie's trailer now!"

"We lost." Nancy grits her teeth. The others have made it back to the real world through the gate in Eddie's trailer. Everyone except Eddie. Dustin tells you how Eddie sacrificed himself to buy everyone more time. His sacrifice was in vain. "Vecna is still out there."

You try to be encouraging. "But we stopped him from opening the last gate."

"For how long?" Nancy asks the question on everyone's mind. "Vecna got away, and Max is still marked. It won't be long before he regains his strength and tries again, or finds another victim. We can't close any of the gates without El."

"El will be here," Max says. "I saw her in my mind. She said something about a piggyback. She fought with Vecna, giving me a chance to get out. I'm sure they're on their way. We just need to wait for them. Until then"—Max holds up the Walkman—"more Kate Bush."

"So it's a stalemate." You sit down and put your head in your hands. The danger is not over. Not even close.

The End

You walk quickly up to Nancy. "Hey, Nance, your mom has been looking for you."

"Oh, okay." She turns back to Jason. "Thanks for the tip. I've got to go."

"Hey, wait a minute," Jason says, stopping you both from leaving. "I don't think I know you."

"This is my cousin from out of town, visiting for spring break."

"Yeah, just my bad luck coming here when all this is going on," you say, trying to aid the story.

"Nice to meet you. I'm Jason Carver." He extends his hand to you. You hesitate before shaking it, and then introduce yourself. Jason grips your hand tightly. "Strange time to be visiting Hawkins, isn't it?" He doesn't let go.

"Nancy," you say, "run." Then you tackle Jason to the ground. You struggle to keep him down before someone pulls you off of him and turns you around, pinning you to the counter. You turn your head to see the others drive away. They made it.

Turn to the next page.

"I refuse to speak without either a parent or a lawyer present," you repeat. After attacking Jason, you were arrested. You have refused to talk, knowing your rights.

"We have tried calling your mother, but no one has been picking up." Officer Callahan leans on the table. "Is there anyone else we can call? Someone in Hawkins?"

"No." Eventually, they will realize they can call the Wheelers since you were staying with them, but you are trying to stall for time. Your hope is that you can keep the police off of the others so they can execute the plan.

"Where were you staying?" Powell finally asks.

"As a minor, I refuse to speak without either a parent or a lawyer present."

Callahan slams the table. "Dammit, kid! People's lives are at stake here. Where is Eddie Munson?" he yells. Powell pushes him back.

"I know for a fact that Eddie is innocent," you say. "He hasn't killed anyone."

"How do you know that?" Powell asks.

You take a deep breath. "I refuse to say more without either a parent or a lawyer present."

Callahan curses again. Powell looks at his watch. "We haven't been able to secure you a lawyer just yet with all the chaos around here."

"Then I guess you'll just have to wait," you say. Powell and Callahan get up and open the door, leading you to a holding cell since you are under arrest for assault. You hear a rumbling sound and then the earth shakes, knocking you over. Tears well up in your eyes. The earth swallows you whole.

The End

Despite your growing curiosity, you can see that you're all unprepared to do anything useful at the Creel house, so you give in. "I guess we should go to Eddie's trailer."

It doesn't take long to make your way back to the trailer. Steve looks around for something to reach the gate in the ceiling. "Eddie, give me a boost."

Eddie laces his fingers together and Steve steps into his hands. He reaches the gate and pulls himself through, then flips and lands perfectly on his feet. He gives a small bow. Robin rolls her eyes. "Okay, show-off, now how about helping the rest of us?"

"Just get a boost from Eddie and then I'll catch you," he says.

"Yeah, but then how do I get out?" Eddie yells. Steve sees his error.

"The gravity changed when you went through, right? Just like the gate in the lake," Nancy says. "If you can get something for us to hold on to and climb, it should hold." Steve leaves the gate and then comes back with some sheets. He tosses the bundle at the gate, and it comes through hanging in the air, just as Nancy predicted. Steve also tosses a mattress on the ground under the hanging sheets for everyone to land on. Robin goes up first. Then Eddie. You step aside so Nancy can go next. She steps forward, then freezes.

"Nancy? What's wrong?" She doesn't answer. You walk around her and see her eyes fluttering and glazed over. "Nancy!"

"What's going on?" Robin yells.

"It's Nancy! She's in a trance! Vecna's got her. We need mus—" Robin runs off before you can finish the sentence. Her eyes continue to flutter, but she hasn't been lifted off the ground yet. Did he detect you all in the Upside Down? Is that why Vecna is trying to kill her now?

Turn to the next page.

Suddenly Nancy falls back. You catch her before she hits the ground. "Nancy! Nancy! Are you okay? What happened?" She is shaking. You quickly help her out of the Upside Down and into the real world.

"Max's trailer is next door. Quick, let's move there," Eddie says. After breaking into Max's trailer, you place a shell-shocked Nancy on a couch. She tells you what she saw. Henry Creel was Vecna, and he killed his own family. Like their friend El, he had powers. El banished him to the Upside Down, and he is seeking revenge.

"He didn't just show me the past," Nancy continues. "He showed me things that haven't happened yet. There were so many monsters. An army. And they were coming into Hawkins, into our neighborhoods, our homes." Her voice breaks. "He showed me four gates spreading across Hawkins."

"How many gates do we know about now?"

"There's the one at Lover's Lake, and one in Eddie's trailer," Robin answers. "So that's two."

"A gate opens wherever Vecna kills someone. Chrissy in Eddie's trailer, Patrick at the lake—" you explain to the others.

"That means there is another gate where Fred was killed. Three gates—he just needs one more. We need to find Max!" You all leave the trailer and hurry back to the lake. When you get there, the others are nowhere to be found.

Go on to the next page.

"The radio Dustin gave us is still in the boat." Robin points over the water.

"I'm not swimming back out there," Steve says. You all agree. Who knows if you'll be lucky again if someone is dragged through the gate for a second time.

"They wouldn't just leave without a reason," Nancy says. She rummages through her pockets and pulls out her car keys. "Something's happened."

"Maybe they went back to your house?" You all get in the car, which is still parked where you left it, and Nancy drives off. When she reaches the cul-de-sac, you see police vehicles outside the Wheelers' house.

"I'll go in, like a ninja." Steve smiles as he gets out of the car. You see him sneak toward the house, climb on top of some garbage cans, and pull himself up to a window on the second floor. Just then the front door opens, and a couple of police officers come out. They see Steve and grab his legs, throwing him to the ground.

"Nancy! Drive!" you yell. But it's too late—officers run out of the house and surround the car. Eddie is pulled out of the car and arrested. The rest of you are ushered into the Wheelers'.

"You don't understand!" Nancy tries to tell the cops as you sit in her family's living room. "He's innocent! Eddie didn't do this. And we're all in danger!"

"We're going to have to take them down to the station too," Chief Powell says to the parents in the room. "On the charges of aiding and abetting a wanted criminal." They take Max's Walkman away.

"No! Wait!" you yell, but it is too late. Max is lifted into the air, and in no time, her limbs break one by one. Lucas screams.

The End

The way Dr. Hatch looked at you as he was leaving made you nervous. As Nancy and Robin follow the guard, you fall back and quietly follow Hatch the way you came. He heads to his office. He swings the door behind him, but it doesn't close all the way. You peek through the crack and listen. Hatch picks up the phone and dials.

"Hello. Can I be transferred to Professor Brantley's office, please?" Your cover is blown! You race back to where you left Nancy and Robin. You need to get out of there.

"And I was sure he would take me, just as he'd taken my Virginia. But then I heard another voice. At first I believed it was an angel, and I followed her only to find myself in a nightmare far worse," you hear a man say, and then he hums a tune. When you reach the others, they are listening intently to Victor Creel. You pull them away. "We've got to go. Now!"

"We can't go—we haven't learned anything yet."

"Listen to me! Hatch is onto us! We need to go!" You lead the way out and race across the garden to the car. You all jump in the car, and Nancy speeds off.

"Code red! I repeat, this is a code red! Do you copy?" Dustin is screaming over the radio. "Come on! Come on!"

"Dustin," Robin answers, "what's happening? Where are you?"

"Finally! Please, please tell me you've figured this out! Vecna's got Max! He's got—" He cuts off. Robin tosses the radio to you and brainstorms with Nancy.

"Dustin? Dustin, what's happening?" You try to get an answer.

"It's too late. She's dead. Max is dead." He tells you to get to the cemetery.

Go on to the next page.

When you get to the cemetery, you find Steve's car parked at the bottom of a hill. You hike to the top as quickly as you can. Lucas is holding Max's lifeless body and screaming in agony, calling Max's name, begging her to wake up. The others are standing in a circle, looking down at something. When you get closer, you see it too. A large, glowing hole in the ground. From far away it looks like lava. Up close you see its fleshy membrane. You all huddle away from the hole.

"Is that . . . ?" Nancy asks. Dustin nods.

"It's a gate to the Upside Down. It opened after . . . after . . ." He can't finish the sentence. You all look at Lucas holding Max so tightly, her eyes completely gone, her face and limbs mangled.

"Should we . . . should we call the police?" you ask.

"And tell them what? That Max was killed by a demon named Vecna?" Steve answers. You all huddle together, trying to think of your next move.

"We can't just leave her here," Robin says. "If she's found, the town will go ballistic. Three gruesome murders in as many days?"

"Then what do we—"

Dustin interrupts you. "Hey, guys? Where are Lucas and Max?" You all turn to see they are no longer there. You look around but can't see them anywhere. Lucas wouldn't have been able to get all the way down the hill that quickly dragging Max's body.

"You don't think he—" He did. He went through the gate. The rest of you follow.

Turn to the next page.

When you follow the others down into the gate, you find yourself reaching upward somehow. Steve helps pull you up. You're in the cemetery, but not. The air is unbearably cold, dust particles float all around you, and the sky is covered in dark clouds with red lightning.

"Welcome to the Upside Down."

"We need to find Lucas quickly." Nancy springs into action. "Remember, this entire world is a hive mind. Don't step on the vines, and don't draw attention to yourselves."

"Where would he take her?" Robin asks. The others discuss options, but something else catches your attention.

"We're still in the same spot Max's brother was buried, right?" The others stop and look at you as if you are mad.

"What?" Steve shakes his head. "Yeah, obviously."

"Then where's his tombstone?" The others look and see the hill is blank.

"What the—"

"Okay, that's something we can look into later. Right now we need to find Lucas." Nancy refocuses the group. "Dustin, know any places that might be important to Lucas and Max?"

"Mad Max," Dustin whispers. He then yells, "We need to get to the arcade!"

Go on to the next page.

The lightning casts a menacing glow on the arcade. Dustin leads the way inside, careful to avoid touching any vines. He walks down an aisle, then pauses. "He has to be here. This is where we first learned about Max. This game right here, Dig Dug, where she beat my high score."

"Okay, spread out and look everywhere. Dustin, if they're not here, you need to think about another place that might be significant to them." You all fan out.

"I found them!" you hear Dustin yell. "He's in the employees-only room!" When you get there, you see Lucas holding Max's hand tenderly. His sobs make it hard to understand what he is saying, but it's clear it's meant for Max. Dustin kneels beside Lucas and wraps his arms around him. Lucas wails on his friend's shoulder. Dustin tries to gently soothe Lucas, holding back his own tears.

"Let's give them some privacy," Steve says, walking out of the room and back into the main arcade. You, Nancy, and Robin follow, finding a place to sit in silence. After some time, Dustin comes out of the room and joins you, his eyes bloodshot.

"He's saying—he's saying his goodbyes." Dustin collapses on the floor next to Steve. Steve holds Dustin as he sobs quietly. You hear the door open and turn to see Lucas emerge, his face and shirt soaked. He looks completely numb. Nancy gets up and leads him to the group, giving him space to sit. Everyone is silent.

"I told her—" Lucas starts. "I told her about everything in that room. About El, about the Upside Down, all of it. She didn't believe me. Maybe—maybe if I stayed away from her like Billy said, she would still . . ." He breaks into sobs again. Nancy holds him tight.

Turn to the next page.

Eventually, Lucas falls asleep in Nancy's lap from exhaustion and grief. The rest of you whisper to each other, trying to figure out what happened.

"Start from the beginning," Nancy whispers to Steve.

"You guys left to see Creel, and Max was out of it. She was writing these letters, one for each of us. She wanted to deliver some letters to her mom and then go to the cemetery. Lucas wanted to go with her to Billy's grave, but she wanted to go alone. We waited for what seemed like forever. When I went up to check on her, she was in a trance. The next thing we knew, we saw her floating."

"It was exactly what Eddie said happened to Chrissy in his trailer," Dustin adds.

"The gate appeared not long after," Steve says. "Lucas pulled her out of the way as it opened. It was exactly where she died."

"Did Eddie mention anything about a hole or a gate?" Nancy asks.

Steve shakes his head. "He said he ran as soon as Chrissy's bones started to snap. If a gate did open up, then he wasn't around to see it."

"What about the grave?" you ask. "Are you sure we were in the same spot in the cemetery?"

"Positive," Nancy answers. "Billy's tombstone should have been there. Whatever is going on, it's clearly connected to the Upside Down."

"Do you think the Mind Flayer is back?" Dustin asks. The others look alarmed.

"If he is, is it safe to be here right now?" Steve looks around warily.

"We can't go anywhere with Lucas like this," Nancy says. "Let's just get some rest."

Go on to the next page.

You try to relax, but you can't. Your heart aches for Max. You hear whispering. Opening your eyes, you see Nancy and Robin walking toward the arcade entrance. They move quietly, clearly not wanting to be noticed. Nancy's hunches have been right before; perhaps this is another one of those. Then again, if some superpowered demon is on the loose, they could be walking into danger.

If you choose to follow Nancy and Robin,
turn to the next page.

If you choose to stop them from leaving, turn to page 231.

You get up and follow them out the door, maintaining a safe distance so they don't realize you're there. This version of Hawkins is abandoned, with the exception of the strange and deadly demobats you see in the distance. If the Upside Down is a parallel universe, you wonder where the people are. There's Spock in the real world, so where is goatee Spock? You wonder if the creatures here were once people. If that was the case, what happened to them to make them this way? Nancy and Robin try to stay under some form of cover as they move farther away from the downtown area. They make it to an old house covered in bats. You watch them, hoping they don't do anything stupid like go in. As if your prayers have been answered, they turn back. You intercept them.

"What were you guys thinking?" you ask incredulously as you make your way back to the arcade with Robin and Nancy.

"We were following a lead," Nancy says.

"Find anything?"

"Whatever killed Victor Creel's family is definitely still there," Robin says.

"Being guarded by those monsters?" you ask.

"Exactly." Nancy nods. "We know that once the family moved into the house, they started having visions and dead animals were appearing—"

"Wait, did you say dead animals?" you interrupt. "You're telling me this killer demon was leaving them dead animals?"

"Yeah, I mean, that seems like the least terrifying thing he did." Robin turns to you. Something about the dead animals nags at you, but you can't figure it out.

Go on to the next page.

When you make it to the arcade, everyone is up. "Where the hell did you guys go?" Steve looks terrified.

"We were following a lead," Nancy answers.

"You guys know how dangerous it is here. You shouldn't be running off—"

"Okay, Mom," Robin teases.

"This is all your fault." Steve steps toward you. "None of this would have happened if you weren't here. Max would still be alive!" His voice grows monstrous.

"It's not my fault! I didn't know! I was just trying to get away from Hatch—"

Suddenly everything around you disappears. You are in a black void; you feel yourself sinking, falling! "I see you've been looking for me." The monstrous voice booms around you. "Nancy was so close. So close to the truth, but then you pulled her away. How was old, blind, dumb Victor? Did he miss me? I've been meaning to check back in, but I've been busy. So very busy." You land in a house. There is a family, a man, his wife, a son, and a daughter.

It's the Creels. You follow them into the dining room. The lights flicker. A radio turns on and plays an old song. The man, Victor Creel, gets up to check on it. Then his wife is lifted into the air. It takes only moments, but her body snaps and contorts, her eyes sink into her skull, and she drops dead on the table. Victor rushes his family to the door but is frozen. Alice is lifted next, snapped apart, and dropped. Then Henry, the Creels' son, falls to the ground, his nose bleeding.

Turn to the next page.

Henry's eyes open and glaze over, then he turns his head to you. "Why don't you take a seat?" Vines reach out and pull you into the now-empty dining room. A hideous creature stands before you—Vecna! He wraps his clawed hand around your head. "I want you to send Nancy a message. Tell her I'm coming for you all. This is the beginning of the end." You hear four chimes.

You fall once more. When you open your eyes, you're back in the Upside Down arcade. "It—" You gasp for air. "It was Vecna! I saw him! He's coming! He's coming for Hawkins! He's going to kill everyone!" Robin tries to get you to slow your breathing. "No! No! We need to get out of here! He knows where we are!"

Steve runs to the window. "Guys! Incoming!" You turn to see bats heading toward the arcade. "We need to move! Now!" Steve leads you all out the back.

"Where do we go? Where do we go?" you yell, tears streaming from your face. This is the beginning of the end.

"The trailer!" Dustin yells. "If a gate opened where Max died, there's got to be one in Eddie's trailer!" You all start running in that direction. You count the others: Steve, Dustin, Nancy, Robin, Eddie . . .

"Where's Lucas?" you yell. You turn back and see Lucas running in the opposite direction, toward the demobats.

"What is he doing?" Dustin screams. He starts to run after him, but Steve pulls him back. It is too late.

Turn to page 228.

You are still shaking in fear, though you are back in the real world. You sit with the other survivors in Nancy's basement. Both Max and Lucas are gone, and Vecna is still out there. After what happened in the Upside Down, Steve snuck Eddie into the Wheeler house from his old hiding place. "Where the hell are they?" Dustin slams the phone. "It's been days, and the line is always busy."

"Something's wrong," Nancy says. She gets up and paces. "This can't be a coincidence. Just when more gates to the Upside Down open, we can't reach El? It has to be connected somehow."

"Okay," Robin says. "Even if it is connected, we can't get in touch with them, so now what?"

Nancy turns to the others. "We have to kill him." She sits down next to you. "Did he tell you anything else? Show you any hint of what he might do next?"

You shake your head. "He said you were close to the truth, but I pulled you away from it."

"Pulled her away?" Robin taps her fingers. "Does he mean from the Creel house? But we didn't even know you were there; we turned back on our own."

"No—" Nancy clenches her fists. "He means Pennhurst, when we were talking to Victor."

"This is connected to those Creel murders, but we already figured that out," Robin says.

"Why them?" Steve asks. "If he's so powerful, why kill a couple of kids and a woman? Why target this family?"

"And then why did he stop until now?" Dustin adds on. "Wow, Steve, you actually helped." Steve doesn't bother hiding his annoyance.

Go on to the next page.

"Look," you say, "I'm as curious as the rest of you, but we've got a more urgent problem. You know, the part where he said he's going to kill everyone!"

"You said you heard chimes, right?" Nancy asks, ignoring your statement.

"Yes, four chimes."

"Three kills in our world, three gates appear . . ."

"You think there's one victim left?" you ask. She nods. "But to what end? As far as we know, those gates just stay there. He could go through any one of them."

"I don't know, but if there's a fourth victim, we need to figure out who it is and fast."

"All the others were seeing Miss Kelley, right?" Eddie asks. "So wouldn't the next person also be someone who was seeing her?"

You're off to the school. When you get there, the streets are crawling with mobs on the hunt for Eddie. You get inside the school easily and head straight to the counselor's office with the others. "Look for files on anyone who has had nightmares, headaches, anything like that," Nancy orders. Everyone grabs a stack of files and starts reading.

Turn to the next page.

"I found one!" Robin yells. Just then a loud noise erupts in the hall. You run out the door to see a gang of teens in letterman jackets running toward you.

"We need to get out of here!" you yell, slamming the door and locking it. "Quick! Out the window!" Glass smashes; there's a mob trying to break in. You're surrounded.

"We can't let them get Eddie!" Dustin yells. "They'll kill him!" The door breaks open. You grab anything you can and start throwing, but it's no use. You're outnumbered.

A blond boy in a letterman jacket seems to be running the show. He goes straight for Eddie.

"Jason, man, listen!" Eddie starts. Jason punches him in the gut.

"Stop! He didn't do anything!" Dustin yells. The crowd becomes violent.

You hear chimes. Vecna's voice calls to you, "It's time." You see Max's face, see Lucas running in the direction of the bats, see Eddie being beaten in the counselor's office. Then you feel your body rising. This is it. This is the end.

The End

"Stop! What do you two think you're doing?" You run past them and block the door. "You can't seriously be thinking of going out there!" You see Steve wake up and come join you at the door.

"What's going on?"

"They were trying to sneak off somewhere," you tell him.

"Are you guys crazy? After what happened to Max—"

"We're going because of Max!" Nancy urges. "We can't sit here and let her death be in vain. We need to stop Vecna, and the answer might be at the Creel house."

"You seriously were going to walk all the way across town to the Creel house?" Steve is exasperated. "Nancy, look, I get it, I'm hurting too. But we can't be reckless, not now, when we still don't know everything that's going on."

"Well, maybe we would have if we got to hear the full story from Victor." Nancy glares at you.

"I got you out of there before Hatch could catch you. It wasn't my fault our cover was blown!" you protest.

"Oh, so it's my fault Max is dead?" Robin balls her fist.

"No, I didn't say that! That's not what I meant—"

"Save it. We're going." Nancy and Robin push past you, and then stop at the door. You see it too: batlike creatures fill the sky. They are flying away from the arcade. "That's the direction of the Creel house. It has to be connected," Nancy whispers.

"We can't stay here. This is our chance to get out," you say.

Turn to the next page.

You all make it to the cemetery with no issues. You follow Dustin through the gate and find yourself back in the real-world cemetery, next to the grave of Max's brother. Police cars whizz past you.

"What's happening?" Nancy asks as she exits the gate last. Steve pulls her up. "We need to follow them!" You jump into Nancy's car with Robin, and Dustin and Lucas go with Steve. Nancy follows the police cars to a rundown diner.

"What's this place?" you ask. You read the sign, Benny's Burgers, but the outside is littered with trash. You get out of the car and watch the cops go inside. "What's happening?"

"Nance?" You turn to see Robin standing in the open driver's side door, shaking Nancy. Nancy's eyes are rolled up in her head, darting rapidly. "Nancy!"

"It's Vecna! He's got Nancy!" Dustin yells, running to the car. "This is what happened to Max. If she is lifted up, she's lost!"

You all frantically try to wake Nancy, but it is no use. She collapses in the seat. Steve pulls her out and helps her rest on the ground. She opens her eyes.

She looks at each of you. "It's over."

"What?" you ask. "What's over?"

"We lost." Nancy's eyes start to tear up. "Vecna just got his last victim. We lost." The earth begins to shake. You're knocked to the ground. You smell smoke and turn to see the diner split apart, screams emanating from inside. The split spreads toward downtown. Hawkins is destroyed!

The End

Nancy gives you a key to her house. "Just take the basement entrance and stay there until we come to get you." You assure her you will, and then set off to take the bus to her place with your suitcase.

When you get to her house, you see the lights are all off. It looks like no one is home. You find a side door and unlock it. The basement looks cozy and well-used, its walls a warm yellow. You're surprised by the *Star Wars* memorabilia and other nerdy items decorating the place. You would never have guessed Nancy was a nerd. After rummaging around, you find nothing of interest. If you want to learn more about Nancy, you'll need to search the house.

You're sure no one else is home, but you go up the stairs quietly anyway. The ground floor looks like the home of a typical suburban family. On the walls you see pictures of Nancy and her family: a mother, a father, and younger siblings, one brother and one sister. You go farther up the stairs. The first bedroom you see is her parents' room. Nothing in there will tell you about Nancy and this obsession with wizards and demons, so you skip it. The next bedroom holds a kid-size bed; obviously belonging to the younger sister. You notice a Lite Brite on the bed, but nothing else sticks out. You walk down the hall and go into another bedroom; this one is clearly the brother's. You notice more nerdy collectibles in this room; he must be the one who uses the basement most. As you leave the room, a picture catches your eye. It is the brother with a girl. The girl looks familiar—something about her eyes. You can't put a name to the face, but you are so sure you've seen her somewhere before.

Turn to the next page.

"Whoa." You let your surprise escape your lips. It's that weird girl in Lenora! The one who stuck her hands out and screamed; you still feel secondhand embarrassment thinking about it. Looks like Nancy's brother knew her. Was she from Hawkins? You wonder what the interview would have been like had you actually spoken to her. You leave and find Nancy's room.

Nancy's room is exactly what you expected: clean, orderly, very preppy. The Wheelers seem to be pretty well-off. You can just picture it: perfect Nancy with her normal family and her boring, ordinary life. No wonder she would want to believe in wizards and demons—anything to escape this drudgery. You open her closet and run your hands over her clothes; everything is soft and well-made. Above the rack you see a shelf holding shoeboxes. You pull one down and open it. The shock of what is inside almost makes you drop it! A gun? Why would Nancy have a gun in a shoebox in her room? Shakily, you close the box and put it back where you found it. You look around the room. You see a picture of her and a boy you haven't seen before. In the picture they look at each other lovingly. Must be a boyfriend. You wonder why he isn't with Nancy now. You see another picture next to it of Nancy with a redheaded girl who is not Max. They are hugging each other and smiling at the camera. Reaching for the picture, you accidentally knock a file over. Newspaper clippings spill out. You quickly gather them to put them back, but a picture catches your eye. It's the same girl! You read the headline: "Toxic Chemical Leak from Hawkins Lab Kills Teen; Officials Attempt Cover-Up." You scan the article and find the girl's name was Barbara Holland.

Go on to the next page.

Barbara died in 1983, but the article you hold is from 1984. You look through the folder for other clippings from 1983; headlines like "The Boy Who Came Back to Life" jump out at you. There is a picture of the boy, who you recognize immediately. His hair is longer in the picture and he is much younger, but he looks mostly the same—it was the boy with that strange screaming girl in Lenora. Now you're sure they're from Hawkins. The article tells the story of Will Byers, who went missing and was presumed dead—after another child's body was misidentified as his—before he turned up, having been lost in the woods. In another article, you see a picture of Will with his family, a mother and brother. You look back at Nancy's desk: the boyfriend is Will's brother. You spend some time perusing the clippings. You don't see the screaming girl's picture anywhere.

A door closes downstairs. Crap! Someone's home. You hastily put the clippings back in the folder, then sneak out of Nancy's room. Peering over the railing, you hear people talking. Nancy's parents, no doubt. You quietly go down the stairs, trying to make it to the basement without being noticed, your heart pounding. You're almost to the door to the basement!

"Oh, hello!" You turn to see a woman, probably Mrs. Wheeler, looking straight at you. "Are you a friend of Nancy's?"

"Oh." You shuffle, then remember the key in your pocket. "Yes, I'm actually here for the conference, but my host family can't house me anymore, so Nancy gave me a key to come wait here while she finishes some work."

"Oh, so you're a journalist too?" Mrs. Wheeler smiles. "How nice."

Turn to the next page.

"Would you like something to drink while you wait for Nancy?"

"We're always happy to have more kids at the house," a man, who must be Mr. Wheeler, calls out sarcastically.

"Never mind him." Mrs. Wheeler shakes her head. "Come into the kitchen and I can get you something. Juice?"

"Just water, please." You have no choice but to follow. You see Mr. Wheeler in a La-Z-Boy armchair, the television remote in his hand, the TV screen reflecting off his glasses. The little blond girl you saw in the family pictures is playing on the floor in the den. The kitchen is large and bright. Mrs. Wheeler fills a glass with water, then hands it to you.

"Do you know when Nancy will be back?" Mrs. Wheeler asks.

"I'm . . . not sure. We were working in the library, and then I got tired so she said I could come here."

"You said your host family couldn't put you up?"

You cough. "Um, yes. The . . . the Bensons. After everything, I thought . . ."

Mrs. Wheeler looks at you sadly. "I understand. It's so horrible what happened to their poor son. Sometimes I just wonder what's going on in this town. Nothing has been the same since Barb . . ."

"Barb as in Barbara Holland?"

"Oh yes, she was Nancy's best friend. They were inseparable until . . . well, until she passed. I'm just glad Nancy's brother, Mike, is safe in Lenora."

You almost spit out your water. "Lenora Hills, California?"

Go on to the next page.

"Oh, do you know it?"

"I'm actually from there." You pause. "I guess I must have just missed him."

"Oh, maybe you know his girlfriend, Jane? She lives there now with Mike's friend Will and his family." You were right— those pictures were of the strange girl and boy you saw on the last day before spring break in Lenora! Just then the door opens, and you hear Nancy's voice.

"Hi, sweetheart!" Mrs. Wheeler calls out. Nancy walks into the kitchen, surprised to see you there. She quickly controls her face.

"Hi, Mom, I hope you don't mind . . ."

"Don't worry, your friend already told me about the hosting situation." Mrs. Wheeler doesn't seem fazed by the gaggle of kids in her home. Nancy is followed by Robin, Steve, Max, Dustin, and a boy you haven't yet met. "How about I order us some pizza?"

"Thanks, Mom, that sounds great." Nancy puts her hand on your shoulder. "We'll be hanging out in the basement." That's your cue to go. You thank Mrs. Wheeler and follow the others downstairs.

"What were you doing?" Nancy hisses. "I told you to stay in the basement."

"I was researching," you say calmly, giving her a knowing look. "Like any good journalist."

Nancy bristles at this. Robin steps in. "Never mind that! We've got bigger problems."

"What bigger problems?" you ask. Everyone looks at you, and then each other. Robin starts talking.

Turn to the next page.

"Well, the good news is Nancy is a genius and the Victor Creel connection was a bull's-eye." You try to hide your surprise, but Nancy notices it and grins. "Victor thought his house was haunted by a demon, which we now think is Vecna. The bad news is . . ." Robin's voice trails off as she looks at Max.

"The bad news is I'm cursed and am going to end up like Chrissy and Fred," Max finishes.

"What?"

"This is why you should have stuck with us," Nancy says. "After we found the Creel connection, Dustin radioed us to meet them at the school."

Dustin continues, "We found out that Fred and Chrissy were both seeing Miss Kelley, the counselor, and had headaches and visions before they were killed. Then Max had a vision and, well . . ."

"Both of them died within twenty-four hours of their first vision." Max sits on the couch, staring blankly. The boy you don't know sits down next to her and tries to take her hand, but she pulls away.

"Who are you?"

"Oh, he's Lucas," Dustin says as Lucas waves. "Right, I forgot there's another problem: some jocks are on a freak hunt looking for us and Eddie. So there's that too."

"Look, we don't have time to waste. Tomorrow Robin and I are going to see Victor Creel at Pennhurst to get more answers. The rest of you will stay here till we get back." She looks pointedly at you. "We should all get some sleep."

Go on to the next page.

You can't sleep. You toss and turn, obsessing over everything you've been told. The world as you knew it is gone, or at least you know now that it never existed. Alternate dimensions, monsters, mind control—it all exists, and somehow you are in the middle of it. You try to fluff your pillow to relax, but it doesn't help; you are still restless. You get up and quietly creep out the side door from the basement. You see a bike on the ground and decide a ride in the cool night air will help.

You ride aimlessly, your thoughts wandering. There were at least two explanations for everything in Hawkins, it seemed. Will Byers was lost in the woods and then found after a case of mistaken identity with some other kid who drowned; or, as you learned from grilling Dustin and Lucas, Will Byers was lost in an alternate dimension called the Upside Down, hiding from a vicious monster. Barbara Holland was poisoned by a toxic chemical leak from the Hawkins Lab that the government tried to cover up; or Barbara was abducted by the same monster as Will and killed. After illegal dealings with the mayor of Hawkins, the Starcourt Mall burned down, killing thirty people, including Police Chief Jim Hopper and Max's brother, Billy Hargrove; or a Soviet spy ring was allowed to operate in Hawkins thanks to the mayor, and the thirty people were possessed by the Mind Flayer, another monster from the Upside Down. Now Chrissy Cunningham and Fred Benson were killed by a teen serial killer named Eddie Munson; or Chrissy and Fred were killed by Vecna, another monster from the Upside Down that has set its sights on Max as his next victim.

Turn to the next page.

In the distance you can see the ruins of the mall. There is graffiti all over the husk of a building. You set the bike down.

"If you're looking for a way in, I can help." You jump and see Robin behind you, holding a bike.

"You followed me," you say, stating a fact rather than asking a question.

"I saw you leave. With everything going on, I didn't think it was smart to let you wander off alone." She lays down her bike next to yours. "Come on, follow me." You quickly scan your surroundings; it doesn't look like anyone else is here. On the one hand, Robin is working with a suspected killer; on the other hand, if she wanted to hurt you, she didn't need to wait until you were inside the mall. You follow her around the back of the mall. "Tada!" She gestures to a roof access door. "The lock on the door to the roof is broken, but we should be able to get in from there, and then I can give you the tour."

Getting inside the mall is as easy as she says. Coming down from the roof access stairway, you are on the second floor of the mall. Robin leads you toward the escalators. From this vantage point, you can see the scorched remnants of the mall. "This looks like the work of a fire to me."

"Well, the government couldn't just tell everyone that the giant pile of human guts and limbs was once a living monster. They burned it to cover the truth."

You look at her. "Why should I believe you?"

Robin smiles. "Come this way, please."

Go on to the next page.

She walks to an ice cream shop, the neon sign barely hanging on. "Welcome to Scoops Ahoy, the place where it all started—for me at least." She walks into the store and leads you to the back. "This is where I first got to know Steve 'The Hair' Harrington and the gaggle of kids he was friends with." She shows you a back room with a table and chairs, a broken whiteboard on the floor. "Here's where I decoded the secret Soviet messages that Dustin picked up on his Cerebro. It's a big radio he built to contact his girlfriend in Utah, Suzie, who we all thought didn't exist for a while."

You pick up the broken whiteboard. Some of the writing is smudged, but you can make out the Russian alphabet written in red marker.

"So there's some Russian on a whiteboard." You turn to Robin. "That hardly counts as proof."

"Like I said, this is only the beginning." She goes through a door leading to a white hallway. "This is where the deliveries were made to each of the stores." She leads you down the hall and out to a loading dock area behind the mall, with large metal double doors and a raised platform—run-of-the-mill stuff.

"Why are we back outside?"

"Just trust me, okay?" Robin pulls on a door handle. "Believe it or not, getting in here the first time was super complicated. Actually, that's how Lucas's sister, Erica, got involved. We needed someone small enough to go through the vents and let us in."

"The vents?"

"Come on." You follow her inside. There are empty shelves and dust, nothing more. She opens a panel by the door, revealing some buttons. "Wait for it."

The room begins to rumble. "Wooo, I'm so glad it worked. Honestly I wasn't sure it would. Hang on!"

Turn to the next page.

You feel your body dropping. You hold on to the bolted shelves, watching the walls behind them move. The room is an elevator! You fall for so long, and then suddenly the room stops and you buckle from the force. "What the—"

"That's not even the best part." Robin hits another button, and the doors open to a long hallway. "Just a warning, it's going to be quite the walk." You stare down the seemingly endless hallway.

"What is this place?"

"The secret Soviet base Dustin was telling you about."

"You were eavesdropping on our conversation."

"It's not like I had much of a choice. The Wheelers' basement isn't that big, and Dustin's voice carries." As you walk, Robin explains what happened to her, Steve, Erica, and Dustin when they first came to the base; how she and Steve were captured and drugged with some kind of truth serum; how Dustin and Erica rescued them. A part of you wants to admit this creepy hallway is proof enough, but you squash it back down.

"Here we are." Robin leads you to a hub with different doors. "We went in here to the comms room, hoping to contact anyone aboveground." She holds the door open for you. Inside you see a control panel and some headphones tossed on the ground. She leads you up a stairway. "This is where the key was. Erica and I didn't know what we were looking at, but Dustin and Steve recognized it immediately."

Go on to the next page.

You see exploded pieces of metal beyond the broken glass of the control room you are in. Robin leads you down some metal stairs; the clanging of your footsteps echoes around you. "The machine was here. It was pointing some kind of laser at the wall right there." You see a crack in the concrete wall. "When we got back up to the surface, we were able to tell the others about what we found. Hopper, our former chief of police, sacrificed himself to destroy the machine. Mrs. Byers, Will's mom, didn't even find a body. He was completely disintegrated. That's how he really died, not some fire." You walk to the edge of the platform and look down. The drop could easily break your bones.

"I can't believe it," you mumble, then turn to Robin. "I mean I do believe you, but—" You're speechless. Everything they told you was the truth.

"And that concludes our tour of the secret Soviet base underneath the Starcourt Mall in Hawkins, Indiana." Robin takes a small bow.

"Why here?" You look around in wonder. "Of all the places in the world?"

"Hopper and Mrs. Byers captured a Soviet scientist—I think his name was Alexei—who told them they had tried opening gates in Russia but weren't successful. So they came to the one place where they knew a gate was successfully opened to help them figure it out."

"And it was your friend El who opened the first gate?"

Robin nods. "From what she told us, I don't think she knew what she was doing when it happened."

"So you're telling me this was all the result of a freak accident?"

Robin shrugs, leading you up to the surface. You get on your bikes and ride back to the Wheelers' house.

Turn to the next page.

"Where have you two been?" Steve pulls the door to the basement open before you can knock.

"We were in the mood for some ice cream, so we went to Scoops Ahoy." Robin smiles. "Anyway, I better get ready to go see Victor Creel." She runs into the basement and up the stairs. You sit on the couch next to Dustin.

"So I saw the secret Soviet base." You suddenly feel very, very tired.

"You believe us now?" he asks. You nod.

Robin and Nancy come down, and Nancy repeats her instructions: stay in the basement and wait for them to return. With that, Nancy and Robin are gone. You find a sleeping bag and rest.

When you wake up, everyone is gone. A radio has been placed next to you. You turn it on. "Hey, is anyone there?"

"You have to say over when you're done speaking. Over." You hear Dustin's voice.

"Where are you guys? I thought we were waiting for Robin and Nancy. Over."

"Max is delivering fail-safe letters. Over."

"What?"

"You forgot to say over. We've got one more stop, and then we'll be back. Just sit tight. Over and out." You get up and open the basement door. The bike you used last night is still there. You grab it and take off in the direction of the Starcourt Mall. Might as well look for clues while everyone else is out doing something.

When you get to the mall, you follow the path Robin led you on the night before to get back to the room with the Soviet gate.

Go on to the next page.

In the control room you stare at the crack in the wall, trying to picture what the gate would have looked like. At first you imagine a neat circular window into a parallel world like something from a movie you saw with your mother years ago. You try to recall the name. *Prisoners of the Parallel Universe?* Something like that. But this massive, jagged crack suggests something more dangerous and violent.

You walk around the control room, not sure what you're looking for. The area is covered in dust and dirt. Your and Robin's footprints from last night are still visible. You go back to the room where she and Steve were captured by the Soviets. You are about to leave when you hear something. Footsteps. It couldn't be the others; they would have called out to you. You pull open a vent and jump down, closing it behind you. Just then you hear the door open. Footsteps come closer until someone is right on top of you. You hold your breath, pleading with the universe that he doesn't look down. Others come in and join them.

"All clear, sir." The first man speaks. "We've checked the premises around the control room, and the gate remains closed."

"Our sensors picked up an entrance last night and again today," another man says. He walks closer, into your line of sight; he's wearing a US military uniform, a nicer one. He must be higher up. "I want a full search. It could be the girl. If you engage with the target, shoot to kill."

"Yes, Colonel Sullivan." The man above salutes. Your heart beats rapidly. You have no choice but to sit there and wait until the coast is clear. After hours of waiting, you eventually fall asleep.

Turn to the next page.

You have no idea how long you've slept for, but it is clear you are alone. You carefully open the grate and take a peek. The room is empty. It was obviously US military you saw, and they were looking for a girl. It had to be the superpowered friend you kept hearing about, Eleven. You quickly make your way back up to the surface. It is nighttime in Hawkins. You wonder if you slept for most of the day. Grabbing your bike, you ride like the wind back to the Wheelers'. When you get far enough away from the mall, you stop riding and pull out your radio.

"Hello? Is anyone there? Dustin? Max? Anybody?"

"Where have you been? Over." It's Lucas.

"Hiding from the US military. Over."

"What?" You hear some static. Lucas's voice returns. "Forget it! Head to Lover's Lake to meet with the others. Do not come to the Wheelers' house. I repeat, do not come to the Wheelers'. Over."

You ride to Lover's Lake but don't see anyone. There is an empty boat floating in the middle of the lake. You call on your radio again. "Nancy? Robin? Where are you guys?" There's no answer. You try again, but still no response. Something must have happened. Despite Lucas's warning not to go to the Wheeler house, you have no other option. Just then you see more military personnel by a cabin and a boathouse. They are taking photographs and searching the grounds. Some are wearing diving suits, getting ready to go in the water; others begin to leave. You tail them.

Go on to the next page.

They drive quietly and slowly, allowing you to catch up as they get farther into the woods on unpaved roads. They stop at a nondescript cabin, park the van, and go inside. You look around carefully before getting closer. The curtains are drawn, but the lights are on. You can hear some talking, but it's not clear enough to make out. You circle the cabin and find one curtain slightly parted. Creeping beneath the window, you poke your head up and squint one eye to see more clearly.

The people are dressed in military uniforms. You recognize the colonel from earlier. Next to him is a board with pictures, names, and locations. You try to read and commit the information to memory. *Eleven, last sighting in Lenora Hills, CA. Sam Owens, last seen at his residence. William Byers, Jonathan Byers, Mike Wheeler, last sighting in Lenora Hills, CA. Joyce Byers, location unknown.* You were right—the girl they are looking for is Eleven. You breathe a sigh of relief that they haven't caught her yet. The colonel gets up from his seat, and the others salute him as he exits the room. You hear the front door creak open and scoop up the bike and pedal for your life! Behind you, you can hear a helicopter taking off. You see it heading west. You then hear shouting, and the sound of running getting closer. You need to leave! With Nancy, Robin, and Steve missing, your only option is to get to the others at the Wheelers'.

Turn to the next page.

You see police cars outside of the Wheelers' house and realize why they warned you away. Pulling out your radio, you signal them.

"What are you doing here? Over," Dustin hisses.

"I couldn't find the others. They weren't at the lake. Over."

"What? They were supposed to search for the water gate. Over."

"The what? Over."

"It'll take too long to explain." Dustin pauses. "I think we found the others. Standby. Over." You wait in the shadows, flinching at every sound. Your radio squeals. "We are rendezvousing at Eddie's trailer. I repeat, we are rendezvousing at Eddie's trailer. The others will be there. Do you copy? Over."

"I copy. Over." You wonder how they knew the others were at the trailer. If they were contacted through the radios, surely you would have heard it too? You see an upstairs window open. A girl you don't know pokes her head out and looks around, then ducks back in. Lucas looks out the window after her and also goes back in. They are planning something. Through the windows downstairs, you can see the cops talking with the Wheelers and some other adults. You turn to see the cars from earlier circling the street. Did the military follow you here? That's a lot of people to sneak away from. Maybe you could help get the others inside a clear path? Then again, you could be caught. If the military followed you here, everyone is in danger.

If you choose to help the others escape, turn to page 250.

If you choose to lead the military away from the Wheelers' house, turn to page 259.

You creep toward the house, making sure to stay low and out of sight. The military's nondescript vans get closer. They slow down outside the Wheelers' house and then drive off. Did they not want their presence known by the police? Circling around back, you see a garden hose and screw it into a faucet. You find a room near where the police are still talking with the adults, and slowly pry open the window. After snaking the hose in, you run back to the faucet.

"I'm so, so sorry, Mr. and Mrs. Wheeler," you whisper, and then turn on the water full blast. You can hear the chaos erupting inside. You run back to the front of the house and see the others climbing down from the window. The girl you don't know stabs the tires on the police cars and then jumps on the back of a bike. They ride off. You grab your bike and follow.

"Where have you been?" Max yells over at you as you all head to the trailer park. "You guys were gone, so I decided to go back to Starcourt. There's another problem—"

"Wait, have you been in Starcourt this whole time?"

"Yeah, since you guys left this morning."

"That wasn't this morning! That was yesterday morning!" As you ride, they fill you in on what you missed. Max had another vision, but thanks to Nancy and Robin's visit to Victor Creel, they figured out that music could prevent Vecna from getting into Max's mind. In her vision, Max had seen something that Nancy figured out was the Creel house. They went to search and found Vecna! Then Eddie's hideout was found and another student was murdered by Vecna. Dustin used a compass to find a gate in the lake, and they were caught by the police and brought to the Wheelers'. You're mostly caught up by the time you reach the trailer.

Go on to the next page.

The gate in Eddie's trailer is definitely not like the circular window you imagined. It oozes and writhes, like organic material: fleshy. On the other side, you see the others. "I understand why you called it the Upside Down."

"Actually, we've never seen this before either." Dustin ties some sheets together. You help the others drag a mattress from Eddie's room and dump it on the floor beneath the gate.

You hear Eddie's voice. "Those stains are, uh . . . I don't know what those stains are." Dustin tosses up the sheets, which go through the gate and are suspended in an equilibrium, creating an escape rope.

"Guess I'm the guinea pig," Robin says, and then climbs up the rope. When she gets through the gate, you see her hair start falling down, the real world's gravity getting hold of her. She pulls herself through and then falls onto the mattress. "That was fun!" Eddie pulls himself through next.

"Nancy?" You hear Steve's voice and look back up. Steve is holding Nancy by the shoulders and shaking her. "Hey! Hey! Stay with me! Nancy! Nancy, wake up!"

"Vecna," Max says. You rush with the others to Eddie's room and scramble through his collection of cassette tapes. Erica runs into the room. "Steve says you need to hurry!"

"What are you even looking for?" Eddie yells.

"Madonna, Blondie, Bowie, the Beatles? Music, we need music!" Robin yells.

"This! Is! Music!" Eddie screams.

"Play anything!" you yell.

Just then Erica returns. "She's out! Nancy's free from Vecna."

Turn to the next page.

In Max's living room, Nancy describes the vision she had from Vecna. He revealed his history to her: that he was Victor Creel's son, Henry; he had killed his family and then was taken by Dr. Brenner, the same scientist who experimented on Eleven, to be his first subject, One; after he killed everyone at the lab, Eleven cast him into the Upside Down, where he became Vecna. He then showed her the future.

"There were so many monsters. An army. And they were coming into Hawkins, into our neighborhoods, our homes—" Her voice breaks. "He showed me gates. Four gates. Spreading across Hawkins. And these gates, they looked like the one outside of Eddie's trailer, but they didn't stop growing. And this wasn't the Upside Down Hawkins. This was *our* Hawkins."

"Try them again. Try them again," Steve says to Max. She turns to use the phone.

"If you're trying to reach your friends in Lenora, don't bother. They aren't there anymore." Everyone looks at you in shock.

"How do you know that?" Max asks. You explain to them what happened when you were trapped in the mall and what you saw after. Their friends were on the run from the military.

"They had orders to shoot to kill," you finish.

"Why are they going after El?" Max asks.

"I have no idea. I just saw that they lost track of them."

"What are we going to do without El?" Steve leans forward on the couch, his elbows on his knees.

"So it's up to us now," Lucas says solemnly. "We're on our own." Nancy comes up with a plan. The first step is to get weapons.

Go on to the next page.

After stealing a trailer, stocking up on weapons, and escaping the horde of jocks hunting for Eddie, you are all preparing for war in an open field. Max holds down a shotgun as Nancy saws off its nozzle. Lucas and Erica build spears. Eddie and Dustin wrestle and joke around in the distance. You walk up to Robin and Steve carrying another canister of kerosene, catching a bit of their conversation.

"I mean, it just doesn't make sense," Steve says.

"What doesn't make sense?" Robin asks him.

"That was Dan Shelter. He graduated, like, two years ago."

"Is Dan important?" you say as you set the canister down.

"Uh, no, it's just some guy we know. Forget about it. Dumb high school crush stuff," Steve says as you sit down to help make more Molotov cocktails.

"The unrequited kind," Robin says as she smacks his arm. You decide not to pry into Robin's crush. "Anyway, in the face of the world ending, the stakes of my love life feel spectacularly low."

"Yeah, I get you there." Steve grabs another bottle. "But I still have hope."

"Not everything has a happy ending," Robin says, filling the bottle with kerosene. She hands it to you, and you place a rag inside the bottle.

"Yeah. Yeah, believe me, I know." You catch Steve looking over at Nancy as he says that.

"I'm not talking about failed romance." Robin pours kerosene into another bottle. "I just . . . I have this terrible, gnawing feeling that it might not work out for us this time."

"Yeah, but what choice do we have?" you ask. Everything is ready. The time has come.

Turn to the next page.

After dropping off Lucas, Max, and Erica at the Creel house, you find yourself back in Max's trailer.

"Okay," Nancy says. "I want to run through it one more time. Phase one."

"We meet Erica at the playground. She'll signal Max and Lucas when we're ready," Robin answers.

"Phase two."

"Max baits Vecna. He'll go after her, which will put him in his trance," Steve answers.

"Phase three?"

"Me and Eddie draw the bats away." Dustin points at Eddie standing behind him.

"Four."

"We head into Vecna's lair and attack," you answer.

"Nobody moves on to the next phase until we've all copied. Nobody deviates from the plan, no matter what. Got it?"

"Got it," you all answer. It's time to head out. You get inside Eddie's trailer, the makeshift rope still hanging through the gate. Steve goes in first, expertly landing on his feet when the gravity shifts on the other side.

"Ooooh, what does he want us to do, applaud?" Robin says sarcastically as Steve walks out of view. He comes back dragging a mattress and places it under the gate. Nancy goes in next, followed by her weapons, then Eddie, then Robin, and then Dustin. You are about to step into the Upside Down for the first, and hopefully last, time. You pull yourself up and climb. When you push through the gate, you feel yourself falling, butterflies in your stomach. It really was fun.

Go on to the next page.

Stepping out into the Upside Down, you see red lightning and dark clouds. Vines wrap around everything. In the distance, you hear the screeching of demobats. Steve stops and turns to Eddie and Dustin. "Hey, guys, listen. If things here start to go south, I mean at all, you abort. Okay? Draw the attention of the bats. Keep 'em busy for a minute or two. We'll take care of Vecna. Don't try to be a hero or something, okay? You guys are just—"

"Decoys," Dustin finishes for him. "Don't worry. You can be the hero, Steve."

"Absolutely. I mean, look at us. We are not heroes," Eddie adds. Steve starts to walk away when Eddie stops him. "Hey, Steve? Make him pay." And with that you walk toward the Creel house.

In the park across the street from Creel house, you see a glowing light in the rocket jungle gym. "Erica," Robin says. You all rush over to the rocket. The bats screech furiously as they scatter around the house. You wait for the go-ahead from Erica.

"Okay, she's in," Erica's voice echoes. "Initiate phase three."

Robin pulls out the radio and contacts Dustin and Eddie. "She's in. Move on to phase three."

"Copy that, initiating phase three," Dustin responds. After a few seconds, you see the demobats fly away from the Creel house in the direction of the trailer park. It's time to initiate phase four. Opening the door to the Creel house, you see vines covering the floor.

"Remember, hive mind. Don't touch the vines," Nancy reminds everyone. Steve leads the way, followed by Nancy. Robin seems frozen. You take her hand.

"It's okay, just go slow. I'll help you," you say as you follow the path Steve sets.

Turn to the next page.

256

You make it to the top of the stairs, outside the door to the attic where Vecna awaits. The earth shakes! You and Robin hold on to each other for dear life, trying to keep steady. You anchor her as well as you can until the shaking stops. Looking down, you are relieved to see that no one has touched a single vine. It's go time. Steve leads the way up to the attic, avoiding the vines there. When you reach the attic, you see Vecna for the first time.

Covered in scar tissue and jagged muscle, he is suspended from the ceiling, frozen. He doesn't register your presence. Nancy points her gun, and the rest of you grab Molotov cocktails. "Flambé," Robin whispers. You start throwing the explosives. Vecna drops from the ceiling, then rises, covered in flames. Nancy steps in front and begins shooting, pushing Vecna back until he bursts through the wall and falls into the street. You all rush down the stairs and outside.

"Did we win? Is he . . . ?" you ask. You find the others staring at a burn spot on the ground. "Where's the body?"

The grandfather clock chimes once. Then again. You all run back inside the house. *Chime. Chime.* The time reads four o'clock. "Four chimes." Robin gasps.

"Max."

The ground begins to shake violently. You all hold on to the banister, your fingers slip, and you fall back, hitting your head hard.

Go on to the next page.

Two days have passed since the rift opened. The newspapers call it a freak earthquake, but you know the truth.

You, Dustin, and Robin are at the Wheelers' house helping to collect donations for people displaced by the "quake." Suddenly, a pizza delivery truck pulls up. The side door slides open and four people step out. A lanky boy and a bald girl hug, and Dustin runs to join them.

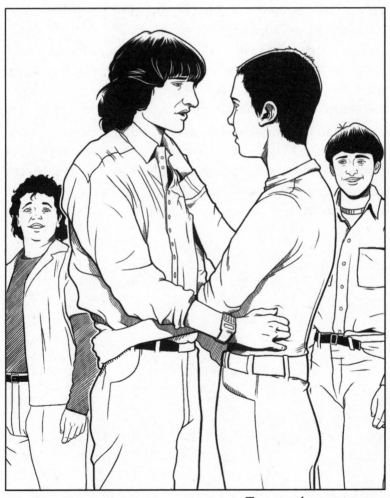

Turn to the next page.

You recognize the van—and the driver! It's Argyle, a kid from your school. He's delivered pizza to your house many times. What is he doing in Hawkins? Has he really driven these people all the way from Lenora?

You slowly piece the story together and identify the new people. The tall dark-haired boy is Mike. You've seen him in many Wheeler family photos. Nancy runs to a boy you know is Jonathan Byers, his photos prominently featured in Nancy's room. The other boy is Will Byers. The quiet girl with a closely shaven head is Eleven.

You stand back as they all embrace. After a moment, you walk over to Dustin, wanting to introduce yourself to the people you've heard so much about.

"Where's Lucas?" Will asks.

"He's at the hospital," Dustin answers. It dawns on Dustin that they don't know what happened. The new arrivals head to the hospital to see Max, while the rest of you get in Steve's car and drive to school. Tomorrow you will be on your way to Lenora while Vecna lives.

The End

Whatever they are doing, you need to have faith that they can handle it. They've been fighting this battle a lot longer than you have. You get on your bicycle and ride past the military vehicles, yelling at the top of your lungs, "I know where Eleven is!" The chase is on! You cut between houses to lose the cars, getting farther and farther away. You know the others are meeting at the trailer park, but you worry about the long ride and potentially being spotted by the military again.

"We're at Eddie's trailer. Where are you?" Dustin's voice comes through your radio. "Vecna is Henry Creel, and he's planning to destroy Hawkins. We found him at the Creel house." Dustin gives you an address. "We're trying to contact our friends, but there's no answer. You need to get here as soon as possible. Over."

"If you're talking about your friends in Lenora, you won't hear from them." You explain what has happened since you escaped the mall. "I can't come to you. I'm compromised. I'm going into hiding. Do not contact me. Over and out." You switch off the radio and bike hard, making it to the one place you are sure the military won't think to look for you: the Creel house. When you arrive, you dump your bike into some bushes and go inside. You find an old musty bed in one of the rooms and collapse onto it from exhaustion.

Turn to the next page.

You are shaken out of your dreamless sleep and see Lucas and Max standing over you. "What are you—" Max places a hand over your mouth to stop you from speaking. Lucas holds up a notepad with *Keep quiet* written on it. You nod, and Max removes her hand. Lucas scribbles another note and shows it to you: *What happened?* He hands you the notepad, and you write back: *Long story. What are you doing here?* Max writes on her notepad and holds it up: *We're going to attack Vecna.* You almost choke. Just then the girl you saw from earlier comes into the room. She holds up a note: *Found Vecna.* Lucas scribbles a note to you: *My sister Erica.* Erica leads you all back down to the foyer of the house. A blue lamp glows on the table more brightly than the ones in Lucas's and Max's hands. Erica holds up another note: *Phase two?* Lucas nods. Just then a fleet of cars screeches to a halt outside, and armed military personnel jump out and run into the house.

"Let go of me!" Max yells. Lucas tries to get them to listen, but they ignore him. You are tossed on the ground, and a man holds you down. Twisting your head, you see Lucas, Erica, and Max pinned down as well. You all are cuffed and then propped up.

"Where's the girl?" a man screams in your face. "Where is the girl?"

Lucas starts screaming. "Give it back! Give it back to her now!" He thrashes wildly. You turn to see another man striding away with Max's Walkman. Suddenly Max is lifted into the air! The military personnel draw their weapons on her, then her limbs begin to break. Lucas screams for Max to wake up, but it is useless. Her body drops to the ground suddenly. Lucas tries desperately to crawl toward her. Beneath Max's lifeless body, the earth opens up. You are dragged away from the rift, along with Erica and Lucas. Lucas cries in agony.

The End

You've been standing in the cover of trees for the last ten minutes, watching the cabin. It's clear someone is in there, and that someone might be a bloodthirsty murderer. . . . You are on your own. You creep as quietly as possible as you get closer. You can hear movement inside the cabin—pots and pans. For a moment you wonder if you've stumbled across a satanic ritual. You shake the thought from your head—now is not the time to lose your grip on reality. It's clear whoever is in there is comfortable. They wouldn't see you coming. You knock on the door, making sure to stay away from windows. The door opens slightly, and you hear a voice. "Dustin?"

You jump and push your way through the door. You see a fishing rod and grab it, swinging it haphazardly. This must be Eddie Munson! He falls back, trying to dodge your swings. You've got him cornered.

"Look, whatever you heard, I swear I didn't do anything! Don't hurt me!" Eddie crouches in the corner. Aside from the puppet and bat tattoos, he looks like an average teen metalhead. You have a bunch of them at your school.

"If you didn't do anything, why haven't you turned yourself in?" You wield the fishing rod as a warning.

"If I did, they wouldn't believe me."

"Why not? You must have seen who did it. You could have just told them, but you ran instead."

"Yes, I ran!" His confession sounds like agony. "But I freaked out. It was crazy!" What he tells you is beyond comprehension. Chrissy was killed by a ghost or demon he couldn't see.

Turn to the next page.

"You're lying!" you yell, wielding the fishing rod like a whip. "Tell me the truth now!"

"This is the truth!" He grabs his hair in his fists. "I swear it's the truth! I don't know how to prove it! If I could prove it, I would go to the police right now, but I can't!" He presses his forehead to the ground, mumbling apologies to Chrissy. He's crying? You lower the fishing rod slightly. Watching him utterly devastated, it's clear that Eddie is no threat to anyone. You think of Lucas at Benny's and his insistence on Eddie's innocence. You can see it now.

"What if you could prove it?" You toss the fishing rod aside and kneel down next to Eddie. "I know you have some friends helping you; maybe they've found a way. They believe you."

"They only believe me because they've dealt with things like this before." He turns to look directly at you. "They had some superpowered friend who is gone now, but they . . . they've seen stuff like this in Hawkins."

"They *what?*"

Bang! Bang! Bang! "Open up! I saw you go in there!" Jason's outside the door! He followed you to Eddie. "Is he in there with you? Eddie Munson, come out here and face me!"

Eddie curses. You pull him up by the arm and move toward the back of the cabin.

"Wait!" Eddie yells, pulling away from you. He runs across the room and grabs a radio. "We'll need this to get in touch with my friends." He follows you out the back, and you start running for the trees.

Go on to the next page.

You run until your lungs are burning before you're sure that you lost Jason. "I—" You bend over, trying to catch your breath. "I didn't think I was followed."

Eddie holds the radio to his mouth. "Dustin, you there? Dustin? Wheeler? Anybody?" There's no answer. Eddie curses.

"I guess we're on our own for now." You straighten up and look at your surroundings. "We can't just stay here all day and hope no one finds us."

"Skull Rock is not too far away." Eddie stands and brushes dirt off his pants. "We could hide there for a while and keep trying to reach my friends." You don't like the idea of sitting around waiting, but Eddie is a wanted suspect and Jason won't be so kind to you if you run into him again. It makes sense to hide. But hiding hasn't really done anything to help Eddie clear his name or solve this murder. "What are you thinking?"

"What if we worked together to prove your innocence?" You pause. Eddie looks at you in surprise. "Let's say I believe you and your friends about this Scooby-Doo stuff going on in Hawkins. It had to start somewhere, for some reason. Maybe, if we could figure out why Chrissy was killed, we could figure out how to beat this ghost."

"It's not a ghost; it's some wizard with powers," Eddie corrects you. "And unless you've been keeping it from me, neither of us has superpowers." Eddie looks determined to stay safe and in hiding. That may be the best thing to do, considering the area is going to be crawling with jocks searching for Eddie. Still, after seeing Eddie's anguish over admitting he ran from Chrissy, you could get him to go along with your plan with a little guilt-tripping.

If you choose to go to Skull Rock to hide,
turn to the next page.

If you choose to investigate the case with Eddie,
turn to page 289.

The walk to Skull Rock is peaceful, despite the gnawing fear of being followed. You ask Eddie for more details about the last time he saw Chrissy, and Eddie holds nothing back. "You still haven't told me why Chrissy was in your trailer."

Eddie looks torn, then sighs and says, "She wasn't supposed to be there. We met at the place I usually make deals."

"So she was a customer. How long was she coming to you for that?"

Eddie shakes his head. "That was the first time." He walks in silence for a bit. "She was really nice. I mean, not fake nice because she wanted something from me, but really, genuinely nice."

"So if you didn't meet at the trailer, why did she go with you?"

"She wanted something stronger, and I didn't have that kind of stuff on me, so we had to go back to my place."

"Did she say why she was buying? Did she maybe buy from other people before?"

Eddie shook his head. "She was so jumpy, it was obviously her first time. I told her we didn't have to do it, but she insisted. I don't know why she was buying, and I didn't ask. I should have asked. Maybe that would have made a difference." You don't know how to answer that, so you walk next to him in silence. Soon Skull Rock is within view.

"I guess we should try contacting your friends again." It doesn't take long for Eddie to get an answer this time.

Go on to the next page.

"The first thing we need to do is get you a new hiding place," Dustin says. Eddie's friends arrive not too long after. Max, Dustin, and Steve broke into the school when they heard Eddie's call. "Nancy and Robin are following a hunch at the library. Hopefully they find something."

"So find a place to hide and then what?" you ask.

Max holds up some keys. "Then we're going to the school to look through some student files. Chrissy was seeing the counselor too, and so was Fred."

"That's right. You two don't know." Dustin's mouth hangs open for a moment. "There was another murder early this morning, or late last night. Fred Benson was killed in the woods near the trailer park when he and Nancy were investigating. . . ."

Dustin's voice fades out as the news of the second murder hits you like a ton of bricks. Was that why Fred didn't pick you up from the airport? But no, you arrived at the Benson house before the murder was reported to the public. Fred must have been killed after. You think of Mrs. Benson. By now she must know what happened to her son. Maybe you should check in with her.

"We still can't get ahold of Lucas either. He radioed us when we were leaving the school. We told him to meet us there, but we haven't heard from him since and it's dark now."

"That . . . might be . . . my . . . fault?" you say sheepishly.

"Where is he?"

Turn to the next page.

It's risky, being so close to Jason and his friends again after being found out, but you owe Lucas at least this much. You turn to the others. Eddie was left at Skull Rock for his own safety. "Lucas is being held in a small janitor's closet back in the kitchen. We'll need to get there, free him, and get out, all without being seen."

"What if I just went in there?" Steve asks. "I was captain of the basketball team. It wouldn't be weird for me to show up and see some old friends."

You shake your head. "Can't do that. Jason knows you're friends with Dustin. I got the address to the cabin when we broke into the video store looking for you."

"Wait, you broke into the store? I'm going to lose my job!"

"Steve, focus." Dustin stares at him incredulously.

"Right." Steve shakes his head. "New plan. I go there as a distraction, while you guys sneak in and get Lucas out. We'll meet back at Skull Rock." Everyone agrees. Steve heads around to the front of the diner, while the rest of you scout the back. You can hear Steve yelling, "What the hell did you guys do to my store?"

The ruckus that follows signals it's time to move. You lead the others into the kitchen quietly and stand lookout while Max and Dustin open the janitor's closet. The knots tying Lucas are tight, and Max and Dustin struggle to get him loose.

"Just grab a knife from the kitchen and cut through the ropes," you hiss at them. "Hurry, I don't think Steve's distraction will last much longer." After some more struggle, Max and Dustin free Lucas. Just then a fight breaks out!

Go on to the next page.

"You guys head to Skull Rock. I'm going to help Steve. Go!" Max and Dustin guide Lucas out the back as you run toward the front. Outside, you see Steve and Jason throwing punches. The rest of the team is standing around them in a circle, cheering Jason on.

"Jason!" you yell. He looks at you and blinks as if he can't believe you are standing right in front of him. Frankly, you can't believe it either.

"You!" Anger blazes in his eyes. "You traitor! Where's Eddie?" Before he can get any closer, you turn and run in the opposite direction as fast as you can. Forgetting Steve entirely, Jason gives chase, his followers close behind. An engine roars behind you. You turn to see Steve's car kicking up dust. Dustin pulls Steve into the car. The engine revs once more, and then the car speeds up directly toward you. The jocks jump out of the way. Max looks fierce behind the wheel. She swerves to a stop, separating you from the jocks. Dustin pushes the door open, and you jump in as Max zooms away.

"What exactly was your plan?" Max says as she careens onto the road and floors it. Soon you're far away from Benny's Burgers. "Just get them to catch you and get beaten to a pulp?"

"Yeah, I didn't really think that through." You lean your head back against the seat, catching your breath. Next to you is Lucas, bruised. You look him directly in the eyes. "I'm sorry, Lucas."

He nods. "Thanks for coming to get me." The car swerves!

Turn to the next page.

"Max! Max?" Steve jumps from the back seat and grabs the steering wheel. Dustin tries shaking Max, but she is unresponsive.

"What's happening?" Lucas yells. Dustin lifts Max's leg off the pedal while Steve steers, yelling at Dustin to hurry up.

"I don't know! I don't know! It's like she's asleep, but her eyes are open." Dustin struggles to move Max out of the driver's seat. Steve tries to steer the car. You lean over and help Dustin pull Max out of the seat, and Steve takes control of the car, bringing it to a stop. Then Max wakes up.

"Holy crap, Max! You almost got us killed!" you yell.

She looks confused and groggy. She looks at the others and asks, "What happened?"

"I don't know. You tell us. One minute you're driving my car—which I specifically told you never to do again, by the way—and then you're just . . . out." Steve turns off the engine.

"I— You guys didn't see it?" She looks worried. "The grandfather clock, in the middle of the road. We almost hit it, and then—" She gets out of the car and walks back down the road. "It was right here!"

Go on to the next page.

When you get to Skull Rock, two others are already with Eddie. They are introduced as Nancy and Robin. Max recounts her vision: a grandfather clock on the road that chimed four times.

"Before break, I saw Chrissy in the bathroom at school. She was afraid, but no one else was there. It was just me and her," Max adds.

"Fred seemed out of it when we first got to the trailer park." Nancy furrows her brow. "The article we found on the Creel murders said the family was having visions too."

"So the only clue we have are these visions," Eddie recaps. "But everyone who had visions is dead, except for Max—"

"Not everyone." Nancy looks at Robin. "Victor Creel is still alive and in Pennhurst. If we could talk to him—"

"Maybe we could get more information on this demon?" you ask.

"Vecna," Dustin corrects you. "We're calling him Vecna."

"Shut up, Henderson." Steve rolls his eyes. "We've got another problem you're all forgetting: where's Eddie going to stay?"

"We could sneak him into the Wheelers' basement, like we did with El," Dustin suggests.

"Wait, I have a better idea." Lucas fills everyone in.

Turn to the next page.

"Home sweet home!" Dustin announces as he leads the way in. The hideout—what the others call Hopper's cabin—looks like a wreck. There's a large hole in the roof and dust and debris everywhere.

"It looks like a war zone," you quip.

"Well, it kind of was." Robin shrugs. "The Mind Flayer became this huge spiderlike monster and attacked El here." While you were filled in on the events of the past three years during the car ride to the cabin, you still feel shock every time you are reminded of the troubles in Hawkins. First there was a Demogorgon that captured one of their friends in a parallel universe. Then the Mind Flayer took over that friend's body and brought down a whole lab with demon dogs—or demodogs, as Dustin corrected you time and time again—and then the Mind Flayer took over Max's brother's mind and created a monster out of the flesh of thirty human beings in town to try to kill their superpowered friend El. So much happened and most of the town doesn't even know it, let alone the rest of the world. After helping Eddie set up a spot to sleep in, the others are ready to leave. You should check in with Mrs. Benson—today she learned her son was brutally murdered. You're not sure how you could help, but you feel like you should say *something* to her.

"Are you okay to be here alone?" you ask Eddie.

"Oh, don't mind me. I'll just spend the night alone in a cabin that was attacked by a killer demon. No biggie." Eddie grins despite the fear in his eyes.

If you choose to stay in the cabin with Eddie,
go on to the next page.

If you choose to go to the Bensons', turn to page 278.

Nancy promises to call Mrs. Benson and let her know that you are going to stay at the Wheelers' for the night and will pick your stuff up in the morning so she can have privacy in her grief. You feel a little guilty dumping that responsibility on her, but you're not sure what to do or say. The others have been keeping secrets like this for much longer than you have. Soon enough, you and Eddie are in your respective corners, ready to sleep.

"What's wrong?" Eddie asks, concerned for you.

"It's . . . I was with Mrs. Benson when Chrissy's murder was reported. Fred was supposed to pick me up from the airport but he never showed. He was hosting me for this journalism conference he was organizing. That's why I came to Hawkins in the first place." You wring the hem of your shirt in your hands. "I guess it's just finally hitting me."

"I get it." He shifts his position. "When it first happened to Chrissy, I couldn't think straight. I was just so afraid. But later it really hit me that she was gone."

"It's stupid for me to feel this way. I mean, I didn't really know Fred at all."

"I hardly knew Chrissy, but it still hurts."

"That's different. You saw it happen; of course that's going to stay with you." You sigh. "I shouldn't be this sad about it. I feel like I'm taking up someone else's grief."

"I don't think it's a competition." Eddie rests his head on his arm as he turns to his side. "We can all grieve." You ponder this until you fall asleep.

Turn to the next page.

You wake to hear Eddie cooking in the kitchenette. The smell of food makes your stomach grumble. When was the last time you ate? It feels like years have passed. What was life like before Hawkins? You can't remember.

"What time is it?" you ask groggily as you head to the table. There are only two seats, the former occupants being only the superpowered friend and her adoptive dad. You wonder what it would be like to live in near isolation for a year as El had to, according to her friends.

"It's late. We slept in." He minds the frying pan. "Breakfast is almost ready." He turns the stove off, shuffles the food onto two plates, and brings one to you.

"So you cook?"

"It's just me and my uncle, so we take turns." He begins scarfing down the food. You pick at your plate.

"I'm going to see Mrs. Benson and get my stuff. What should I say to her?"

"I don't know." He looks up at you but almost seems to be looking past you. "If I could talk to Chrissy's parents . . . I'd say I'm sorry."

You nod. The rest of breakfast goes quietly. Soon you are ready to head back into civilization.

"Hey," Eddie says, standing in the doorway, "be careful out there. Jason's still on the hunt."

Go on to the next page.

You rest Fred's bike against the side of the house and take a deep breath before knocking. Mrs. Benson opens the door, her eyes red and puffy. "Mrs. Benson, I—I am so sorry about what happened to Fred."

"Thank you. I brought your suitcase down since you didn't get a chance to unpack. Come in; your friend is waiting for you."

"My friend?" When you step into the house, you see him sitting in the living room. Jason winks. "What are you doing here?"

"I'm helping you move your stuff, remember?" The veneer of friendliness in Jason's voice is thin. "We can't just let you walk around with your suitcase. What kind of friend does that?"

"It's okay, I've got it handled. But thanks."

Jason's face turns stern. "It's no problem at all. Besides, we need to talk." Your heart is thumping hard in your chest.

"I think you should go with him," Mrs. Benson adds. "After what's been going on, it's not good to be out alone. If my Fred hadn't wandered by himself, maybe—" Her voice catches. "It's safer, my dear."

You can't let yourself be taken by Jason, but if you cause a scene, Mrs. Benson might get suspicious. On the other hand, you've seen what Jason is capable of, and you're no longer on his good side.

If you choose to lie to Jason, turn to the next page.

If you choose to make a run for it, turn to page 277.

"Actually, I already have a friend meeting me here to give me a ride." Once Jason leaves, you can excuse yourself from the Bensons' house and get away.

"Oh, that's right, you're staying with Nancy Wheeler now." Mrs. Benson smiles. "She was always a good friend to my Fred. It would be nice to see her." Your heart drops. Jason didn't know about Nancy's involvement, and now Mrs. Benson has just exposed her to Jason's wrath.

"Nancy Wheeler, huh?" Jason's eyes are cold and calculating. "Doesn't she have a brother named Mike in that Hellfire Club? How is he doing?"

"I don't know, I haven't met him. He's not in Hawkins for the break."

"Too bad. I would have loved to talk to him." Jason's jaw clenches. "Well, it would be good to see Nancy; maybe we'll just wait a while."

"I'm sure you have other things to do, and we don't want to inconvenience Mrs. Benson—"

"Oh no, it's all right. I'd prefer to know you kids are somewhere safe while you wait." Mrs. Benson smiles, clueless of the fact that she just ruined your chance to get rid of Jason.

"Thank you." You try to remain calm. "Would it be all right if I used your phone to call the Wheelers and see if Nancy is on her way?" Mrs. Benson leads you to a phone. You pull out the piece of paper with Nancy's number on it and dial, your heart pounding. A woman answers.

Go on to the next page.

"Hello, may I speak to Nancy, please?"

Mrs. Wheeler informs you that Nancy and Robin left earlier that morning, and Steve left a little later with Max, Lucas, and Dustin. You're on your own.

"When they come back, could you please tell them to call me at Mrs. Benson's? Tell her Jason Carver and I are waiting for her. Thank you." You hang up the phone. Not only was Nancy exposed, but your last chance of getting out of here without Jason is gone too. You need to do something quick, or Jason will insist on driving you when Nancy doesn't show up. You walk into the living room where he is still sitting. "Looks like Nancy is on her way." You smile, keeping up the lie. You take a seat opposite Jason.

"Wonderful," Mrs. Benson says. "If you don't mind, kids, I'm going to excuse myself. Feel free to use the TV and help yourself to anything in the kitchen." You can see Mrs. Benson is worn out; she heads up the stairs. It doesn't take Jason long to start grilling you.

"I know you helped Sinclair escape. What I don't get is why. You were the one who ratted him out. Or was that a distraction so you could get to Eddie first?" His fists clench, and he gets up.

Turn to the next page.

"I haven't told the cops about you and Eddie yet, but don't think I won't." His grin is sinister. He gets closer. He wouldn't do anything when Mrs. Benson is right upstairs, would he?

"You would have already done it by now, Jason. You want to get to Eddie before they do. I think you should leave, or I'll tell the cops what you did to Lucas."

"You'd only make things worse for yourself. Besides, they won't care about Lucas when I tell them I saw you with Eddie."

"Do you have any proof that I've even met Eddie? I'm from out of town, remember. And I arrived here after Eddie already fled." That wipes the grin off his face. "It's your word against mine."

"Wrong." He pulls out a knife and holds it to your throat. "You're going to tell me where Eddie is, and then you're going to tell the police everything yourself." He grabs you by your shirt and pulls you up, the knife never leaving your throat. Then he turns his head and says loud enough for Mrs. Benson to hear, "Nancy can't make it? Well then, why don't we go now?" He walks behind you, keeping the knife at your throat. "Don't forget your suitcase." Soon you and your suitcase are locked in Jason's car with him. No one is coming to save you.

The End

"Oh, I forgot. I left Fred's bike outside. I should put it in the garage." Before anyone can react, you leap out the front door, jump on the bike, and take off, yelling apologies to Mrs. Benson over your shoulder. So much for getting your stuff. You don't look back, knowing Jason will be chasing you. Instead, you pedal harder. You need to get back to the cabin to hide.

Eddie gets Dustin on the radio. "Yeah, we're fine now, but Jason's looking for us."

"Well, it's good we found a new hiding spot," Dustin answers. "We're leaving the trailer park now. Max has one more letter to deliver, then we can rendezvous with you. Still no word from Nancy and Robin."

When Dustin signs off, you sigh. "So we're just supposed to wait and hide?"

"I mean, that's all I've been doing." He takes a seat next to you. "It's not so bad."

"If I had just let Steve handle Jason, then I could be out there with the others. I could be doing something."

"If they need us, they'll come get us. For now, we're in a place where no one can find us, and that's a good thing. Can you imagine what would have happened if we got caught by Jason?" You know he's right, and at least you have company while you wait. Eddie offers to teach you about Dungeons and Dragons to pass the time. After a while, there is a knock on the door. It must be Dustin and the others. When you open the door, a jock knocks you down. You were followed!

"Game over, Munson!" Jason yells.

The End

278

You are up late, unable to sleep. When you got to the house, Mrs. Benson was grateful for your choice to stay elsewhere, and you were able to give her your condolences and then get your stuff. Now you are in the Wheelers' basement, tossing and turning. You wonder if Eddie is awake. You get up quietly and take the radio into the bathroom, closing the door behind you.

"Hey, Eddie, it's me. You up?"

"Yeah, can't sleep." His voice is hoarse. You both want company.

"Tomorrow Nancy and Robin are going to see Victor Creel. They think they might find something."

"I'll take anything at this point." He sounds defeated. "But Vecna killed his family too. How are we supposed to stop him when others couldn't?"

You try to reassure him. "I don't know, but everyone here said they've fought things like this before and won, so maybe there's a chance."

"Yeah, maybe."

You spend the night talking about random things. Eventually, you fall asleep on the bathroom floor with the radio next to your head.

Go on to the next page.

Max shakes you. "Hey, wake up! Nancy and Robin are almost ready to leave." You sit up groggily and wipe the sleep from your eyes.

"To Pennhurst, right?" You yawn. "Okay, okay, I'm getting up." You greet the others in the basement, then Nancy and Robin come down the stairs.

"Stay here until Robin and I get back," Nancy tells the rest of you before leaving. Max spends the morning writing letters, while Dustin, Lucas, and Steve watch her with concern. Hours pass, and then Max suddenly gets up and hands out letters. Before you know it, you're in Steve's car. Max has other letters to deliver, and she was able to convince Steve to make it happen.

You are at the cemetery waiting for Max to deliver her last letter to her brother's grave, which sits on top of a hill. You are in the car with the others. Steve looks agitated.

"It's taking too long," he says impatiently.

"Give her time, Steve," Lucas answers. Steve gets out of the car and heads up the hill before anyone can stop him. He begins to shake Max.

"What's happening?" You open the car door.

"Something's wrong!" Lucas yells. You, Lucas, and Dustin run up the hill. Steve is still shaking Max, yelling her name. Max sits still, her eyes rolled back into her head. It's Vecna! Dustin runs back down to the car to contact Nancy and Robin. He returns clutching a Walkman and some cassettes.

Turn to the next page.

It's the next morning, back in the Wheelers' basement. Max is listening to music on her Walkman. According to Robin and Nancy, music keeps Vecna away. It was how Victor Creel survived Vecna's attack on his family all those years ago. Nancy comes down the stairs, followed by Dustin and Max.

"We need to go to the Creel house," she announces. The others are ready to go.

"What about Eddie?" you ask. "Shouldn't we check on him after Max's latest vision?"

"I don't think Vecna is targeting Eddie," Dustin answers. "I think he was just in the wrong place at the wrong time with Chrissy. Vecna's not targeting him."

"Still, shouldn't he be told about what's happening?" you say. They agree someone should be with Eddie. Besides, there's more than enough of them to search the house.

Go on to the next page.

You and Eddie sit by the radio, waiting to hear from the others. It's dark out. You've updated Eddie on everything that happened since he had to leave Coal Mill Road.

"What time is it?" you ask during a pause in the conversation. He shows you his watch; it's around 9:30 p.m. The radio comes alive.

"You guys there? Is everything okay?" It's Max.

"Yeah, we're fine. Why?" you answer.

"We found Vecna," she responds. "Something happened over here. We'll fill you in tomorrow."

The next day, when the others arrive at the cabin, they explain what they found at the Creel house. Vecna was there, but also not. He was on the other side, the Upside Down dimension. Then in the attic he did something that made the lights burst. You don't really understand, and you regret not being there to see it for yourself. "So what do you think that was?"

"When the Demogorgon appeared, the lights would flicker. Whatever Vecna was doing was much more powerful," Nancy answered. "Will used lights to talk to his mom when he was lost in the Upside Down."

"So was Vecna trying to communicate with you?"

"I don't think so. But he was definitely up to something." You hear police sirens screaming in the distance. Everyone except Eddie runs to the car to follow.

"It was Patrick," Lucas says as he walks back from Benny's Burgers and the surrounding police presence. "Vecna attacked him like he did Chrissy and Fred sometime last night."

Turn to the next page.

"The lights." Dustin turns to Nancy. "You don't think what we saw was Vecna's attack?"

"So Patrick was killed last night?" You straighten up. "This is great!"

"What? How is Patrick being killed great?" Lucas looks angry; Patrick was his teammate. You should have been more sensitive.

"No, that's not what I meant! I mean that Eddie's in the clear now. I was with him all last night; he has an alibi. Maybe we can convince the police that he's innocent and he can come out of hiding."

"Do you think Powell will accept that? Eddie is his only suspect right now." Robin looks unconvinced. "If you tell him, he'll know that we know where Eddie is hiding. We can't take that chance."

"Right now the only people who know Eddie is a suspect are the police, Jason, and us," you say. A commotion draws your attention. News crews are setting up around the chief of police as he gets ready to make an announcement.

"Last night another murder of a Hawkins High student took place here at Benny's. The deceased has been identified as Patrick McKinney. The manner of death—" Chief Powell goes on.

"Three murders. He's going to have to give the press more information," you say, worried.

"If he tells the news it was Eddie, it's open season on him," Max says. It's now or never. You can clear Eddie, but that might get you into trouble. Then again, if you say nothing, Eddie is in even more danger than before.

If you choose to interrupt the press conference, go on to the next page.

If you choose to stay quiet, turn to page 286.

You run toward the conference, yelling at the top of your lungs. "I need to speak to Chief Powell! I have some important information about the murders! Move!" The camera crews and reporters, stunned by your outburst, make way for you. Powell is as shocked as the others. "Sir, please, I need to talk to you right now!" Powell looks at the reporters, then back at you. "Please!"

"I'm sorry for the interruption, but we will have a town hall today that the public is invited to attend. I will answer your questions then." He pulls you aside. "Come with me."

"He's innocent," you say as soon as you and Powell are alone. "Eddie Munson can't be the killer."

"The first murder took place in his own home, and he has not been seen since." Powell looks unconvinced. "What makes you so sure?"

"I—" You hesitate, remembering Robin's warning. Too late now. "I know because I was with him all last night when Patrick was murdered."

"You were with Eddie Munson? So why hasn't he come to the police to explain what happened? Why has he been hiding?"

"Because he was afraid you wouldn't believe him."

"Well, if you tell me where he is, I can talk to him myself." Powell is no fool. "If he has nothing to hide, he should talk to the police."

Turn to the next page.

"Did anyone witness Patrick's death?" you ask. Powell is surprised by the change of topic. "Someone did, didn't they? There were so many people at Benny's helping Jason look for Eddie, someone did see something. What if I told you that whatever that witness told you is exactly what Eddie said he saw happen to Chrissy?"

"I don't know what you mean—"

"Eddie said that Chrissy froze. He tried to wake her, but she wouldn't react at all. Then she was lifted into the air, and that's when her bones started to break. I bet that's exactly what your witness told you happened to Patrick, and it's probably what happened to Fred Benson as well." The stunned look on Powell's face tells you you've hit a bull's-eye.

"You need to tell me where Eddie is," Powell answers after a long pause. He's not listening; maybe Robin was right after all.

"I can't do that," you say. "Not if you are still treating him as a suspect."

"Then you are under arrest for assisting a criminal and harboring a fugitive." Powell pulls out a pair of handcuffs. Robin was right.

Go on to the next page.

It's been weeks since the earthquake, and you are waiting for your sentencing. You have been tried for harboring a fugitive. Eddie is still wanted but hasn't been seen. In their visits, your friends have told you what really happened. Eddie died trying to save the city from Vecna. Max is now in a coma because of Vecna's attack. The earthquake was actually Vecna's mega gate being opened, and he has since disappeared. You know he'll be back, though.

"You are hereby sentenced to one year in state prison." The judge slams his gavel. You are immediately taken from the courtroom. Your mother, who spent all her savings to be with you and pay for a lawyer, wails behind you.

The End

Eddie is now public enemy number one after Powell's press conference. You sit with the others in the cabin trying to figure out the next move.

"Hopper hid El here for a year," Nancy tries to reassure Eddie. "No one is going to find you."

"Meanwhile, we're no closer to knowing anything about Vecna and his plans. We don't even know why he's killing random teens." You are frustrated by the lack of progress. "What do we have? We know Vecna probably killed the Creels, and then he decided to stop for some reason. We know that Vecna is in the Upside Down. And we know he can kill using his mind powers. Is he just planning to kill one by one until he gets rid of the entire town?"

"You're right." Robin sighs. "Even with the Russians, we figured out that they had a key here in Hawkins. We know nothing about Vecna, really."

"Okay, so we start from the beginning," Nancy says. "Beginning with Chrissy's murder."

"I've already told you what I saw." Eddie looks defeated. "I don't know how my uncle can stand being in that trailer."

"He's not," Max says suddenly. "He's not staying there. When we went to drop off my letters, the trailer was still empty."

"That's impossible. Where could he go?" Eddie asks. "That trailer and his truck are all he has."

"If he's not staying in the trailer, there must be a reason." Nancy furrows her brow.

"So what's in that trailer?" you ask. Finally, you have a lead.

Go on to the next page.

The trailer door creaks open, musty air coming out. You all see it at once. "That's exactly where Chrissy died," Eddie says, looking at the large red membrane on the ceiling of the living room. Dustin pulls out his compass and shows it to everyone.

"It's going crazy. This has to be a—"

"A gate," Nancy finishes for him. "If a gate opens every time Vecna kills someone, then that means there are three gates already—one here, one where Fred died, and one at Benny's."

"In both visions I had from Vecna, the grandfather clock chimed four times." Max grips Lucas's hand. "Four times exactly."

"Four chimes, four gates," Lucas whispers.

"If he's planning to come here, doesn't he just need the one gate?" you ask.

"Unless he's not coming alone. The Demogorgon, the demodogs, the Mind Flayer, who knows what else is on the other side." Dustin's voice is hoarse. The trailer has become a cocoon of fear. "End of the world."

"Fire worked on the Demogorgon and the demodogs, right? Can we just burn it?" Steve asks.

"When Jonathan and I went to the lab, Owens showed us how the burning kept the gate in check, but didn't close it. The only one who could close them was El." Nancy pulls you back from the gate. "Hopper and Mrs. Byers were only able to close the last one because they destroyed the Russians' machine and Hopper died. We should get Max out of here." You look at the gate; if burning it could stall Vecna, wouldn't it be worth doing?

If you choose to burn the gate, turn to the next page.

If you choose to leave with the others, turn to page 291.

You go into the kitchen and rummage around. "If all we can do is keep this thing in check, maybe that's what we should be doing until we figure out a better plan. Burn this gate, the one where Fred died, and the one at Benny's. Maybe that will stall Vecna." You find the matches. "I need something to light. I don't think a tiny match is going to do much damage to that thing."

"Okay." Nancy steps forward, taking charge. "Okay, let's try it." She goes into the bedroom and returns with some sheets and starts ripping them apart. "We'll need something to reach it."

"Like a stick or something? I've got it." Steve runs out of the trailer, then comes back holding a baseball bat with nails in it. "Will this work?"

"You kept that?" Nancy's face is a mix of emotions.

"Came in handy against Dustin's demodog—"

"Hey, keep D'Art out of this," Dustin protests. "He let us go in the end."

"Fine, fine." Steve rolls his eyes. "Let's do this. I'll light the bat and hold it up to the gate."

"No way." You take the bat from him. "It's my idea, so I should be the one to do it." The others stand back as you wrap the ripped sheets around the bat and then light it. Standing on a chair, you lift the flame to the gate. It sizzles and releases a putrid smell. "I think it's working!" A vine bursts out of the gate, knocking you down. You feel it grip your leg and lift you up. Eddie tries to grab on to you and pull you back down, but it's no use. You're pulled into the gate. The vine wraps around your neck and squeezes.

The End

"So you just left Chrissy to die and then went into hiding like a coward." You look Eddie straight in the eye.

"I was freaked out. What was I supposed to—"

"You could have tried to help her!" you yell. "You didn't then, but maybe you can help find her killer instead of making your friends do the dirty work for you." You've got him now. The first stop is back to the trailer, the scene of the crime.

"That wasn't there when Chrissy died." Eddie looks up at the hole in the ceiling of his trailer. "But that's exactly where she died." You stare at the spot in disbelief. You have no idea what you're looking at. You step closer, pulling a chair behind you so you can reach it. It's slimy to the touch, and cold, but somehow feels alive. Eddie pulls out his radio. "We should tell the others." You're only half listening. You push your hand through and a burst of liquid splashes your face. You and Eddie both scream. It's in your eyes, your mouth!

"Dustin! Dustin, come in now!" Eddie speaks into the radio frantically. You wipe the slime from your face and look farther into the hole. You hold your breath and push your head through. Suddenly you are upside down staring down at the trailer's living room, but this one is covered in vines. "Dustin! Dustin!" Eddie yells in the background. You pull your head out to tell Eddie what you see. Suddenly a vine grips your arm and pulls you up. You feel Eddie tugging at your legs, but it's no use.

Turn to the next page.

The vine lets go and you drop flat on your back, staring up at the hole from the other side. Loud, high-pitched screeching deafens you, and the trailer begins to rock as though something is pushing it. You look out the window to see giant bats attacking the trailer, trying to force their way in. "Eddie, help me!" you yell, jumping up to reach the hole. The bats burst through, whipping you with their tails. A vine knocks you down to the floor and the bats pounce, digging their sharp teeth into you. You scream in agony.

"Just hold on! The others are on their way!" It's Eddie, here to help you. He grabs a chair and swings it at the bats. You start to feel dizzy—you'll lose consciousness soon. You try to tell Eddie to run, but all that comes out is a croak and blood. The last thing you see is him being overrun by the bats.

The End

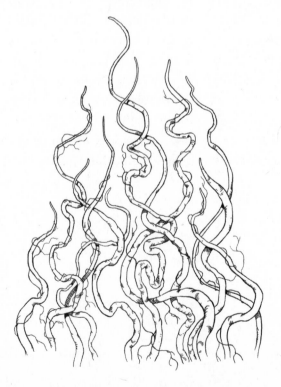

After checking out both the road where Fred died and Benny's—which has been cleared of all jocks—the theory is confirmed. Vecna has three of his four gates. You rub your forehead, trying to process everything. "As long as Max keeps listening to music, doesn't that mean that Vecna can't complete his plan?"

"Unless he gives up on her and kills someone else." Robin shakes her head.

"So what if I stop listening to the music?" Max asks.

Lucas grips her arms. "Max, you can't be serious!"

"I am serious. If I'm the last piece Vecna needs, then we've at least got something."

"You want to use yourself as bait." Nancy purses her lips, considering Max's proposal.

"We lure him to attack Max, and then what? Watch her die?" you say. "How does that help?"

"If you guys get the music playing, I can escape again," Max says. She is resolute.

"It's too risky," Lucas protests. You can see Nancy is torn. The decision is going to come down to her.

Dustin backs Max. "We know Vecna is in the Upside Down at the Creel house; he attacked Patrick from there. If we can get to the Creel house through the Upside Down, maybe we can—"

"Are you nuts? What would stop him from attacking us when we get there?" Your frustration begins to rise. Every step you take gets you closer to defeating Vecna, but it's still not enough. You feel like some key information is missing.

"Nancy?" Steve rushes to her side. "Nance!" Her eyes roll into the back of her head.

Turn to the next page.

You're all back in the Wheelers' basement. Nancy woke from her vision with the last piece of the puzzle. Vecna was Henry Creel all along. After El banished him to the Upside Down, he couldn't hurt anyone, until El opened the first gate. Now Vecna was coming for revenge.

"I guess Vecna got tired of waiting on us to figure it out. . . ." You try to inject some humor into the dark situation. The others just glare at you. "Sorry, bad joke."

"You think?" Robin raises an eyebrow. Nancy is still shaking from her encounter with Vecna. "Should we try calling the others? El, Jonathan?"

"The line's been busy for days." Max still has her music playing. "Joyce is always on the phone for her job."

"No," Nancy finally says. "Whatever is going on in Lenora has something to do with this. It can't just be Joyce."

"Wait, Lenora?" You're taken aback, it's been so long since you thought of home. "You mean in California?"

"Yeah, El and the Byerses moved there after Hopper died," Steve answers. "Nancy's brother Mike is there visiting. Why? You know it?"

Go on to the next page.

"I'm—" You let out a chuckle of disbelief. "I'm from there. I can't believe this."

"Do you know Jonathan Byers?" Nancy asks, her eyes wide. "Or maybe his friend who delivers pizzas? Ar—"

"Argyle? Yeah, he usually delivers to my place. I don't think I've met Jonathan, sorry. But I can try to reach Argyle. Maybe he knows something." You race to the phone and dial the number for Surfer Boy Pizza, then ask for Argyle. He's not there. "Can I get his home number? Please, it's an emergency." The person on the other end gives you the number. You hang up and then dial Argyle's home line. After a couple of rings, there's an answer. Still no luck—Argyle isn't there. He's been on a road trip with some friends. You ask if one of the friends was named Jonathan. Thanking the person on the phone, you hang up. "Argyle is with Jonathan and I'm guessing the others. They're on some kind of road trip."

"No, Jonathan wasn't going anywhere for spring break. I was supposed to go see him." Nancy starts pacing. "Whatever is going on there has to be connected to this."

"So what does that mean for us?" you ask.

"It means we're on our own." Nancy runs her hands through her hair. "If we do nothing, Vecna will destroy everything. We need to take the fight to him before it's too late."

"How?" Eddie asks. "He's got incredible superpowers, and we've got . . ."

"We've got knowledge." Dustin perks up. "When El uses her powers to see the Upside Down, she's vulnerable. I bet Vecna's powers work the same way." A plan is formed.

Turn to the next page.

"So what should I expect in the Upside Down?" you ask as you stand below the gate in Eddie's trailer. "I don't like the idea of going in with little to no intel."

"The only one here who's been is me, and I was busy running from the Demogorgon. We're all Hawkins has right now." Nancy hoists her sawed-off shotgun on her arm. Steve and Robin carry backpacks filled with Molotov cocktails. You, Dustin, and Eddie hold makeshift spears and shields made out of trash can lids with nails sticking out. "Just remember, the whole thing is a hive mind. Don't touch anything, not even a vine. We make our way to the Creel house, and then signal Lucas and Max to set the trap. When Lucas tells us Vecna has taken the bait, then we go in."

Steve hoists himself through and makes a perfect landing on the other side. The view of Steve standing upside down on the other side almost gives you vertigo. Soon the rest of you follow. The world flips as you fall through the gate, landing on a mattress. Eddie helps you up. All around you are vines twisting around the walls and floor of Eddie's Upside Down trailer. "I can't believe I'm in another dimension."

"Freaky," Eddie says, looking around. Steve leads the way out of the trailer and through the woods to the Creel house.

Go on to the next page.

"Demobats." Dustin gasps as you all stare at the Creel house from the safety of tree cover. Giant screeching bats sit on every inch of the roof.

"Why didn't you mention those?" Fear builds steadily inside you.

"Because we've never seen them before," Dustin answers. "Demogorgons, demodogs, the Mind Flayer, those we know. This is new."

"We can't just go in there," Steve says. "We'll never get past them."

"Did we really come all this way for nothing?" You let out a breath.

"No." Nancy shakes her head. "No, we just need to improvise. We need a distraction, something to get those demobats away from here. We can't turn back now."

"Maybe we should," Robin says. "I have a really bad feeling about all of this. Like, really bad. Lucas and Max won't start until they hear from us. We could just go back to the trailer." Everyone starts to debate the two sides. Eddie and Robin want to go back. Dustin and Nancy want to keep going. After going back and forth, Steve sides with Robin and Eddie. You can either make this a deadlock or give the majority to Team Go Home by joining or abstaining from voting.

If you choose to side with Nancy and Dustin, turn to the next page.

If you choose to head back, turn to page 297.

"I think I'm going to regret this, but we can't go back now. We need to find a way to get in there." Eddie, Robin, and Steve look nervous, but then nod. You are all Hawkins's last hope. If you don't do anything, no one else will.

"So we need a distraction," Eddie says resignedly. "I think I have an idea, but I'll need to go back to my trailer."

"Take Dustin with you," Steve says. Dustin protests, but Steve cuts him off. "Look, you two distract them for a few minutes and then get out of here. Got it?"

Eddie pulls Dustin toward him. "Yeah, got it."

"Tell us when you get there. We'll let you know over the radio when to start." Nancy tosses him one. "Don't do anything until then." You watch as Eddie and Dustin start their journey back. It won't be long until the final showdown.

Turn to page 257.

"I'm with Robin." You take a deep breath. "We're in over our heads. We didn't even know about these bats. Who knows what else might be in there?" Dustin and Nancy are upset, but the majority rules and you make your way back to Eddie's trailer.

Nancy contacts Lucas and Max over the radio when you are out of the Upside Down. "Lucas, the plan has changed. Come in." There's no answer.

"Something's wrong." Dustin grabs the radio from Nancy and tries to get an answer. Outside, you can hear the sound of engines revving.

"They wouldn't have started without the signal from us. Something else must have happened." Robin goes to the window. "What the—?" You run to the window. A trail of cars rips through the trailer park, filled with adults carrying bats, crowbars, and even guns.

"Freak hunt." Eddie pulls the curtains shut.

"It looks like the whole town is out there. We need to get you back to the cabin." You see the fear in Eddie's eyes.

"Guys, I can't get ahold of Lucas and Max." Dustin is frantic. "Do you think the mob got them?"

"Eddie!" a voice yells from outside. You peek through the curtains and see Jason. "Eddie, come out now. We've got your acolyte, and you're surrounded." The crowd behind him parts to reveal Lucas tied up. You can't see Max. You hope she's somewhere safe with her Walkman. When the earth rumbles, you know Max is gone.

The End

ABOUT THE AUTHOR

Portrait by Rana Awadallah / instagram @rana.theartist

Rana Tahir was born in Pakistan and raised on the beaches of Kuwait, where she first learned to love writing. When not at her desk writing or researching, she can be found jumping into lakes and rivers during long hikes, even though she always forgets a bathing suit and must sit in the car in her cold, wet clothes on the ride home. She is a Cancer sun and moon, so she never regrets being in the water. She lives in Portland, Oregon, with her husband and two cats.